MEOW MAYHEM

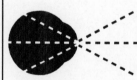

This Large Print Book carries the
Seal of Approval of N.A.V.H.

FANCY CAT COZY MYSTERY, BOOK 1

MEOW MAYHEM

LISA J. LICKEL

THORNDIKE PRESS
A part of Gale, a Cengage Company

Farmington Hills, Mich • San Francisco • New York • Waterville, Maine
Meriden, Conn • Mason, Ohio • Chicago

LIBRARY OF CONGRESS CIP DATA ON FILE.
CATALOGUING IN PUBLICATION FOR THIS BOOK
IS AVAILABLE FROM THE LIBRARY OF CONGRESS

ISBN-13: 978-1-4328-6250-3 (hardcover)

Published in 2019 by arrangement with Pelican Ventures, LLC

Printed in Mexico
2 3 4 5 6 7 23 22 21 20 19

MEOW MAYHEM

1

I jolted alert to the rude 2:48 AM summons of my business phone. Fumbling for the receiver on my nightstand, I squinted. The name and number was unfamiliar. I frowned. In the middle of the night? This must be a crank call. I hoped it wasn't an angry-at-the-world abusive type. I was tired and not in the mood to be professionally pleasant. I held the headpiece next to my ear and answered. "McTeague Technical Services. This is Ivy. How may I be —"

"mm . . . get . . . help . . . call . . . mmm —

"Don —" I couldn't make anything out through the crackling static and so I got out of my nice, cozy warm bed and went to stand by the window, hoping for a clearer signal. A burst of static rocketed me backward and I held the phone away from my ear. "Oww!"

I sat on the end of the bed and checked the phone, expecting smoke. The background was lit, but the call disconnected. I got back into bed but switched on my bedside light. I searched the caller ID and came up with Chicago. Summersby Building.

A chime indicated an incoming call from the same number.

"Hello? Who's there?" A soft buzz sounded and then a distinct click. At least the recorder had been on.

I yawned. Summersby Building was probably a construction company doing work for one of the new businesses coming to Apple Grove. That's why I was here, too, invited on behalf of the mayor's new community growth incentive. I yawned again, turned my business phone to silent and pulled the covers up to my chin.

The next evening, after my third attempt to reach my friend Donald, the mayor of Apple Grove, Illinois, I ran my fingers across the screen of my personal phone, to view photos of my cat from last year at Christmas at my home in Maplewood. I usually found pictures cheerful. Comforting. But not the holiday ones which reminded me of all I hated about Christmas.

Now, in the twilight on the cusp of summer in a new and unfamiliar home, the images made me homesick.

When I'd moved here two months ago, April Fool's Day to be exact, the week after the annual spring CAT convention, the phone and cable companies wondered about how I could make McTeague's Services work with my three servers. I showed them Donald's letter of reference and the preliminary approval of the exception to the zoning ordinance in this quiet little neighborhood.

My business was dedicated to tech for non-techies, computer set-ups, web design, personal computer lessons. I supplemented that with other home-based requests that sometimes went along with my home visits, such as pet, houseplant, and mailbox sitting for those going away for whatever reason. Small businesses needed web maintenance. I also offered letter and blog writing services and help with forms. In this day and age of rapidly changing informational systems, everyone needed help.

I toyed with the phone. This evening, I couldn't shake the feeling that Donald's silence was not a matter of choice. I needed to help my friend. I looked up a phone number and tapped it out.

"Apple Grove Police. Officer Ripple. How can I help you?"

"Hello. I . . . I need to report a missing

person. Maybe a kidnapping."

"Name?"

"Ivy Preston."

"Right. High Vee? Could you spell that, please."

"I–V–Y. Preston."

"And where are you now, ma'am? Can you see any weapons? Do you know the name of your kidnappers?"

"Oh, no, Officer. It's not me. It's the mayor."

"Mayor? Got that. First name?"

"Donald."

"Donald Mayor. And is he a relative? Is there a note?"

"No . . . you've got it all mixed up. I'm calling about somebody possibly kidnapping Mayor Donald Conklin."

"You think someone's kidnapping the mayor? That's a pretty serious charge."

"Not doing it. I think they already did."

"We'll send someone over to talk to you. What's your address?"

"Three-twelve Marigold."

"Ah, yes. The Pagner house. And you have some sort of evidence?"

"Well, I received the strangest call last night on my business line and now he won't answer his private number. I'm worried."

"Business line?"

"I own the new tech services business in town. McTeague's. Donald invited me."

"OK. Sit tight. I'm sending Officer Dow over to you to take your statement."

"Thank you." I hung up and wondered what kind of a statement I was expected to give. I had the recording, but unless one understood the context, it could mean anything. Maybe I should call someone. How did I know I can trust the police here? On TV sometimes the bad guys aren't who people would think. My mental contact list was pretty slim. My neighbors, whom I didn't know that well. Mom — who lived a couple of hours away.

A knock on the door saved me from a slide into self-pity. I let in Officer Ann Dow, and smiled politely at the little blonde who looked as if the wind would carry her away if she hadn't been anchored by her sturdy shoes and even sturdier holstered, shiny black weapon.

"Thank you for coming." I'm not a giant, but I had a couple of inches on her. I refrained from telling her I could take point if things got dicey.

"So, tell me about this alleged kidnapping." The officer got out her pad and pen. She shushed her shoulder mic.

"The mayor is missing."

11

She didn't say anything at first. "And you believe that because . . . ?"

"I received this strange call late last night. On my business line. Donald asked me to move my tech services business to help Apple Grove. Now he's not answering my calls."

"I'm not privy to the mayor's office practices," she said, straight-faced.

I ignored her implication and instead got out my office phone, explaining she could hear for herself. "This call came in, but it was all static-y and garbled. I couldn't make out much except 'Don,' and 'get.' "

She listened. "Get what? 'Don'? And you think it came from the mayor?"

"I don't know for sure. The caller ID said Summersby Building in Chicago. I just thought you should check it out."

Officer Dow tapped her pen on her pad. She shook her head and returned to the kitchen, me following like a lost puppy. "I'll make a report," she said, reaching for the door. "Maybe you should notify the FCC. If you get threatening calls, you should call the telephone company. We'll talk to Mrs. Bader-Conklin, who's been in the office today covering for her husband who's on a business trip. If that's all, I'll let you get back to . . . what you were doing."

"Thank you. But —"

Click. The door closed. She was gone.

And I thought Apple Grove seemed like such a nice town.

I let out a sigh of pure exasperation and tapped my size seven and half sandal on the tile floor. Last night's phone call . . . I just couldn't get it out of my head. I get mistaken numbers, of course, but I had a funny feeling. And that was a new one — Donald's wife had been in the office? Why had he called my business line?

Calling the police wasn't the best first move. But what else could I have done?

Maybe I should have been mad at him, instead of concerned. With my ringless fingers I tucked a loose spiral of my dishyblah, frizzy hair back into its sloppy bun. Donald would never have ignored me this long. And he'd want to talk about the next CAT convention coming up. That's Cat Association Titlists — the group where we met years and years ago. We both owned purebred Egyptian Maus, the only spotted domestic cat.

I have never been a whimsical person and uprooting myself to move to a new town was a major deal, not something I would have done under normal circumstances, but I'll get to that later. Let's just say his request, that I move my business and myself to Apple Grove, happened at a good time. That's me — Ivy Amanda McTeague Preston — of McTeague Technical Services.

If the police thought Donald was perfectly safe I should just wait until tomorrow and then see if Mrs. Bader-Conklin had some notion about what was going on. I could go visit her at the office and ask, casual-like, if she'd heard from him. And offer to work on the city's website.

My next hint that something was wrong was that Donald's assistant, Marion Green, was not at her usual post. If the mayor's office was open for business, Marion at least should be here, even if she supposedly had the week off. Donald joked that she was the one who really ran the town. The stern-looking, black-haired woman who infringed on Marion's space made me wait fifteen minutes. Donald usually came out of his office when he heard my voice. The light was on. I could see it shining under his door. I supposed Margaret — Mrs. Bader-Conklin — could have been making an urgent call.

I heard a distinct sneeze from inside the office. Then the tap of high heels.

Why had I waited so long before getting concerned enough about Donald to call the police? Final registration for CAT was in two days. Donald never missed. He hadn't registered yet — I checked. We all register as early as we can for the next year to make sure we saved the date, even though the convention is always at the start of spring. He'd take his cat, Tut, out of his wife's hair for a while, since she was allergic to animal dander. He never said anything negative, but I got the impression the vacation was a three-way blessing between him, his wife, and Tut.

A woman opened the door to the mayor's office. I recognized her from a photo that Donald once showed me: Margaret. She studied me over half-glasses perched on a razor-thin nose, thin-penciled eyebrows raised toward her curled-under bangs. I shivered.

"Sorry to keep you waiting, Miss Preston. Please." She gestured to me to follow her. And then she invited me to sit in the ugly, straight-back chair on the opposite side of Donald's desk instead of the comfy one in front of the computer. Donald had never done that.

I warily started a conversation. "I hope Marion isn't sick."

"I gave Mrs. Green a few days off. My personal assistant is with me." The wife of the mayor of Apple Grove leaned back in her husband's leather chair. "Now, what can I do for you, Miss . . . Preston?"

I swallowed hard. "Uh, well, Don — the mayor — isn't returning my calls, and he hasn't registered for our — the — CAT convention yet. I wondered . . . if you've heard from him?" Dang, I tried hard not to squeak with nerves at the end. I couldn't help it, yet instinct told me that I must not show fear. I hoped she wouldn't get the wrong impression at my lame excuse to see her.

"What is the nature of your business with the mayor?"

I took a deep breath. Maybe I'd sounded a bit strange. "The mayor asked me to bring my tech services business to Apple Grove."

Margaret sneezed again and took out a dainty lace handkerchief. "Something in the air," she muttered, sniffling. "You must have a cat or a dog at home. I'm allergic."

"Oh?" I said, stopping before I mentioned I already knew that. Wrong impressions, and all.

"I recall Donald speaking of you," she said. "From that little group he goes to, right? So, did you?"

"Did I what?"

"Get him signed up."

16

"Well, that's something people usually do for themselves. Conference fees, and so forth . . ." I muttered.

"Oh, just send me a bill, then. Was there anything else?"

"So, your husband is around? He's all right?"

"Of course, he's all right. Why wouldn't he be? He just needed a day to . . . ah, get ready for that cat thing after . . . ah, meeting with company officials. Letty can handle business."

Letty must be the scary woman up front. Margaret stood, and I followed suit. She was taller than me. I supposed if I wore heels instead of tennies, I could have stared at her nose instead of her chin. Three black hairs sprouted under her makeup. I pressed my lips tight to hold in the grin while she turned to open the door to her office.

"How's Tut these days?" I asked, testing her out on a whim.

"Tut? Oh — fine, just fine."

Mmhmm. "Mem's just fine, too."

"Mem? Memo? I don't underst—" She glanced over my shoulder. "Oh, ah, good to know. Excuse me while I, ah . . ."

I followed her line of sight to see Letty in the doorway, frowning, while her left hand came to rest on her folded elbow. We locked

17

stares. Her brown irises had weird little gold flecks in them. She blinked first. She went back to her desk.

Margaret pushed forward, forcing me to move to the door. "Thank you. If you'll excuse me, we have a great deal of work. Good-bye, now. Take care."

I nodded to Letty on my way out. I got turned around in the maze of staircases and hallways and ended up leaving city hall by the back door. In my muse I dodged a dark-colored delivery van squealing right up to the exit before I found the walk that went around to the side parking lot where I'd left my car. What on earth would Mrs. Bader-Conklin do in her husband's office? Especially if he was in town and getting ready for the conference? But if he was getting ready why did he need me to register for him?

How I got home, I'm not sure. I don't think I ran into anyone on the way. I paced my tiny kitchen, three steps forward and back, as the evening wore on, deciding how much further to get involved in this business.

Judging by the officer's response to my initial phone call, I wondered if I would ever rate any respect for my theory that the mayor needed help. I needed to find a better way to explain my dilemma to the police if I had the urge to call again.

I could talk to someone else. Of course! Someone else. Adam! He'd know what to do. How could I have left out Adam Truegood Thompson, Donald's other pet project. I grinned. Adam had moved to Apple Grove a week after I did. Mea Cuppa, his little bookshop and fancy coffee joint, needed more prep time than my machines, so he'd only recently opened. I spent an odd hour or two helping him sort merchandise and stock shelves.

I drove through downtown, chased by an occasional scrap of newspaper or leaf swirling in the spring breeze riffling up from the river through alleys. I knocked on the front door of the closed coffee shop. I didn't think Adam heard me at first, as he took some time coming down from his apartment.

"Ivy. What's wrong? Come on in. Sit down."

A solid comfort, Adam. I babbled. "I don't know where else to turn. Will you hear me out?"

"Of course, I will."

I glanced around, feeling vulnerable through the huge plate glass window. Anyone passing by could see us clearly. "Not here."

He seemed unfazed. "OK. Come on up. I wasn't exactly expecting visitors, though."

And clearly, he wasn't. He tossed aside a pile of towels and picture hangers and bade me sit on his recliner while he went to fix tea. I grew antsy. There was little room to pace with the floor covered with boxes and bubble wrap. I could barely tell the color of the carpet.

He smiled and put a steaming cup of ginger tea in my hand. "I told you it was a mess."

Ginger-mint. I inhaled. "Thank you."

He surveyed the room and grimaced. "Let's go in the kitchen, shall we?"

His kitchen was a different world. Neat and cozy. I could see where Adam felt most comfortable. We sat. I sipped while appreciating his patience. I mulled over a couple of ways to tell my tale and decided direct was best.

"Donald's missing. I think he's in trouble." I stopped and took a deep whimpering breath.

Adam put one of his gigantic warm hands over mine and anchored me with his calming gray stare.

I had no idea what he thought, but I trusted him.

"Ivy. Donald told us that he would be

coming and going while he courted more businesses."

"This is different. His wife is running his office."

Adam's eyebrows went up with a comforting incredulity. He shook his head, his eyes narrowed. "What do you mean?"

I twisted my mouth and jiggled my foot. "Um, well. If there's an emergency, doesn't the city council president take over? But Margaret didn't say anything about an emergency. She said he was here — well, in town. And Donald hasn't registered for CAT yet. He planned to go, so I tried his personal number. Three times. To remind him. He didn't answer. Then, later, I received this strange, garbled call — I could only make out what sounded like 'Don,' and 'get' from some number in Chicago — it must have been Donald asking me to get help."

Adam sat back, not saying anything. Finally, he got up and walked over to the sink.

I admired his height and flexed back muscles, the efficiency of movement, but also his deliberation of thought before speaking. He was older than me — I'm almost thirty-two and single, thanks to my ex-fiancé Stanley — but I wasn't sure how much older he was. His wavy black hair was slightly salted at the temples, and his nose looked as if it had been broken at one time and fixed, but best of all, he wasn't married.

The tone of his voice led me to believe he wanted to take me seriously but was finding it difficult. "Donald's scheduled business trip yesterday wasn't to Chicago. What do you think might be going on?"

"I don't know. Donald is our friend. If he's in trouble, I want to help."

Adam's mouth twitched. "What kind of help?"

I sighed, thinking how ludicrous my actions had been and not ready to admit the call to the police. "Yeah. So, I thought I'd just go over to city hall and visit Margaret. You know, just ask if she'd heard from Donald. So, I did. But Margaret wasn't talking. Marion wasn't even there."

"She might not spend all day in the office if Donald is out," Adam reminded me.

I took another deep breath. "She said he was all right. But there was someone else there. Someone I didn't recognize, sitting at Marion's desk."

"Ivy, you wouldn't know many people here, anyway, remember? We just moved."

I liked the "we" part of his comment.

"Right. But did you know that Margaret's allergic to cats? I thought she just hated them."

"That's one of the reasons Donald was so interested in that new company he hopes to bring to Apple Grove. Happy Hearts Bioengineering. They're working to produce a hypoallergenic breed of animal."

"I thought he was . . . well, maybe I hadn't been paying attention. I thought he was going after a pet food company. Fel-feli—"

"Feli-Mix. He told me they'd signed an 'intent to build' contract based on getting the zoning approval."

"Oh. Good." I scratched my ear. Isis wandered in from a dark hallway to curl around Adam's ankles. Adam's Mau smoke female was daintier in appearance than disposition. My Mem had been at the receiving end of her ferocity since they'd been introduced two years ago at a convention. Poor Mem had only tried to be polite.

Adam nudged me back to the present topic at hand. "What did Margaret say?"

"She wouldn't talk to me."

He wiped a hand over his face.

"I didn't think I was nosy. She asked me to get Donald signed up for the convention and send her the bill."

"Oh?"

"Don't you think that's a little odd?"

"It's unusual, but she could have just been trying to help Donald if he's distracted with town business." He smiled gently. "You're still worried."

"Yes, about him and Tut. I wish now I hadn't called the police."

He raised his brows and took a deep breath. "What exactly did you say to them?"

I grimaced. "That I wanted to report a . . . a kidnapping." My voice dropped to a too-low whisper on the last word. I sounded perfectly ridiculous.

"Based on a phone call you couldn't understand? And after the police officer stopped laughing?"

"He didn't laugh at all! He sent a lady cop to check on me."

"And?"

"She said she'd file a report."

Adam uncrossed his arms and got up from the table. He gently removed the mug from my hands and raised me to my feet. I liked the feel of those hands. I liked the confidence he exuded even more. "Ivy, I can tell you're concerned about this. Why don't you let me go talk to Margaret tomorrow, see what I think. OK? I'm not dismissing you, but I have to think about this."

I nodded. "It sounds wild. I need to do

something, but I'm not sure what."

Adam walked me to the door and down the steps. The moccasins he wore silenced his path across the floor of the shop. "You drove. You want me to take you home?"

I appreciated his thoughtfulness. "I'm all right." I caught my reflection in the window of the door. My corkscrew hair flew in all directions — I looked like a nutcase. No wonder he had been concerned I couldn't drive. I stopped and turned. The top of my head came to his shoulder, giving me a good view of his throat. His turtleneck shirt hid most of the scar that snaked around his neck and across his right shoulder. I never asked about it and I was too shy around him yet to pry, but I hoped that would change in the near future. "Thank you for listening. I hope it's just some kind of mental lapse on my part."

"We both care about Donald. I'll talk to you tomorrow." He flashed a grin and closed the door behind me, staying at the window to watch until I sat safely in my car.

I did not expect to sleep much, so after checking my client list and the current work orders in my office, I settled on the couch with my pet, Memnet, nearby, and popped a movie into my player.

Mau owners often give their friends names popular in ancient Egypt for obvious reasons. Mem was a beautiful, black-spotted, registered silver male running past middle age. We garnered tons of compliments for his personality and outstanding looks, and he was as devoted to me as I was to him. He had been a staunch friend when Stanley decided he did not want to marry me — after we'd ordered the invitations and my dress, rented the hall, and the organist.

Memnet's scratching woke me sometime later.

Cold and stiff, I came to my senses abruptly when I heard a loud crack and tinkling sound from the kitchen.

Mem was not as cautious and streaked toward the sound, a silver shadow in the blue glow of the television screen. His screech was primeval.

My hand shook as I dialed the number of the police department with a legitimate complaint this time. After being assured they would send someone immediately, I peered into the kitchen to see the broken window panel of the door and the swinging chain.

Mem sat guard, his tail twitching and ears forward, his paw resting on top of a stone with something tied to it.

"What have you got, Mem?" I crouched, wary of glass. With a low growl pulsing from his furry throat, he reluctantly let me examine the rock. I supposed it was evidence, but it was in my house. And Ripple had laughed at me earlier, after all. With one eye watching for the police car, I hurriedly untied the string and read the attached note.

"Busy-body's don't belong in our town."
I hated misused apostrophes.

2

Donald should concede one point to his opponents of community growth: the crime rate was going up.

Mem never left off his fearsome stare — not even when the strobe lights of the police car pierced the house.

After the excitement of the photographs, fingerprinting and sampling of the streak of blood left on the door frame, I was allowed to clean my kitchen. Thanks to Memnet, the creep had not gotten in. At least, that was the reason according to the police.

"We'll send someone around frequently, ma'am, to check on you. We've searched the premises. Is there someone I can call to stay with you? Or would you be more comfortable going away for the rest of the night?" Hopefully Officer Ripple didn't recognize my name from my earlier call to report Donald's kidnapping. "In case there are any lurking kidnappers."

OK, so he did recognize my name. I gave him a tight little smile. But his comment made me wonder if this incident was somehow related to Donald's disappearance. Absence. Whatever.

Memnet and I made our own search through the two bedrooms, the hall closet, and my second-story office.

I carried a bat as menacingly as I could. After the adrenaline rush leached from my veins, I realized I was too tired to think about it anymore and went to bed.

In the morning I called the insurance company and then my mother, assuring her that I was all right. She had been concerned about my move to Apple Grove, but since Stanley's little maneuver of dumping me practically at the altar after five years of empty promises, she understood my need to start fresh. Her spring session wrapped up and she was planning to visit. Mom taught two classes of criminology at Maplewood, a little community college near the house where I grew up, on the outskirts of Chicago.

I stood at the kitchen sink after lunch. I didn't change the décor when I moved in, and loved the sunny yellow the former owners had painted in this room, and the black and white checkered floor. My towels even matched. I dried a coffee mug while I watched Adam, who wore a serious expression, stride up the sidewalk. I heard his knock at the kitchen door and I went to invite him in.

Threads of silver at his temples emphasized the lines fanning out from his eyes. It occurred to me that nothing of Stanley's features had anything remotely distinguishing about them. When Adam stopped to wipe his feet at the door, I restrained myself from throwing my arms around him in appreciation of his consideration.

"I just heard about what happened here last night," he said. "I'm sorry I didn't call right away. Are you OK?" He set his hands on the back of a chair and hunched slightly.

I nodded. "Yes. Thanks to Mem, here. He scared away the intruder."

"The police don't have any theories about who would do this?"

"None they're sharing with me." I invited him to sit in the white wooden chairs at my tile-top kitchen table.

He drank from the cup of coffee I placed in front of him and tried to practice the same of kind of patience he showed me last night. "The note called you a busybody?"

"It was a general note about busybodies. I wouldn't have thought it was personal, except that it had been thrown through my window."

We both turned to look at the plastic and duct tape covering the broken pane of my kitchen door. I think they made yellow duct tape that would match my walls. I'd check it out.

Finally, he sighed and stared straight into my eyes. "Ivy, I'm sorry to be so blunt. I admit I was skeptical of your story. I went to meet with Margaret fully prepared to discount your concern."

I could not turn away despite my disappointment.

"That dark-haired woman, Letty, was at Marion's desk."

I nodded.

"She said Margaret could spare me about five minutes if I could come back at eleven fifteen. I did. The conversation was strained. She asked about Mea Cuppa's opening, how the store was doing, that kind of thing. I asked how the plans were coming for some of the other businesses. She seemed surprised that I knew anything about it, until I reminded her that was one of the reasons I chose to accept her husband's invitation — because of the potential growth." He took another drink.

I waited.

"I asked when I could meet with Donald, and she told me that the mayor would be out of town longer than he'd originally expected. Then I tested her, just as you did. I told her that Isis missed Tut, and we should get them together." He swallowed and spoke into his coffee cup. "She gave one of those fake laughs and said she would have to check her appointment book about when I could bring my little girl over to play with Donald's kitty."

I sat on my hands. "She thought that Isis . . ." At the sorrow on his face I let my voice die out. There were a lot of things I didn't know about Adam.

Isis had been Grand Champion in her class last year at CAT. Even though she hated my Memnet with a ferocious feline passion, she tolerated Donald's cat, Tut.

"So, you agree that something strange is going on?" I asked, growing a little faint.

"I don't know what exactly to think. Unless Donald's had some kind of accident or something," Adam replied. "I don't understand why Margaret thought I still — why I had a daughter."

Ah, the reason for the sorrow. With amazing self-restraint, I reined in my nosiness. Curiosity. Abnormal need to know things that aren't my business. Not yet, anyway.

"Maybe we should follow up on her invitation," I said.

"It would give us a reason to check on Tut at least."

"Us?" I added mentally — and spend more time together. Heat crept up my neck.

His eyes twinkled.

Mem put a paw on his leg and leaped into his lap.

"Mem!"

"That's all right. As long as he doesn't think I brought Isis and start a fight."

"Hey, Mem's a perfect gentleman. Isis is the one who decided . . ." I let the argument die as I realized Adam was goading me.

His grin invited me to join him in a smile.

Mem circled and sat in a graceful pool of spotted sleekness.

Isis and Mem attacked each other if they got within sniffing distance. Isis would ignore me if she got a hint of Mem on my clothes. In Mem's case, any aggression was usually self-defense. Neither animal had been declawed. Did I mention that Maus are outstanding animals? They look like leopards from the back and were worshiped by the ancient Egyptians. They're referred to by their color — silver, bronze or smoke — but they come in varieties with bluish or black characteristics. Donald named his cat Tut. Nice guy, Donald, just not very original.

They say that pets and their owners begin to look alike after a while. I'm not necessarily saying this about myself, but I definitely think it's so about Adam Thompson. Even his eyes were the smoky color of Isis's pelt.

"Maybe this is none of our business," he said, breaking into my reverie.

"Donald had big plans that involved us." I'd grown impatient. "Maybe I was ready to make a change in my life and pick myself up and start all over in Apple Grove." I snorted. "A place where I don't know anyone and where I'm not even sure I can develop enough of a customer base to pay my bills. But how about you? Were you ready to take a chance like that? What about family? Friends? Donald made promises that involved tax breaks, don't forget. I need that."

"We don't know that the mayor changed his position on that," Adam said. But I could tell he was troubled. He stroked Mem, who rubbed the side of his head on Adam's knee.

Although I'd known Donald for all the years, eleven, that Mem and I attended CAT, it was only last spring while we were

34

waiting in line at the photo booth in Minneapolis, he started chatting about his town, Apple Grove. He was the mayor of a small city, but he rarely spoke about it. He always said he came to CAT to get away from things, and we never talked much about our work. Back then, I could tell he needed to talk. Apparently, Apple Grove was just shriveling up. Dying. Rotting, so to speak. He wanted to attract new businesses, more jobs, more people. He battled with his city council over this. I could see the whole thing weighed heavily, and I felt sorry for him and wanted to help.

"You have your records, don't you?" Adam said. "About the promises Donald made?"

"I normally make sure I have important papers filed. Everything's a mess right now with the move, though. I'll have to sort it all out." I relaxed.

Adam continued to stroke Memnet, who showed his appreciation with his throaty imitation of a laughing purr.

I stirred my coffee, remembering when Donald introduced me to Adam last year at the convention. Adam's molten eyes drew me in and made me hot and cold at the same time.

My mental image of Stanley faded. He

only called once, three months after the wedding that wasn't. Before I let my apartment and hired the moving van. He said he was sorry, but I could tell he didn't really mean it. I wished him well and promptly threw out his new number and address.

Mem plopped to the floor as Adam stood. "Ivy, I've been thinking. I like the idea of going over to the Conklins' house on the pretext of visiting Tut. Can you get away for a couple of hours? Bob was to help me with some shelves but canceled just before I came here."

Bob Green was Donald's secretary's husband. He was Apple Grove's barber, and his shop was next door to Adam. Mea Cuppa had been an antique store before Adam moved in and renovated the place. He'd given Bob an ancient barber pole he'd found in the basement.

Adam reached for his jacket. "As I was leaving, I overheard Letty talk about getting lunch at home before they catch a flight. I bet they're there now."

"Catch a flight? You want to go to the house right away? What if they're busy? Who'll run the city while they're away?"

He laughed and shrugged as we left the house. "Got me. We'll only need a couple of minutes." He opened the front door of his later model, retro-blue pickup truck for me.

I adjusted my seatbelt and the visor. "Donald and Margaret have a farmstead, I believe. I've never been there, but he told me about their renovations."

I gave in to a moment of vanity when I noted in the mirror that I'd smudged mascara under one of my muddy green eyes. Not exactly exotic. I sighed. I had my dad's high cheekbones, but my mom's pale coloring. With my wild, ash-brown hair that would never do what I wanted, I wondered, just for a moment, how Adam really saw me. Stanley told me I looked nice. A couple of times.

Go on with you, girl. I took a deep breath, loving the smell of the box of books behind me. I noticed the radio was set to the local public channel, and I didn't detect any cigarette smoke. Not that I thought he was the smoking type, anyway. Isis left her presence with a few shed hairs.

"I have the address." Adam squinted at a paper stuck up on his visor. "Do you know a quick way to get there?"

We worked out a path through the crooked streets and maze of downtown parking. I pointed to a red brick building at Main and Second. "There's New Horizons, the church I'm thinking about joining." I tried to sound casual. "Do you go to church?"

"It's been a few years." He met my gaze briefly before turning onto the county road along the edge of Apple Grove. "This way, right?"

I respected his change of subject. "Yes, down" — I checked a mailbox — "about two more driveways, I think. Yep. There's their number on the gate." Which was thankfully open.

We drove to the large house, complete with two-story, crisp white fluted columns. Margaret, or whoever did their lawn, had the plantings around the stone portals military sharp, with lush red impatiens in neat rows.

Adam pulled up to the front step, his mouth tight as he slammed his door shut. I followed suit, but more slowly, noting the circle drive around the back of the house and the outbuildings, a detached four-car garage with steps to a windowed apartment above, a small building that must be the old carriage house, and a playhouse-size mock Egyptian temple which I assumed was Tut's domain. Donald told me long ago that Margaret would not tolerate pets in the house. Parked next to the little structure was a navy blue, paneled work van with no rear windows. It was parked at an angle, so all I

38

could read of the small lettering along one side was ". . . rity" and the line below it: "ace of mind."

We climbed the red brick steps and walked through those imposing columns.

"Some farmstead," Adam muttered from the corner of his mouth. He rang the bell.

A cloud went over the sun, and a chilly gust blew along the long porch. We checked one way, then the other while we waited. Finally, Adam rang the bell again. We heard it echo through the house. Footsteps, click-sliding on a wooden floor. The door was opened by the dark-haired woman from Donald's office.

"Hello, Letty," Adam said. "We hoped Mrs. Conklin was at home."

Letty's mouth did not change from its scimitar shape. "Mrs. Bader-Conklin is not receiving visitors at this time. Whom shall I say called?"

"So, she is home?" I asked in my best polite voice.

Letty did not even glance in my direction. "She is unavailable."

The curtain to Adam's left twitched. I brushed his arm.

"Could you please tell her that two old friends of her husband's came by, Ivy Preston and Adam Thompson?" Adam bobbed his head. "Ma'am."

"Wait! Um, Mrs . . . Letty, is Tut here or did Donald take him? Who's taking care of him?"

"There's no cat here," Letty said. "The mayor took his animal with him."

"But —"

Adam pulled me down the steps with him as Letty closed the door.

"Hey! Did you —"

He cut me off with a warning pinch while he opened the passenger door for me before going to the driver's side. He started the engine with a twist of the key and drove out.

"You saw what I saw behind the curtain?" I asked, once we'd turned on the road into the mighty suburbs of Apple Grove.

"That wasn't him in the window," Adam replied.

I didn't understand what he was thinking. Clearly, he was on a mission as he drove past my turn.

"But who — what — if they're leaving town, who's running Apple Grove? And what about Tut? If Donald has him, why did Margaret say that you could bring Isis over to play with him? And in the window? Are they hiding some man?"

He gave a snort of impatience. "Could be

the gardener, for all we know. I aim to find out." Adam pulled up at city hall with a rocking stop and jumped out.

I caught my breath as I tried to keep up with him. He raced up the stairs to Donald's office, I watched, undecided for a moment while I contemplated the elevator. The mayor's suite was on the fourth floor. When the doors opened in front of me and spilled out its riders, I jumped in. I met up with Adam at the door marked "Mayor" on frosted glass.

He pushed it open and I followed. Donald's office light was on. How had Adam guessed there would be someone in the mayor's office? I narrowed my eyes. Or had he guessed?

"Hi, Marion." I greeted the blonde woman who stood between us and the inner office. She was not much older than I, but had married and had kids in a more timely fashion.

She jumped. "Oh, Ivy, hello. Mr. Thompson. What's going on?"

Adam wasn't even breathing that heavily after his jog up the steps. "I hope the mayor isn't too busy today. We just stopped back in to see him. I wanted to double check on some information he had for me earlier, about investing in Happy Hearts."

41

I gave him my best wide-eyed "what in the world are you up to, but I'm with you" expression.

Marion turned away and picked up a piece of paper from her desk. "I don't know what to tell you folks. I hope it isn't anything urgent, because the mayor won't be able to see you for a while."

"Oh?"

"I just got in. If you were here earlier, you remember that Mrs. Conklin's assistant, Letty, was here. She called and asked me to come back to work the rest of today and tomorrow. Normally, I would never admit to being unsettled, but well, frankly, I'm not sure what's going on." She held out the paper.

Cancel my meetings and appearances for the next week. I'll be working with the Happy Hearts people in Madison and Washington. The deal's a close one, Marion, and you understand what it will mean to Apple Grove if we can convince them to come here. Of course, I can rely on your discretion in this matter.

Adam and I stared in puzzlement at each other.

"What's got you unsettled?" I asked. "And, since we already knew about Happy Hearts, your discretion is intact." I wrinkled my brow. "But the CAT conference is coming up. He didn't mention that?"

"No," Marion replied. "But, about this message — for one thing, it's typed. Donald doesn't type. Never learned, never wanted to. Said his fingers were too clumsy."

My throat closed up. I suddenly got the dizzy-sick premonition that I wouldn't see him again.

"What else is bothering you?" Adam asked her.

She hitched her skirt and sat on the corner of her desk. "It's just a feeling. I've worked for the mayor since I was in high school. At first, I ran errands, and then after I went to school for office training, he hired me when Regina retired — oh, eight years ago, now. A person in Donald's job has to be careful. Tough, but respectful. Not everyone can do it well."

"I'm sure Donald is a great boss, Marion," I cut in when she took a breath.

She raised her brow. "Donald wants to do something to make Apple Grove a better place to live. But convincing the life-time residents to change their ways and vote to spend money to attract business and families is an uphill battle. We need more people like you to come in and support the community. But more people means spending

43

more on schools and that sort of thing. The businesses and families would bring in more tax money, of course, but the old-timers don't see the issue from that angle. I helped the mayor with some grant applications."

She folded her arms and sighed. "There's a lot of money at stake. Anyway, Donald wouldn't have typed that note. He would have left a voice message and fairly detailed instructions for me. I know most of what I should do — that's not what bothers me. But the fact that he didn't do it, or even leave contact information or his itinerary, makes me feel — well, suspicious on some level."

Adam rocked on his heels, ready to jump ahead. "You did know about Happy Hearts, though, right? Can you tell me what you know?"

Marion gave him a curious glance. "Part of Donald's plan. Happy Hearts is a bioengineering firm that's developed the technology to breed cats that are hypoallergenic."

I blinked. That's what Adam said earlier. "It's for real?"

"Yup. Has something to do with proteins and saliva. I didn't quite catch it all, but Donald was enthusiastic. He said it would be a major boost to get them to settle here."

Adam jumped up. "Thanks, Marion. And

no, we didn't have any urgent business."

"I heard that you're planning a grand opening fairly soon, Mr. Thompson. I'm sure he'll be here for that," Marion said. "I've been instructed to review your settlement claims and get the checks ready."

Donald dealt with my relocation by paying the mover and the telecommunication people for the initial hookups directly. He also promised to cover a certain percentage of my advertising bills and showed me a list of where I could place my ads. Marion had a large file of prepared folders with specific information. One whole file drawer to the side of her desk was marked "Business Growth" in a bold new font.

I liked Marion, having met her the day Adam and Isis moved to town a couple of weeks ago. I admitted to some jealousy that Marion could so easily practice a teasing, small town chat, coaxing information from Adam that I had been too shy to discover. No, he was not dating anyone in the Windy City. He owned four other shops and was planning more. When the heat of carting boxes up the steps got to be too much, Adam had unbuttoned and rolled the sleeves of the plaid shirt he wore over a faded blue T-shirt. Not even Marion dared ask about the puckered scars that coiled around his neck and right arm.

"Thanks." I echoed Adam. "I was also wondering where his cat, Tut, is now."

"He always takes Tut with him. I assume he did this time, too."

"Marion," I asked, "Do the Conklins have a gardener?"

"Of course."

I walked to the door. "OK, we'll be in touch." I thought of something else. "Oh, hey, Marion? Do you have a photo of the mayor — you know, smiling, or something? I was thinking about . . . hanging one in my office."

Adam gave me a raised eyebrow.

Marion frowned. "There are several pictures around. Let me see." She held up two laminated pages and a framed photo.

I took one. "Thanks."

Adam accompanied me in the elevator. "What was that about?"

"The picture? Just in case."

After we got in his truck, he hesitated. "Ivy, you're not thinking of doing anything dangerous, are you? Busy-body-ish, perhaps?"

"Who, me?" I grinned at him from behind the seatbelt. "I wouldn't even know where to start."

3

The little two-bedroom bungalow I bought in Apple Grove was perfect for me. I had gotten most of the money back from reserving the reception hall, and even took my wedding dress back, so I'd had some money I could use for a down payment. I owned a home! There was a sweet little living room and kitchen on the ground floor, besides the tiny bedrooms, and a finished room at the top of the stairs — like a garret. I wished I were an artist of some kind.

It took Mem four days after the move to get used to our new digs. For the first time, he could wander in a yard with a real lawn and trees, and the old boy was living it up, discovering green grass and all kinds of new scents.

The tech and personal computer business, or maybe it was me, was a novelty in Apple Grove. Although folks remained somewhat cool, things picked up once they realized the benefits and saw my advertising. I suspected that was natural in a small town. At least they were willing to pay me to keep other people from knowing their personal computing issues.

People who were away, busy, didn't like or trust technology, or just preferred to keep a personal touch to update their home equipment or websites used a service like mine. I made house calls. It was more common than people thought. I never wore pearls, or dressed in polka dots, well, almost never — about the pearls, that is — but I did use several incoming telephone and dedicated electronic mail lines. Faxes, too. Amazing how few people faxed from home. Once a customer punched in the code, I could have anything he directed sent through my system. I kept electronic mailboxes from becoming too full, a feature customers loved, and I wished more would use.

I managed to make stiff acquaintance with Yolanda Toynsbee, the publisher of the local twice-weekly newspaper, the Apple Grove Gazette. I did not know enough other people to declare her the crotchetiest citizen of Apple Grove, but right now she topped my list.

When I sailed through the Gazette's front door on Thursday afternoon, she barely glanced up, half-glasses perched on her knobby nose. I needed to update my ad and I was determined to keep the newspaper in my favor. I stood in front of the desk, staring past Yolanda's hunched shoulders and gray mop to the big clock on the wall.

She made me wait for two minutes and twelve seconds. She slashed at something with her blue pencil then reluctantly gave me her attention. "Yes? Miss Preston? What do you need today?"

Three questions. I breathed in through my nose first. "Right, it's me, Ivy." I had tried to get her to call me by my first name since day one, but she never bought it. "And I'd like to update my ad, please." There, polite enough and offering to provide food for her table.

She reached under the counter and pulled out a manila folder, seemingly by touch. She set it between us and flipped it open, all the while staring at me.

I tried to smile, but my lips trembled.

She was the least nosy newspaper person I had ever come across. I tried to engage her in conversation. "I suppose it seems strange that my last name is Preston and my business is McTeague," I said and leaned over the tear sheet of my last design.

Yolanda sniffed. "None of my concern."

My next comment was interrupted by a crash somewhere down the hall.

Yolanda's face changed expression, then she turned to rush toward the sound. "Jennifer, Jennifer Jean, what are you up to?"

Unburdened by a lack of curiosity, I followed.

A tiny girl with curls almost as wild as mine lay tangled in a folding chair she had apparently tried to pull to the water fountain located near the back door. She appeared to be debating whether or not to cry.

"There, there, Jenny Jean, Gramma's got you." She bent to pull the little girl's pink sandals from under the rungs and seemed grateful when I gently tugged on the other side.

Jenny took several wobbly breaths and stuck her forefinger in her mouth while giving me a doubtful look.

"Hi, there. You must be Jennifer. I'm Ivy." I put on my sunniest smile.

Jennifer rolled her face into her grandmother's stomach. Yolanda patted her shoulder. Jenny peeked out with a shy giggle.

"Thank you," Yolanda told me. She escorted the child into the office and then brought her a paper cup half full of water. "Gramma's got a little more work to do, then we can go home. Be good for a little longer, Jennifer. Can you make another picture for me?"

"I'd like one, if you please," I put my two cents in.

"OK. I got a giraffe in me," Jennifer said. She got on her knees on the seat of the desk chair and went to work.

Yolanda led me back to the main room. As I rounded the big desk, she seemed to consider whether I was worthy of her confidence. Apparently, I passed the test. "My son's child." She sighed, squared my ad copy with both of her hands while staring at it absently.

"Jennifer seems like a sweetheart. Not in school yet, apparently?"

"Mornings with early kindergarten," Yolanda said. "But out for summer as of next week."

We reviewed my ad copy while I told her what I wanted to change. We discussed pricing and size for a minute, and then I ordered small posters, too. She tallied my bill. While I ripped out the check, I happened to notice the blue-penciled article Yolanda had been working on when I first came in. The picture showed Margaret Bader-Conklin shaking hands with somebody. The caption read "Mrs. Conklin greets representatives of MerriFood, the pet food company."

51

"Yolanda, is this an article for the next edition?" I asked her.

She nodded, peering at me over her half-glasses.

"May I?" I indicated the article. She didn't say anything but turned away. I got the impression that she wanted my opinion but couldn't bring herself to break the code of revealing the news before it went to print. I scanned the text and took one more glance at the picture. "Yolanda, you know that Mayor Conklin invited Feli-Mix to move here and signed contracts. You broke the story after the talk about incubator businesses and the special loan funds. It doesn't say in the article, but is there any chance MerriFood is the parent company to Feli-Mix?"

"I don't believe so," she said, her back still turned.

"Is there enough room in Apple Grove for both companies?"

"I can't imagine how that would work. The employment base is non-existent as it is."

"Was Donald aware of this, Yolanda?"

"This article was faxed over from Mrs. Conklin this morning, with instructions to publish it in the next edition of the Gazette."

"Well, don't you need the other side? Feli-

Mix's side? And Donald's side?"

Yolanda faced me. "We have a strict policy to publish fair and unbiased information in the Gazette. And this article will not be published until we can gather the correct information from all parties involved."

I smiled. "That sounds like the Gazette I've come to love." I glanced around the room, then lowered my voice. "Yolanda, what do you really think is going on?"

Jennifer came into the main room, clutching two pictures. "Gramma, can we go yet? I'm all done with my drawings."

Yolanda picked the child up. Jenny thrust one wrinkled piece of paper at me. "Here, Ivy. I made a kitty picture for you. I just knew you liked kitties."

A number of snappy cat comments came to my mind regarding Yolanda Toynsbee's expression. All of them involved satisfaction.

"Thank you, Jennifer. I'll stop at the store on the way home and get some refrigerator magnets, so I can put your picture up in my kitchen. And yes, I do have a nice kitty named Memnet. I hope your grandma will bring you to meet him soon."

Jennifer nodded her curly head up and down with enthusiasm and sent a pleading look at Yolanda. I suspected Yolanda needed an excuse to visit me.

I went out onto the sidewalk, the jingle of the door clashing with the striking chorus of my own cell phone. I was naturally a techno-geek. When people found out, they either start talking jargon a mile a minute as if they were afraid I'd vanish or gave me that look of feigned sympathy as if I'd sprouted gills or a third eye.

My mother, Geneva McTeague Preston, taught me to appreciate electronics. She raised me on her own after Dad died when I was six — not much older than Jennifer back there. Whenever Mom visited she somehow got hold of my phone and programmed a new personal ring tone for when she called. I used separate tones for my customers — repeats, urgents, faxes coming in at home. She liked to know she was more important than business. The tinny rendition of the "Hallelujah Chorus" she'd somehow found was teeth-gritting. A couple of passers-by stared at me as I ducked into a shadowy entry to answer.

"Mother. Hello. Honestly, I'll have to change that chorus. People are staring."

"Sweetheart, I have been so worried. I nearly called that mayor's office myself. You didn't answer my e-mail yesterday or today."

"I saw it late last night and I've been a

little busy this morning, Mom. How are you?"

"Now, dear, it's not me we should be worrying about. You're sure you're safe? People don't realize that small towns can harbor such villains. Villains." The last word was said with a sinister hiss.

"You should know." My mother, who appeared as fragile as a mayfly, could talk villains with the best of them in her criminology courses, so I wasn't being facetious. But I did regret making my present situation sound so melodramatic.

"I have all the details worked out on my end. Sophie's taking care of things at the condo, and the class lists are in and the labs arranged, so I have a week free."

"That's good. I have your bedroom all ready."

"I can't wait to see your new place. And you're sure you're all right, now?"

"Yes, Mom. Day after tomorrow. You have the directions? We'll go to church on Sunday."

"Good, dear. Of course, I don't want to interrupt any plans you may have already made."

I grinned. "I understand. You won't. I'll see you Saturday. Love you."

"I love you, too, darling."

Yes, I was eagerly anticipating my mother's visit. She had a strange kind of trimester schedule that had a spring, summer, and fall sessions, with fieldwork requirements. The local police stations all shuddered when it came time for student field placement, for it meant an interruption in their routines so they could show students how to work crime scenes and put an investigation together. In return, though, it meant more college-trained police officers and detectives, if the students decided to go into that area of study. All the cop shows on TV kept her courses filled.

Anyway, I wanted to put our heads together about this issue with the mayor and my break-in with the ungrammatical note. I almost convinced myself I was just making things up — until I saw that unpublished article from Margaret about MerriFoods on Yolanda's desk. There must be some connection. I had only been half kidding when I'd told Adam I couldn't run an investigation because I had nowhere to start.

Adam was setting out his "Open" sandwich board sign across the street. He gave me the smile that meant he was in business mode.

I waved and sauntered over. I waited in line for a mocha latte and was truly glad to see him attract so much business, even if it was curiosity-seekers checking out the new store. Framed stills of Isis decorated the brick wall by the couple of glass-topped tables set on the wood floor near the big front window. I listened idly while he explained about her to the two young women who were ahead of me.

"Oh, I've had Isis about six years, now," he said.

That surprised me, since he had only been part of CAT for the last two.

"A fire," Adam said patiently, and then wished them a pleasant day. "Next."

That was me. They had asked him about his scars. I met his steady gaze with a sympathetic twist to my lips. "I suppose you get that a lot," I murmured.

He grinned back. "Yes, people ask about Isis all the time," he said. "Cup of coffee?"

I surely did not need the extra calories of the mocha latte and agreed to the plain coffee. "Thanks." I took my wide blue pottery mug to one of the stuffed loungers he had placed around a low table and sipped cautiously. He added the creamer I liked, and I was grateful for small favors. Fire. I shivered. He'd had Isis for six years. He was not married or dating. He'd apparently had a daughter. Where was she now?

I picked up the county shopping paper to distract myself. Adam Truegood Thompson's personal life was not my concern, much as I wished that someday it would involve me. I saw my old ad for McTeague's Technical Services in the shopper and realized I needed to change that, too. Mom and I could go for a drive to the small office of the County Shopping News in Colby next week. She would like that. After I finished my coffee the place was quiet again.

Adam sat in his open-door office at his computer.

I perused the old books section and found a classic I always meant to read but just never got around to. He met me at the register when I walked up. "And are you willing to put up advertisements?" I asked, showing him a copy of the poster I was having printed.

"Sure." He indicated a bulletin board by the door after he rang up my book, giving me a healthy discount. "You can also put your business card in the fishbowl here for a chance drawing on Mondays. Winner gets a free daily coffee for the week."

"Good deal." I dropped in my card and leaned across the counter. "I need to tell you something else I saw at the newspaper office."

He cocked his head while waiting for me to explain.

"Yolanda Toynsbee showed me an article that had been faxed to the office. The article is about Mrs. Conklin inviting a competitor to Feli-Mix to build in Apple Grove. Complete with picture."

"Do you think Donald knew about this?"

"I asked. Yolanda didn't know. I can't imagine how he wouldn't. Feli-Mix was already awarded a building permit and a tax grant."

The door chimed as an elderly couple came in.

"Hello, there," Adam called to them. "Let me know if you need anything." They waved and headed for the travel section.

"I have to get back to work," I said. "My mother's coming to visit." I cleared my throat. "Would you like to have dinner with us one night?"

It was a tough decision for him, I could tell by his hesitation.

I decided to rescue him. "Of course, you're busy. Things are different now that the store is open. That's all right, I understand."

Lines crinkled around his eyes as he smiled. "Seeing as I'm hiring help, that won't be a problem for me, Ivy. I'd love to have dinner with you and your mother. Just tell me when."

"OK." I did not realize I was holding my breath until I was out on the sidewalk. *Well, well, Ivy Amanda McTeague Preston. If you didn't think you were nuts before, you certainly are now. Asking a man to dinner. With your mother.* I walked the few blocks home thinking about Stanley and the distant memory he had become. I had never been so straightforward, asking a man to dinner. Then I groaned and smacked my forehead. With my mother! I let myself in the side door. "Hello, there, my Memnet. Did you miss me?"

With a chortling Mem on my lap in my upstairs office, I got to work, sorting through the incoming, outgoing, and junk electronic and voicemail. One of the new orders for web redesign service was from city hall. Again. I called Marion to confirm and got official voice mail. I debated three seconds whether to call her at home to find out what was going on. I dialed her number thinking I could always pretend this was just a friendly chat. "Hi, Marion. It's Ivy — Ivy Preston."

"Hi. You got the work order, right? To redo the city website? You can work from home, can't you? Margaret says she and the mayor will be out of town. And the council said I only needed to go in once a day to check on things, like the regular mail and any other business. My family will appreciate that. You can reroute the email, too? How does that work?"

I thought a dam had burst as she pattered, asking questions and not waiting for me to answer. Or she was nervous about something. "So, Marion, how about Mrs. Conklin? Does she usually take over when the mayor's away? The atmosphere was like a lull before the storm."

"What do you mean?"

I chewed my lip. I couldn't tell her how I found out, but I sure wanted to talk about Margaret and MerriFood. "With the new pet food business starting up, I just thought things would be busy."

"Oh, so you heard," she said. "Cat's out of the bag, then."

I groaned dutifully.

She giggled. "Yes, Feli-Mix is moving in," Marion confirmed. "They'll be renovating part of the old feed mill and adding on. Those plans have been in the works for a while. But I thought you were aware of that."

"I am, Marion. But I thought there was another company coming, too, with a different name."

"If you mean Happy Hearts, you know that's not pet food."

"Right." I felt confused enough myself by that time and decided to drop the matter of Margaret and MerriFood. "Well, enough about business. My mom's coming to visit. Do you have any thoughts about what to do with her for a week?"

Marion named a few local events and places she knew about. I thanked her after a few minutes and hung up.

MeriFood, Feli-Mix, Happy Hearts . . . happily-ever-after. Until the next edition of the Gazette came out and spoiled the Feli-Mix plan.

Mom came in time for lunch on Saturday. The past couple of days had been rainy, so I was glad the afternoon was nice. School was winding down. I had enjoyed seeing the yellow school buses and the kids who walked. Several young families lived on my block, and we were slowly getting acquainted.

After the grand tour of my cottage, which took about three minutes, she unpacked her cases in the guest room. I had the other downstairs bedroom, having decided to take over the upstairs room for the office. I figured going up and down the stairs would be good exercise.

I started to fix lunch when Mom joined me. People probably wouldn't guess my mom's age from her appearance. She kept her short hair dyed pale gold. She'd had laser surgery on her eyes and only used glasses at night. I hoped I would be as trim when I got to be her age.

She perched on a chair, watching me. "So, are you happy to be in Apple Grove?"

Direct as usual. I did not have to think about it. "I am, Mom. There are nice people. Business is picking up. I think things will be all right."

"Did you tell Stanley you were moving?"

"Why? He's history." I brought our sandwich plates to the table and opened the fridge for the pitcher of iced tea I had made earlier.

Mem wandered in and sniffed at Mom's leg. She put her hand down and he rubbed against it. Then he sat in a pool of light and began a bath.

"And you? How do you feel about that?"

I put her off with a little meal time prayer and took a bite. Washing down the turkey salad with tea, I took my time. "I'm surprised at how easily I've moved on. Everything in that other life feels as though it never happened. I hardly even think about him. Or us."

Mom put a hand over mine. "Enough of that. Do the police have any idea who tried to break into your house? What's the latest?"

I was glad she didn't want to waste any more time on Stanley. "I haven't heard any news about the case, Mom. It will be a while before they can analyze the blood, let alone find out if it matches any criminals in the police database."

She sighed. "Backup is such a problem everywhere. So many criminals, so few good folks to catch them. Do you feel safe?"

"Everyone asks that. But yes, I think we're OK. Once the neighbors heard about the break-in, they reformed a neighborhood watch group they had started years ago and never needed. We're all keeping an eye out for each other. I don't think the guy would get away with something like this again. At least not around here."

I was wrong.

While my mother and I visited Colby the next afternoon, someone who was apparently more careful than the first crook, who obviously knew my house better and who definitely had more thievery skills, managed to cut the glass to the downstairs window, sneak up the steps, smash my computers and take my router, along with my temporary lock box with the new hard drives. Those external hard drives had all the backups of work I had done and had in progress since moving to Apple Grove.

Memnet was stuffed in a burlap sack, drugged, and tossed under the stairs.

4

"You're sure he'll be all right?" I asked the woman for the sixth time.

She placed a gloved hand on my beloved Memnet, tiny stethoscope to his chest.

Mom grabbed my elbow to steer me away from the exam table back into the waiting room, casting the too-young-looking veterinarian an apologetic glance.

"She's gotta be younger than I am, Mom," I said. "I can't trust Memnet to somebody who is that much younger than me. How can she possibly know what's going on? I don't know what's going on." I felt hysteria burbling up, and I could tell Mom thought so, too.

"Now, Ivy." Mom used the firm tone she once used on me in high school when I tried to find a reason for breaking curfew. "You're not helping the situation with this kind of behavior. Doctor Bailey appears to know what she's doing. She came in special for us. Come, sit."

I could not sit, so I paced. The long, narrow room smelled of dog and disinfectant with an underlying hint of peppermint, which I realized, after passing it on my eighth lap, came from an air freshener plugged into the outlet behind a hexagonal side table. The police allowed us to rush Memnet over to the vet's office as soon as the preliminary check was done. We promised to give a full statement tomorrow.

"Miss Preston?" The doctor stood in the connecting doorway, holding a limp Memnet in her arms.

He tried to greet me and made a weak attempt to come to me. I took him with gratitude and hid my tears in his coat. Mem's wheezy purr ratcheted up a notch.

Dr. Bailey stroked his ears. "Generally speaking, Memnet's in very good health," she praised us. "He's getting up there, of course. He's eleven years old, you said? He's doing pretty well, then."

"Do-do you know much about Maus?" I asked, while getting control of myself.

Mom stood at my other side.

The doctor smiled. "The mayor brings Tut in regularly." She looked at us with narrow-eyed curiosity. "He told me he hoped to bring more Mauists into Apple Grove and I should be ready." The woman swished her long ponytail over her right shoulder. "I didn't think my first encounter would be with a beauty like Memnet. I wish I could be more specific about what he got into, but at this point, the substance seems to have cleared most of his system. I took a blood sample to send to the lab. Update me on how he's getting on, say, in two days. Otherwise, don't hesitate to call if you need anything." In response to my apparent expression of panic, she pointed to the pocket of my shirt. "You put my card in your pocket." She winked at us, then. "My daughter is in high school. She's developed a keen interest in Egyptian Maus since getting acquainted with Tut." Dr. Bailey walked to the door with us and let us out. Up close I could see that she was not that young. There were plenty of silver hairs streaking that blond ponytail.

Ivy, get a grip.

Mom drove so I could hold Memnet. Usually a contented rider as long as he was in his carry box, today he was too exhausted to notice scenery whizzing by.

"I think Memnet scared your intruder away the first time. The thief realized he had to knock out your attack cat if he wanted to steal anything on this attempt,"

Mom said.

"But who would do something like that?"

Mom hmm'd. "You must have gotten some information someone needed to be kept quiet. Perhaps someone in the town just wants to frighten you away. You were the one who wanted to move away from the big, bad suburbs, remember? And I believe you said not everyone in Apple Grove is ready for an influx of newcomers."

I ignored her subtle hint. "Or Mem annoyed someone."

"What do you suppose the doctor meant when she said the mayor thought she should be ready?" Mom asked.

"For more cats like Tut and Mem?"

"Or their owners."

"Ha! We're all just a bunch of troublemakers, right?" Mom didn't have any pets. She pulled into my narrow gravel drive up to the one-car garage painted a zesty yellow to match the trim of the cottage. "You should come home with me." She put a hand up to halt my protest. "I said 'should.' I know you don't want to, but won't you please think about it, at least until you feel safe?"

"I do feel safe, Mom. I'm not sure why, exactly, but the person could have easily killed Mem and he or she didn't. The thief obviously got what he came for, although pawning my equipment won't be easy since it's all marked."

"The thief obviously wanted more than the equipment alone, then. What about information?"

"Who would care about Netty Drumm's flower blog she commissioned me to design? Or that Bernice's Hobby Shop will be closed for three days next week due to having the place fumigated, which I'm not supposed to mention, and I'm to put announcements on their website? Or Gina Ebersole's babysitting service that's supposed to block assignments from the Wayland Murphys? What kind of high school kid orders a message relay for unwanted business?" I shook my head. "Mom —"

"Your business can't be that mundane." She held her tongue as we took Mem inside where he sought a patch of sunlight in the living room and made himself comfortable. Messages on the answering machine I kept for my private line were waiting: the LCD indicator flashed three.

"I'll just go freshen up," Mom said as she carried her purse into the guest room.

The first message was from Officer Ripple who wanted to set up a time to interview my mother and me.

Easy enough. Mom would be here all week. We could surely squeeze in an appointment for such an important opportunity to discuss why Apple Grove was suddenly turning into a hotbed of intrigue since I moved here. They had, of course, taken our initial statements earlier; dusted for fingerprints, took photos, combed poor Mem, and taken the sack he'd been tied in.

Dale Robbins from next door said he'd assumed the van in the driveway, the one that advertised something about security systems, was there on business for me; and no, unfortunately he hadn't paid any more attention to the company name or license plate number.

We definitely needed to work on the neighborhood watch details.

The next message was from some family member of Netty, wondering about the cost of the funeral flowers. I had not been kidding with my mom about the nature of my work. I wondered how the family member got my personal number, since I don't give it out readily. The third message was a hangup. I frowned, perplexed. My machine did not record hang-ups unless there was some other accompanying sound. I reached to press the replay button.

"OK, honey. All set for lunch? Anything I

71

can help you with?" Mom came back to the kitchen with her "determined to keep Ivy upbeat" expression.

I let the puzzling last message go and turned to explain about the police request for an interview.

"Of course, I'll help in any way I can. They do know about my coursework, don't they?"

"Um, I doubt it. For some reason, the subject hasn't come up." To thwart the astonishing news I had a lapse of judgment in not relaying to the police the very important information that my mother taught criminology, part time, at a community college, in another city, I distracted her with the first item that came to mind. "I've invited a friend over for dinner later in the week. I hope you can help me cook."

Her eyebrows went up. "A friend?"

I planned to regret this later. "Yep. I have made a bona fide friend. His name's Adam Thompson and he just opened the new bookstore. In fact, tomorrow we'll get a cup of coffee there."

"I thought you said this man owned a bookstore."

I squirmed and gathered the strap of my purse over my shoulder. I jiggled the car keys. "He also does fancy coffees and gifts.

Memnet seems fine for now. Let's go out for lunch."

"Sounds intriguing."

I wasn't sure if she meant the friend, the cat, or the lunch.

We sat in Officer Ripple's cramped office at City Hall the next morning. Mom settled in, comfortable in the presence of law enforcement as much as I was not. I didn't feel guilty or anything, I just wasn't as fascinated by high crimes and misdemeanors as my mother. She had made a niche for herself studying criminal behavior and passing that knowledge on in her college classes, the workshops she put on for community neighborhood watches, and even for local police departments and schools. She possessed a natural poise I assumed I would have by the time I reached her age. Trouble was, I never seemed to reach her age.

"So, Miss Preston, Mrs. Preston." Ripple shuffled the typed pages of our earlier statements on his desk. "As I understand, you both were out of town —"

"That's right," Mom said. "We went for a drive in the . . . country."

"And neither of you heard anything earlier in the day or evening? Saw anything or anyone out of place, say, in the neighborhood? Heard any strange noises you couldn't identify?" Ripple asked.

"Officer, my daughter has barely settled in. Everything is strange and out of place to her. Perhaps I could offer my assistance," Mom said.

Ripple threw his pen on the pile of pages and then leaned back in his creaky chair.

I swiftly gathered a breath. "Thank you, Mom." I shifted to meet the resigned, closed expression of the officer in charge of me — my case, that is. "We didn't see anything out of place. The neighbors came and went at their usual times. This has to be related to the earlier break-in, right? Only this time they were prepared for Memnet." At Ripple's speculative glance in my direction, I closed my open mouth, then gave a faint negative shake of my head. I could just imagine his thoughts: no wonder this one's crazy. Check out the parent.

"We can't jump to conclusions, Miss Preston," Ripple said. "Until we have clear evidence linking the two, we're treating this as a separate incident."

"Detec— ah, Officer Ripple," my mother inserted suavely, uncrossing her legs and leaning toward him, smile wide and deep. She tapped the pile of papers on the desk. "You've applied for promotion, I see. You'll make a wonderful detective."

Officer Ripple actually preened at my mother's non-accidental slip.

I felt my mouth pucker and stifled the smirk at her tactics.

"Do you believe this theft has anything to do with Ivy's allegation that something might have happened to Apple Grove's mayor?"

Ripple laughed, but quickly smothered it. "Absolutely not! Mayor Conklin is on a business trip. In small towns like ours, the mayor's job isn't often a full-time position. Donald keeps regular office hours, but he's been away a lot recently, working on behalf of bettering the community. Outsiders will have to adjust to not having the mayor at their beck and call."

Ouch. OK, I'll probably always be considered an outsider. I was unprepared for Mom's next move and needed to hustle to keep up with her.

She stood in one fluid movement while somehow managing to snag her handbag at the same time.

I grabbed and missed my bag a couple of times, and then, red-faced, clumsily pushed out of the broken-sprung chair.

Mom held out her hand over Ripple's desk.

Ripple lurched forward to grab it, while trying to stand as well.

"Thank you for your time, sir," Mom cooed, as if we had not been the invitees. She smiled brilliantly, doing her magic best to put him at ease.

I often watched her do it with recalcitrant students, obstinate potential suitors, and bullying neighbors, and stood back to admire. Although why she catered to this guy, I couldn't tell. I followed her out the door, to the elevator.

"Do you mind if we go up to the mayor's office, Ivy?" she asked.

"The office will probably be locked up if the mayor is out," I replied. "But, sure, we can see if maybe Marion's there. She said she would stop in a couple of times to catch up on the mail." After the elevator doors closed I started in. "Mom, why —"

She held up a hand, her warning sign, and made a nice smile at me. It was her way of asking me to wait before speaking. I suppose she thought the elevator might be bugged or something. As if Big Brother was concerned that terrorists might be planning their attack strategy in an elevator in Apple Grove, Illinois. Honestly.

As I suspected, the door marked "Mayor" was locked tight and the place was dark.

Mom still peered through the window and rattled the door. Then she looked up and down the hallway.

On the fourth floor the only other enclosed spaces in this wing were restrooms and two large conference rooms. The area was cut off from the police side of city hall by a wall, with the elevator and stairs being the only inside access. An emergency fire escape snaked up one side of the wall past windows.

"I've been told the old holding cells are in the basement. With the rats. Wanna go check those out, too?"

"No, thank you, darling. Some other time," Mom replied calmly.

I despised the childish anxiety that rose from my gut. "Let's go get that cup of coffee." Seeing Adam would definitely perk me up. Pun intended. I grinned.

"What's so funny?" Mom asked, as she headed toward the elevator.

"Oh, nothing much." I reached out and hugged her. "I'm glad you're here."

We turned to walk back the way we'd come.

Mom stopped and glanced back.

"What's wrong?" I asked.

"Why would the men's room light be on, when there's no one here?"

I shrugged. "I'm sure someone just forgot. Maintenance will take care of it."

"But the mayor's suite is the only one occupying this floor, right?"

I double-checked the felt board at the end of the hall. "Yup."

"And if only the mayor's wife and female assistant were here . . ."

"Then what? Mom, there's bound to be a lot of people coming and going."

"Not if the mayor's out of town."

I could have kept going with the rationalization, but I wanted to see Adam. I knew where this was headed, so I heaved my best drama queen sigh and straight-armed the door open.

I suppose I should have called out first, but Donald was in no state to protest.

5

Mom sniffed the air before proceeding cautiously into the chilly, tiled room. "The mayor, I presume?" Her voice echoed.

I already started to tear up. Donald did not deserve to be seen like this. I blinked. I sniffed. "Um, yes. Mom! Don't go in there!"

She walked up to him. Donald was slumped unnaturally in one of the stalls, the door wide open. At least he was fully dressed. "Just checking. Why don't you go tell the police, darling?"

"O-OK. Wha-what do you think happened? Is he . . . is he . . . ?" I sniffed.

"I'm afraid so. There's rigor, which means he hasn't been gone all that long. But . . . judging by the way he's angled, it's as if his body has been put here . . . as though he was just set down . . . see? His hands aren't natural. I don't think he died here. Hmm . . . hard to tell. His neck is so swollen. I wonder . . . there are scratches on his hands and cheek."

"Don't touch anything! Maybe he's contagious."

"Of course not."

I returned double-quick with Officer Unhelpful Ripple and his female cohort.

Dow introduced herself to Mom, who was standing guard at the closed restroom door. The officers nodded, and then walked inside. Dow reappeared and called for an ambulance, although everyone realized it could just as easily have been a hearse.

We were back in Ripple's office giving statements, again. I think I was in shock, for I didn't remember how I got there or what I said. I sniffled, stated what I had seen, then sniffled again.

Mom took my hand while she spoke. "Officer, I'd like to take my daughter home, now. She's upset."

"Of course," Ripple told Mom, as though he were granting her a great favor. "I'll be in touch."

When we go to the front door, we had to stand aside for Yolanda Toynsbee. The Gazette's owner was a little late. At least she didn't seem to realize we were the ones to find the body.

"I'd rather go for a cup of coffee," I told Mom.

80

She looked critically at me. Brushing back my hair with a comforting hand, she agreed.

Mea Cuppa, Adam's store, was down the block so we walked, leaving my car in the municipal lot.

The weather was pleasantly warm, peaceful. Summer would official start in a couple of weeks, unless people went by the school year and knew it started the second the last bell rang. Leaves had unfurled, and the grass greened up nicely. Why was everything so alive when poor Donald was not?

In the shop three customers were absorbed by books while two older ladies sat at one of the tables enjoying a chat and coffee. Most of the regulars at Tiny's Buffet, kitty corner from Adam, already had their daily dose of gossip and cholesterol and weren't quite ready yet for a fancy cappuccino or book browsing.

Adam and a young lady I didn't recognize were behind the cash register. Adam smiled, then sobered when he saw my face.

Mom took her time checking out the store and, surreptitiously, its owner.

We made our way over.

He closed the cash register. "Hello, Ivy. And you must be Mrs. Preston. How do you do? I'm Adam Thompson. This is Colleen Bailey, my new assistant. Her mother is —"

"We met your mother earlier when she took care of Memnet. The vet, right?" I asked.

Colleen wasn't quite the stunner her mother was. She was more down-to-earth looking, tall, but with a heavier structure than the doctor.

Colleen gave a shy smile, showing crooked front teeth. "Mother mentioned she knew another Mau that was different from Tut. And, did you know — Mr. Thompson, here, has one, too! Isn't that just insane?"

I blinked.

Adam opened his mouth, then closed it again. He took a breath and said, "Colleen is working for me Monday and Wednesday afternoons after swim practice and Saturday mornings when she doesn't have a meet. She's a junior at Memorial High School, and, obviously, loves cats."

I pressed her limp hand.

"Geneva Preston," my mother said. "Ivy's mother, come to visit for a few days."

"Adam . . ." was all I got out before the tears started again.

Bless my mother, who began to chat with Colleen. "I'd like a latte." She drew Colleen away from Adam and me. "Can you show me how it works?"

"Is that OK with you, Mr. Thompson?"

Colleen strode confidently to the machine, set in a corner away from the cash register.

"Sure." Adam touched my shoulder and peered into my face. He led me to his office and closed the door. "What happened?" he asked.

I sat with him on a black leather sofa set against the exposed brick wall. "Someone broke in again a few hours ago and this time managed to steal some of my equipment and tried to hurt Mem." At his steady expression of concern, my tears streamed in earnest. "He's fine. Dr. Bailey checked him over. Then, Mom wanted to see Donald's office after our report to Officer Ri-Ripple. We went up there and we — we found — we saw Donald — de-dead!" I hardly noticed how nice his arms felt around me as I bawled into his shoulder. After I managed to gain control, I took his big white handkerchief, but stayed pressed against him. I hoped he didn't mind, but I was afraid that if I moved away, everything else in my life that I thought was solid would turn out to be vapor.

I felt his breath in my hair. "That must have been awful for you. Can you tell me what happened?"

I sat up and wiped my eyes. "We don't know. Mom said his neck appeared swollen and he had some sores on his hands and face."

"Where did you find him?"

Him — not his body. What a nice man Adam was. "Um, in the men's room near his office."

He never asked what we were doing in the men's room. So very nice.

"The police?"

"Said they'd be in touch."

"I wonder why . . . who . . . how he got there."

I shivered. "Mom thought he hadn't been gone that long, but what if he'd been there all week? And no one knew? We just kept passing by, all the while . . ."

"Maintenance would have said something, Ivy."

Of course. "What'll happen now?"

He got up and walked to his desk, shaking his head. "The one thing we don't want to do is let Donald down, right? We carry on with his dream to bring Apple Grove back to life."

I got up, too, determined to do my part. "And make sure no one gets away with murder in this town."

Adam's eyes widened at my statement, but my indignation fueled my renewed obligation to make sure Donald's plans for Apple

Grove went as he desired. I opened the office door and walked out to find Mom. I took a deep breath and forced a smile. Not much I could do about red eyes.

Adam followed and touched my arm. We stood in each other's warmth, side by side, looking out over his store and acting nonchalant. At least, I tried to. "I'm glad your mother is with you right now."

"Yes. Speaking of whom, can you make it tomorrow evening to eat with us? We're cooking." The last part came out like some kind of special announcement. When Adam and I had our previous rendezvous of casual dinners, we met in public, or had a pizza delivered while we worked putting up shelves and stocking them with books and magazines. He probably didn't even realize I could cook.

"That would be nice," he said.

"See you at 6:30? You close by 6:00, right?"

"Right. And with clean up and tallying, that should work fine. Can I bring something?"

"Not this time," I replied, and walked away before I could read his expression, afraid of what it might reveal. We had a lot to talk about. Maybe the police would know something by then, too.

85

I met my mother halfway to the register, walking with Colleen, whom she had engaged in a conversation about college. And pretty nearly talked into attending Maplewood Community College, where she taught, by the one-sided gist I overheard.

Colleen nodded enthusiastically.

"I'll just talk to your mother some more about it before I head back, how's that?"

Colleen nodded harder, like one of those bobblehead dolls.

"Here we are, Mr. Thompson," Mom plunked her paperback on the counter.

"Call me Adam," he said, while he rang up her order.

"Thank you. And I believe we'll see you soon?"

He inclined his head. "Yes. Ivy invited me for tomorrow."

Colleen watched this whole proceeding, obviously fascinated with the adult nuances.

I pursed my mouth and hurried my mother out of the shop before she gave the rumor mill any more feed.

"What's your hurry?" Mom disliked being hustled.

"I just don't like being gossip fodder."

"There was no one left in there."

"Except for Miss Bailey, who grew up here, and who probably knows everyone in town, and can't wait to tell her mother, who will then tell all of her clients."

"Oh, Ivy. What did he say when you told him about the mayor?"

"Mostly that we need to do all we can to make sure Donald's dream of making Apple Grove a better place to live comes true." I narrowed my sore, weepy eyes. "And make sure that if someone hurt Donald he or she pays." Time to change the subject. "So, what shall we cook for tomorrow?"

Between menu planning, shopping, and calling the insurance company, our day was full. I tried not to dwell on poor Donald, but naturally it was hard not to. What had he been doing in the bathroom anyway, when he was supposed to be out of town? And how did he die? I hoped the police would have the courtesy to tell us. After all, we found him.

Life went on. At least, ours did. Mom disappeared for a little while the next afternoon while I got caught up on some calls. When she returned I didn't think to ask where she'd been as we were busy getting ready for supper. I spruced up the place a bit while she set the table. I hoped Adam would like my simple meal of country ham and, to go with it, a green salad and cantaloupe.

He arrived promptly as the clock chimed

the half hour.

We went through all the cordial formalities of greeting and finding out how we all were. We were fine, and all had a nice day. Whew. I guessed we weren't ready to bring up the other subject yet, which was fine with me.

After dinner Mom managed to turn the conversation toward a full-blown investigation, conspiracy theories and all. She jumped right in with the business of the mayor's death. "Ivy told me about the case. What can you tell me about Donald?"

Adam set his napkin by his empty plate and picked up a china cup, cradling it in his hands. He sipped and stared at the bay candles amongst daisies I arranged as a centerpiece. I could not tell if he mulled or stalled. He seemed to make up his mind when he leaned his elbows on the table to speak to us.

"The Donald Conklin I knew was passionate about this community, and he cared deeply what would happen in Apple Grove unless there was revitalization." Adam put the cup down and favored my mother with a calculating expression. "I'm a businessman, and so is the mayor. As a businessman, I am somewhat cautious. I don't know what he told Ivy to encourage her to pick up everything to move to Apple Grove. Donald told me about the tax grants straight up, and the funding he was able to secure, which was geared toward small town development. It's a sizeable sum of money. Donald, as the grant fund distributor, also unusual in a community with an active town council, had the biggest input as to how the funds would be distributed."

Mom nodded from time to time, absorbing Adam's statements.

I understood about the tax grants, of course, but hadn't made it my business to find out how they affected anyone but me. I was impressed. And chagrined.

Mom cut to the chase. "I think I understand you to say that if someone were to control the mayor's office they would also be able to control a hefty sum of money? And this sum of money is tied up in bonds, I assume, and directed at particular aspects of building and development."

"No. Donald showed me one of the grants. It's a straight-out sum of five million dollars paid to the municipality of Apple Grove, cosigned by the mayor, to be used for advertising and attracting new business to settle inside the city limits of Apple Grove. There are two other similar grants, used for different aspects of attracting business and building housing for the needed work force. A smaller grant, which is a bond, is strictly for additional water and sewer upgrades, to be finished within five years."

"How much does it add up to?" I asked.

"A total of twelve million dollars," Adam said.

"Men have been killed for considerably less," Mom commented. "Who else knows about this?"

Adam studied a spoon, turning it this way and that. "I got the feeling Donald didn't have a lot of . . . trust in people around here. In fact, he mentioned there was opposition to his plan from the council itself. But he was determined to help Apple Grove. And I believe, as a businessman, that his plan was sound. He wasn't rushing headlong into things and had researched the companies and people he wanted to introduce." Adam smiled at me and my lips automatically responded.

Mom cleared her throat.

I shook my head. "How much do you think Margaret knows?"

"That's Mrs. Conklin?" Mom asked.

"Bader-Conklin. Margaret comes from old money," he said. "I hear a lot of things in the shop."

"Maybe she wants more," I muttered. I

told her our impressions and also about Margaret's assistant acting as guard dog the day I went to check on him.

Adam told about our visit to the Conklin house.

I mentioned the news article about Meri-Food, the rival of the company Donald had invited to move to Apple Grove. "And Tut," I said. "Don't forget about him. If Donald had him, then where is he now?"

Mom said, "Spoken like a true cat fancier. I work best on paper. Let's make a chart."

I got the large pad of drawing paper I move from place to place, thinking that someday I might actually learn to sketch. Now that I had a garret . . .

Mem leapt onto my lap, so I could stroke him. I was glad he felt better, but he didn't leave my room at night.

Mom and Adam filled a page with boxes and arrows and time references.

Mom glanced at me at one point. "What do you think?"

I inadvertently peeked up the staircase where my system used to be. There were gouges in the drywall and chips in the wood trim where the thief hadn't been careful with my equipment. I heaved a sigh and went to check out their drawing. They'd made a note of the two attacks on my house.

"Busybody." I wrinkled my nose at Mom. "They're calling me a busybody? Thanks."

"Why would anyone attack you twice?" she asked. "What would they have to gain? Was there anything strange about the messages you took for the mayor's office?"

I stared at the box labeled "Chicago." Something stirred. "You wrote this because . . . ?"

"I overheard Margaret's assistant talking about going there, remember?"

"Yes . . ." I wrinkled my brow.

"What is it?" Mom asked.

"I had a strange call a couple of nights before you got here. A lot of static. I couldn't hear anything, really. Then a hang-up. But the caller ID said Summersby Building, Chicago."

Adam tapped the pen. "Right. You told me about that and that you had notified the police."

Mom asked, "You did? Who did you talk to? What did they say?"

"Ripple. And he said he'd do me a favor and consider it a crank call."

"Hmm." Mom studied the chart again. "Adam, write 'Summersby Building.' We'll do a search and see what comes up. You didn't recognize the voice?"

Had I? "It might have been a man . . . but

I couldn't be sure. I can't replay it for you since my . . ."

They both hmm'd again, absorbed in their task.

The phone rang. Mem sprang down as I stood and reached for it.

"Yeah, swell," Marion Green replied to my standard query. "My boss just died and I'm heartbroken. But other than that . . . I'm mad as a pressure cooker with a leaky gasket. We're gonna get 'em, Ivy, I promise. No one's gonna get by with murder in my town."

"Huh?"

She didn't even pause for a breath. "Listen, you know how Mrs. Conklin has her own office and assistant at city hall? Like she's co-mayor, or something? I've been in her office, as a favor to the mayor, upon occasion."

"Sure, Marion."

"All these years. I can't believe I never studied it closer. Maybe I thought it was fake. Maybe I just didn't care."

"Care about what, Marion?"

Mom and Adam stopped their plotting to stare at me.

"You know how people sometimes put their diplomas and certificates in frames on the walls of their offices?"

"Yeah, so?"

"Mrs. Mayor has one. Fancy wood frame. I just never really read it."

"OK."

"So today I did take a good look at it. What do you think her degree is in?"

"Political intrigue?" I guessed, not a huge fan of word games.

"No. Pharmacology."

"You're kidding! Wow. Mrs. Conklin has a diploma on her office wall that says she has a degree in pharmacology? The study of the effect of drugs and chemicals on living beings?" I recapitulated for Mom and Adam.

They both came close to the phone, as if they could take part in the conversation. Neither of them needed me to define pharmacology. Mom, as a criminology teacher, understood the implications, and Adam, I assumed, was well educated, or at least well read.

"What do you think about that?" Marion asked.

"Oh! Um, what do I think about that?" I repeated, stalling for time while Mom made frantic slice-across-the-neck motions at me. "I guess I have to revise my opinion about good old Mrs. Conklin."

Mom's narrowed eyes and folded arms

94

gave me the feeling she was putting together a plan.

"So, what do you think about it, Marion?" I asked her, ignoring Mom.

"I never thought of her as anything but Mrs. Mayor, you know, giving parties and welcoming important people and going on trips. Of course, I wouldn't have paid much attention to her earlier life, like whether she had a job or not, when I was growing up."

"You mean that you don't believe she worked in her field?" I asked her. This could lead somewhere.

Mom stopped her "cut" signal.

"I'm saying that I just don't know what she did," Marion said, reluctance in her voice.

"You don't know for sure whether or not she was some kind of druggist, or researcher, or held some kind of job like that," I relayed for my listeners.

Adam stroked his chin. Memnet placed a paw on his leg, begging to be picked up. Adam reached for him.

I turned away and took deep breaths at the sight of someone else, a handsome, eligible male in my house, caring for my cat. So long, any vestigial memories of my erstwhile fiancé, Stanley, who had avoided Mem.

"I could ask around," Marion said in the meantime.

I forced my daydreams back into the recesses of my brain, so I could pay attention to the current crisis. "I'm not sure that would be the best approach at this point, Marion." I shook my head when Mom grabbed my elbow, mouthing 'what?' at me. "She just lost her husband. She's got to be pretty upset."

"And that's another thing. No one knows where she is."

"You're kidding. She and her assistant were planning a trip to Chicago."

"She's not at the hotel she booked. You didn't hear this from me, of course. But what about Memnet? Your cat? Wasn't he drugged?"

"Yes, Memnet was drugged." I changed the subject back to Margaret. "What do you mean, no one knows where Margaret is? How would she find out about Donald?"

Marion met my lob and volleyed back. "She's no longer registered at the hotel, and isn't answering her private cell, which has been terminated. Don't you think drugging Memnet took some expertise? Like from a pharmacist?"

Marion was persistent. I got the sense she wasn't too keen on having Mrs. Mayor around, even if the woman had just lost her husband and deserved to be informed.

My thoughts bounced as much as Marion's back to Memnet. A vet would certainly have that information, too. Now I wanted to hang up, so Mom and Adam and I could talk about this. "Thank you, Marion. Can I think about this for a while and call you back? Say, tomorrow morning? Good. It has to be morning because you have to take minutes at the council meeting tomorrow night. They didn't cancel despite Donald's death. Sure. Fine. And, thanks for telling me this. I know. You won't say anything except to Bob for now. Yes, fine. Talk to you tomorrow." Another thought occurred to me. "Oh, wait! Marion? Do you know anything about Summersby Building?"

"Never heard of them. Why don't you search for it on the internet? Or, try the online business directory."

"Thanks, Marion." I hung up and turned back to the sight of Adam and Memnet, envious of the attention my pet received.

Adam held Mem in one arm while he went back to the chart. He bent over the table, adding a note in another box, which he placed between columns headed "businesses being courted by Donald" and "criminal activity." "Margaret. Pharmacology," he wrote.

Mem's tail twitched back and forth, lazily. He was king, receiving his due attention, and he knew it.

I just wished I wasn't jealous. "Margaret hates cats," I said, with some acidity. A memory reasserted itself. "Adam? Do you remember when we went to the Conklins' house? There was a work van parked by Tut's house."

"Yes, I recall. Dark-colored. I didn't catch the advertising."

"Me, either, something about 'peace of mind' or at least, that's what I assumed. I couldn't actually read all the words."

Adam wrote "van" and "peace of mind" on the page.

Mom turned to a clean page and began listing our speculations.

We sat at the table and commented out loud about motives and suspects.

Mem jumped to the floor and went exploring.

When Mom finished writing, we sat back to review our work.

"Donald wanted to revitalize Apple Grove," Adam stated. "He managed to get twelve million dollars to do it."

"But he needed both people and businesses to make it work," I said.

"Some of the townspeople are against the revitalization," Mom said. "Going back through the papers, we know that the city council president, Rupert Murphy, and the city engineer, Georgine Crosby, are opposed."

"In public opinion, at least. I think we can say the newspaper is neutral at this point," I said.

"Marion has access to the grant money?" Mom asked.

"She indicated that she was preparing payments the other day, didn't she, Ivy?" Adam asked.

"It sounded as if she just typed checks for the mayor to sign."

"Hmmm," Mom mused. "All right. How concerned are you about this business plan?"

"I had my lawyer go over it and the plan appeared sound. I had no reason to believe the contract wouldn't be honored."

"Then the mayor reports," Mom said, "that a pet food company and a bioengineering company have indicated interest in locating in or near Apple Grove. Ivy discovers evidence that the mayor's wife is dealing with an unrelated pet food company. The mayor's secretary indicated she felt something odd was going on at the office." Mom glanced up at me. "What has she said to you?"

"Donald left the office without giving his usual instructions and she worried about how his absence would affect the Feli-Mix deal."

Mom nodded. "Going on, then: Ivy — no. Ivy's business was robbed. Would a thief believe you have vital information relating to the funds in your computer system?" Mom asked.

Adam raised an eyebrow in my direction.

I snorted. "I don't know why. Except that I downloaded a few messages for the mayor while the website was under redesign. Mostly just neighbor complaints, and the like. One cancelation of an appointment, lots of vendor calls."

Mom capped the marker with a snap. "OK. That will give us a good start. By the way, darling, can you find places for three students for, say, a week? Near the end of the month?"

"What?" I asked.

"I usually have them do their twenty hours of field work after the classroom time is complete, but this is an emergency. They only have two of the required trimesters finished. I'll have three of my advanced students come to help you out. I've already arranged it with the police department —"

"Aha! So that's where you disappeared to the other day."

"— who graciously agreed to allow job shadowing. We won't mention that they're really here to investigate all the sinister implications."

"Mother! That sounds like the title to some ludicrous mystery novel."

She patted my hand. "So, I assume at least one or two of them could stay with you."

"I have an extra room, too, for a male student." Adam added. His forehead wrinkled. He stood with his arms folded, as if undecided about the whole thing.

"Thank you," Mom said. "In the meantime, perhaps the next best step would be to find out what the city council is aware of. Didn't Marion say a meeting was scheduled tomorrow?"

"What about her offer to ask about Margaret's prior work history?" Adam asked.

Mom twiddled her pen. "Openly questioning people might damage our accountability. Or interfere with the police."

Now she doesn't want to interfere with the police?

"Let's make up an excuse to attend the council meeting," Mom said.

"We're citizens. We don't need an excuse," I said. "Besides it'll probably be so crowded with the news and all. Everyone will want to be there."

Adam laughed, humor apparently restored. "That's the only reason people will go. You know how many citizens attend these meetings just because it's our 'constitutional right'? OK. None." He had a point. "I have a legitimate concern about what will happen to my business if I can't count on public safety, especially after the mayor's suspicious death. If I can get on the agenda."

"You certainly don't want to antagonize anyone," Mom said. "They'll need to call a special meeting sometime later to discuss the mayoral situation."

Adam nodded. "Yes. It'll still be a madhouse, though. I think I can easily get away with asking, as a new business owner, about the future upgrades to the water and sewer systems, and if the fees are going up any time soon."

"That sounds perfect," Mom replied. "We could get a feel for the engineer's responses at the same time."

"So, then," I said, eager to change the subject to a more sociable one. "How about some coffee?"

We retired to my living room with the cocoa brown leather sofa and two tan leather wing chairs I had splurged on when I moved to Apple Grove. The old set from my grandparents had done its duty. I always wanted a room with quiet, moss-green walls and an oak chair rail. I ignored the line of spackled nail holes just under the railing on the short wall where I had measured wrong. Besides, if I didn't point it out, no one would know it was there.

Mom and Adam and I talked about the state of the federal government and gas prices and the weather.

When he was ready to leave, I walked him out to his car.

He leaned against the driver's side door, key in hand. "Thank you, Ivy, for tonight. I enjoyed talking to your mother, even if the conversation could have been about a more pleasant subject. She's certainly methodical. You're all right with her plan?"

I was touched. Stanley would not have strung so many words together at one time. I took a step toward Adam. "Yes. It seems harmless. Adam — do you think you'll stay here, now that Donald is gone?"

Adam thrust the keys in his pocket and reached for my shoulders. I stepped willingly into his embrace. It felt like home.

"Donald wasn't the main reason I came."

"I am glad he introduced us," I said into his collar. Adam gave me a little squeeze and let go. It felt like a promise, not a brush off.

"So am I." His smile lingered. "In a way that makes me feel responsible for you and your safety. Hopefully we'll get some insight into who understood what Donald was trying to do here — who had his back and who had it in for him." He let me go and opened the car door. "I'll pick you up at quarter to seven tomorrow night."

6

The next day I spent haggling with my insurance representative regarding the robbery.

After supper, Mom told me that she would not attend the meeting.

"I don't want the council to think we're ganging up on them," she said. "And I want to pick your brains about your impressions of the council members and audience when you return."

I spent fifteen minutes, a record stretch of time for me, trying to decide what to wear that evening. I opted for nice gray slacks — I managed to stay size ten, even though my job required I sit a lot — and a soft peachy blouse; even a necklace.

Mom gave me the once-over, a speculative gleam in her eyes, but refrained from commenting.

I wondered if I would feel different, meeting Adam tonight after that hug he left me with last night. I had been awake longer than normal afterward, ready to test the romance waters again, but not sure how to go about it.

When Adam came, I went out to him. He wore a leather vest over a white shirt and black jeans. A scarf at his neck hid much of the scarring, but I could see where the raised and mottled flesh curved along his arm under the rolled-up sleeves.

Mom never brought up the subject of his burns. She was pretty good at deciding what was her business, and sometimes, what wasn't. By the way she spoke to him last night, and worked on the chart with him, I could tell she trusted him.

I trusted her. And those instincts helped me feel comfortable now in his presence. "How was the shop today? Colleen seemed like a quick learner," I said, as we drove the few blocks to city hall.

"She wasn't in today," Adam reminded me. "But you're right, I think she'll do fine. Have you been in touch with the insurance agent about replacing your equipment?"

I spent a couple of hours that morning at the police station faxing copies of the report to my company. I had filed a claim after the electrical storm a few months ago. They had covered half the replacement value of my machines. I could have hit the off button on the surge protector, I knew that, so the accident was half my fault. Robbery was not my fault, and after two hours, e-mailing photographs, and having Officer Ripple speak to him at one point, the agent said he would call for a second estimate on replacement value and make sure I had a check or a store credit at the nearest electronics outlet by Monday. "We finally made a deal," I told Adam. "I should be up and running again on Monday."

"In the meantime, what will happen? You've got open cases, I assume."

His thoughtfulness made me want to place my head on his shoulder and lay claim. "I've got my personal phone and answering machine. I can use a computer at the library to access my website and e-mail. It's not a tragedy. The mayor's office had been my most pressing need, but now . . ."

"You're welcome to use my office at the store," Adam offered.

I was grateful. "Thank you. I'll think about it."

He whistled low at the amount of traffic when we got close to city hall. "Do you mind a walk?" He found a spot two blocks away and parked. As we closed our doors and met on the sidewalk, he asked, "All set?

Do you plan to speak?"

"No. They won't have room for everyone. This is wild." I followed him into the building to the council chamber on the first floor.

Standing room only, like a rock concert or ball game, only in a 1970s-style cement block and fake paneling, plastic yellow curtain-kind of way. An inadequate few rows of tan folding chairs had been set up in front of curving tables outfitted with microphones and cups of water for the council members representing the four city wards. Other city officials were there to report, as well. Name plaques rested in front of each place. I nodded at Yolanda, who was apparently representing the newspaper. She smiled briefly, then resumed her professional, detached expression and fidgeted with a recorder and a notepad.

Adam picked up a copy of the agenda at the door and we noted when the public would be allowed to speak. "At the end, there," he pointed out.

"Good. Then we'll be able to hear the city engineer's report first," I whispered against the quiet murmur of the crowd.

Council members settled in.

I wrinkled my nose. What was that smell? Was somebody grilling burgers in the corner? I wouldn't have been surprised. I waved at Marion, who sat next to Donald's empty seat.

Rupert Murphy called the meeting to order precisely at 7:00 and led the pledge of allegiance and a moment of silence in honor of our dearly departed elected official, Mayor Donald Conklin.

Marion called the roll.

Then the circus began.

The overhead shine reflected in whatever goo Murphy used to slick his black hair. "I call the meeting to order. The first item on the agenda," he said in his nasal monotone.

"Say, Rupert, why doncha cut to the chase and tell us what in tarnation's going on around here? Who's the new mayor gonna be?"

He jerked his head up at the interruption.

I couldn't make out the questioner.

Murphy frowned as though he hadn't expected that one. His mouth twitched. He held a hand over the mic as the council member next to him, Jeff Hanley, leaned over and whispered.

"The special meeting to discuss the replacement for Mayor Conklin will be held on . . ."

Marion spoke up. "July first."

"Why so long?"

I still couldn't see who spoke, but I agreed.

So did the crowd.

Murphy had a hard time making himself heard. "We have to go over the constitution and bylaws with the city lawyers. We've never had this kind of thing happen before, and we want to get our ducks in a row. Tonight's meeting . . ."

More "aws," "boos," "shushes," and "gwan's" squelched Murphy's rehearsed speech.

Another voice boomed above the crowd, one that I recognized.

Yolanda in full reporter mode. "Can you answer just one question?"

Murphy looked at her with an expression that clearly said, *No, I don't want to.*

Yolanda stood, pen poised. "Why did you sign a work order telling maintenance not to clean on the fourth floor last week?"

Murphy paled to nearly the color of his dress shirt, a stark contrast with the nondescript, standard dark suit — public official male dress code. "No questions at this time."

The crowd took a collective breath before voicing its cumulative displeasure.

Adam squeezed my arm gently and took a slightly more protective stance.

Officer Ripple's boss, Chief Gene Hackman, no kidding, stood up at that point.

"People! This is the regular monthly meeting of the Apple Grove City Council. I understand you have questions. President Murphy told you they'd be answered in a few days. If you cannot control yourselves, I will have to call in some of my officers to help you out of the room. Do you want that?"

"So, you're saying nothing about Conklin tonight?" someone asked.

"No," Murphy said. "Just regular business. And our deepest condolences to the family."

"How can you conduct business without the mayor?"

I had wondered that myself, until Adam whispered in my ear a reminder that the mayor reports to city council.

About a third of the crowd pushed out the door after that.

Adam stood in front of me and took most of the jostling.

Murphy called a recess until those people left.

We scrambled for vacated seats just before the real meeting began.

Chief Hackman reported on public safety. My robbery was duly noted. All eyes in the crowd were on me for that moment. I folded my arms and stared right at Murphy.

The representative for Public Utilities reported on water flow, sewage treatment, roadways, and upcoming snowplow season projections.

I yawned through my nose to appear polite and not breathe in any more body or spoiled grease smell, and re-crossed my legs.

Finally, public comments were next.

I admired Adam who sat, apparently serenely, through the whole thing, while I struggled to sit still.

"Audience comments. Please keep it brief," Murphy called, with an eye on the clock. "Come to the microphone in the aisle, there, state your name and address first," he instructed. He gave the collected group a raised-brow glance, as if threatening to cut off the first person who spoke past thirty seconds.

A heavy-set man dressed for a morning behind a deli counter, and the proud owner of the rancid oil odor I noted as he brushed past me, ambled across the industrial blue carpet to the microphone. "Tiny Alnord, one-oh-one Lombardy Lane. I wanna know what you're doing, lettin' in all kinds of competition for us little guys. What did I ever do to deserve this?"

"What're you talking about, Tiny?" Murphy asked.

112

No wonder he smelled like — I blinked when Granger turned to point a beefy paw in our direction. "Him. Been taking my business left and right."

"Tiny, you own the buffet. Since when did you start selling books?"

"Ain't books. Coffee. Mister highfalutin' over there's been stealing my coffee customers."

A couple of guffaws issued from the head table. "Is that what you call it, Tiny?" Council member Jeff Hanley spoke up.

"Time we had something we could recognize as coffee in this town," Hanley's neighbor, Stewart, said.

Murphy slapped his gavel once. The remaining audience members had been recruited by Tiny, apparently, as a perturbed-sounding buzz of underlying comments about strangers and expensive coffee and a general shuffling started up.

"How can he say that?" I heard someone whisper loudly from behind me.

"So, what're you gonna do?" Tiny asked. "He's using up more water, and that'll make the price of everything go up, or our antiquitated system break down. I can't afford —"

"Antiquated. Tiny, I never saw so many people downtown as I did last week, come

113

to shop and check out a new store," Murphy said. "I had to wait to get a seat at your diner."

I received the benefit of his attention next.

"Well, then." Tiny pointed, "Her. Used to be a body didn't need any fancy messenger. You just came in and pretty soon everybody knew what was going on. Who needed work, who had to shut down a day and what for, when —"

"Don't be ridiculous." Murphy rapped the gavel.

I sat up straight.

Adam touched my arm.

"Next," Murphy called.

Tiny shuffled away, but not far enough. By sheer will I ordered my nostrils not to dilate.

The audience rustled and muttered, but no one got up to defend Tiny.

No free coffee tomorrow at the buffet, I'd bet.

Yolanda had not bothered to make notes about Tiny's complaint.

Marion adjusted her tape recorder.

Adam walked to the microphone.

"Mr. Thompson, welcome," Murphy said first.

"Adam Truegood Thompson, one-eleven Main." He spoke in a friendly voice. "Thank

114

you." He turned to Tiny. "Mr. Alnord, I certainly don't want any bad blood between us. In fact, my question tonight deals with the aging water and sewer plant in Apple Grove."

Yolanda tightened the grip on her pen.

Adam faced the council. "I understand that Mayor Conklin, God rest his soul, went to considerable effort to secure a grant to update the municipal services. The fact that the mayor was willing to go to such lengths for his city is one of the reasons I decided to branch out from the Chicago suburbs. I just wondered when the updates to the system would begin."

I counted four council members who stared at their microphones, including Hanley, who was the chairman of the sewage commission under the auspices of the Public Utilities Committee.

The murmur from the crowd rose.

Murphy pounded the gavel. "Mr. Thompson, where did you come by this privileged, confidential, and unconfirmed information?"

"From Mayor Conklin himself. Three months ago, when we sat down to draw up a business agreement with the tax credits he offered, also by way of grant." Adam stood at the microphone, calm.

"I told them." Georgine Crosby twisted in her seat to fix Murphy with a laser glare, "It would be foolish to upgrade when we need a whole new plant. And that will raise taxes. That's why I voted no. And so did you."

"I understood the mayor said you were given five years to complete the work," Adam added helpfully.

"From when? Rupert Murphy, I demand an explanation!" Crosby's face seemed to swell. Two bright red patches appeared on her cheeks.

Three elderly audience members stood up.

"What do you mean, raise my taxes? I can't afford no more," a white-haired gentleman called out.

"Now wait just a minute!" Tiny was on his feet again, raging in odoriferous glory toward the council table. "Tax credits! To strangers! You gotta be kiddin'. How'd Donald get money for the sewer and not for us who live here?" He halted near Yolanda. "You better be putting this in the paper, Yolanda!"

Marion's eyes grew huge, her mouth gaping in surprise. Mayhem on the Apple Grove city council apparently was a rarity.

Six people left the room, shaking their heads. The phones would be busy tonight as people passed on the news. Other audience members advanced on the head table, demanding information. Hackman got up and demanded the people keep back. The noise of the gavel grew fainter under the volume of shouting that erupted.

Murphy yelled, "The tax credits are for the taxpayers, you idiot!"

Adam threaded his way back and grabbed my arm. "I think we have our answer." He hustled us out of the room as Yolanda's camera flashed.

We made it out to the parking lot before I started giggling. "Who knew a dozen old folks could make such a racket? It's like an attack scene from the movies, or something," I managed to get out. "Aren't you glad we moved to Apple Grove?"

He pulled me into his arms. "I sure am." He held back to look at me, sober in an instant. "It's hard to imagine any of those folks would have killed the mayor, no matter how much they want to keep Apple Grove the same."

"How did someone like Donald end up here? With his business acumen and talent, he could have settled anywhere in the world. And married to someone like Margaret . . ." I shuddered. "I find that the hardest thing to believe."

"Twelve million dollars is a lot of money.

You saw as well as I did that at least four people on the council besides Murphy thought something was going on. I wonder about the city engineer," Adam said, as he released his hold, escorted me to his truck, and opened the door.

"Thompson!" A gruff male voice spoke from the shadow of the building not touched by the streetlight.

I stood close to Adam, who took a casual step back with me, placing us behind the car door.

"Yes? Who's there?"

"Someone who's got his eye on you and your girlfriend, there. This is just a friendly warning. Don't get mixed up in things that don't concern you. In fact, the both of you should pack up and leave Apple Grove. The Conklins don't need your interference."

"We don't believe you," I shouted, foolishly brave, clutching my big, strong Adam by the shirt front. "What if we don't want to leave?"

Smarter than I, Adam gripped my elbow and encouraged me to duck into the passenger seat. He moved quickly to get into the driver's side and start the engine. He pulled away from the curb.

I held my breath, waiting for a reprimand. When none came, I stared at him.

His mouth quirked. "The Conklins?" he said. "All of them? I think this has gone on long enough. Something about that van at their house still bothers me. Remember — when we went to visit? You recall it was backed right up against the little building Donald had for Tut?"

I nodded, sad about Tut and poor Donald. With the mayor dead and his wife out of town, what had happened to his cat? He deserved to be cared for. But how did a van fit in? "You think Tut might be there, forgotten?"

"Or stolen. It's time to go back there and check it out."

I closed my eyes and nodded. "Maus aren't that valuable, are they?"

"Not just any Mau," he said. "Donald's Mau. You told me Margaret didn't answer you when you asked if you could care for him, and then Letty said there was no cat there."

"I hope we're not the only ones worried about him."

7

The gates to the Conklin property stood ajar, casting eerie shadows on the lawn from the flickering jets at the top of the posts on either side. They weren't inviting. Moonlight wavered as clouds passed.

I glanced at Adam in apprehension.

He only nodded. "I have a small flash-light," he said, as if testing my resolve.

"Good."

He turned off the headlights and drove into the circular drive, stopping behind the miniature Egyptian temple I assumed was Tut's. Adam turned the interior light switch to "off" before we opened the doors. Good move. I was impressed. We opened our doors quietly but didn't close them all the way to avoid the click. He grabbed my hand and we tiptoed around to the door of temple. It was locked.

Adam shone his light into one of the four windows, which didn't open, either. "I don't see anything moving," he whispered.

"Like a cat?"

"No. I think . . . there's Tut's bed."

"We just have to get in. What if he's been left in there, and no one's come to take care of him?"

Adam handed me the flash. "There really shouldn't be any reason for Donald to lock this door," he muttered, and studied the lock. With a glance in my direction, he reached in his hip pocket and pulled out a card. In about two minutes, he had the lock jimmied.

I didn't ask any questions but followed him inside.

The air was fetid, but not as bad as Tiny's aroma. I immediately put a hand across my nose, breathing shallowly until I adapted.

Adam hesitated by the door, sweeping his light across the place. The large litter area Donald kept for Tut was clean.

I hoped and prayed the odor wasn't anything . . . serious. I heard a rustle and squeak and jumped. My hand brushed the wall and I accidentally activated a switch.

The central chandelier glowed down into a room decked out like an exhibit I had once seen recreated in a museum. Scratching-post pillars lined the walls. A sleeping couch and miniature bench low to the ground held Tut's feeding and water bowls, where Adam now stood.

He gave a low whistle.

I followed with a lame "wow" and didn't bother to shut off the light. The damage had been done. Surely if anyone else was around the Conklin place, they'd have heard us by now. I ran my fingers along a smooth gold-painted plaster cast of a cat, one of a pair flanking the door, each with a paw reaching up and forward. Along a glass-enclosed wall were framed awards and pictures. Another wall held shelving for his scrapbooks which had been tossed willy nilly onto the floor.

I picked up one that had fallen open to a clipping with only vague information about Adam's accident and how much Isis helped in his healing. The clipping was undated, which accounted for why Margaret would have thought Adam had a little girl who liked to play with kitties. I set the album down.

There was no evidence of the cat in residence. What had happened to Tut?

Adam ran his hand over a number of decorative collars hanging on a hook near a column. "These are pretty fancy."

I recognized one from last year's CAT convention and picked it up. "Tut wore this last year."

He took it from me. "These can't be real stones."

"Diamonds? I don't think so." But I looked again, puzzled. The settings were quite sturdy for a run-of-the-mill pet collar. The whole thing was heavy, come to think of it. "Um . . . well, now you've made me wonder." I checked out the others. Nothing else seemed unusual. Except for the one with the hidden pocket on the inside. I held it up. "What would anyone put in here?"

"Change. Keys, I suppose," he replied. He seemed edgy, and I followed him to the door. "Let's go back to your place."

I flipped the light switch and locked the door, taking a moment to savor a grin at Adam's expense. I wondered what other tricks he had in his repertoire of petty criminal activity we could call upon.

He shrugged, then drove us home.

The first thing I told Mom about was the mysterious warning we received after the meeting. I shivered.

"I want to hear all about it, but first," Mom closed the door behind us. "I'll get us something to drink. Adam? Can you stay for a little while?"

"I'll get it," I said, when he agreed. I bustled to make lemonade while Mom ushered him into the living room.

"And he threatened you," Mom was saying as I brought a tray out. She picked up a glass.

I sat next to Adam.

"The coward didn't bother to show himself," I said, restraining the "hmpf" that begged to follow.

"Do you want to involve the police?" Mom asked.

"No. We weren't assaulted, and we have no evidence."

"So, how was the meeting?" Mom asked, abruptly changing the subject. Or was she?

I told her how Murphy and Hackman shut down the questions. "The leftover crowd at the meeting seemed to be mostly Tiny Alnord's buddies from the buffet. They thought Adam shouldn't be allowed to use up all the water and clog the old sewer pipes downtown."

She grinned. "Bookstores are known for that, aren't they?"

Adam toasted her with his glass of lemonade, grinning back.

"I can't wait to read what Yolanda writes in the paper," I said. "She didn't make a big deal about Tiny's complaints, but I saw her taking pictures after the crowd went wild."

"Did you get a look at the reactions of the council members?" Mom asked.

"Four of them stared at their microphones and the others appeared surprised when they found out Adam knew Donald raised money to fix the sewer and water system," I said. "Mr. Stewart, the chairman of Public Utilities, and his friend Hanley acted as if they knew about how the money was supposed to be used. In fact, Hanley even seemed as though he enjoyed the fact that Georgine Crosby was opposed."

"Why do you think the mayor didn't listen to the engineer's report about needing a new sewage treatment plant instead of upgrading the old one?" Mom asked.

"I don't know." Adam shrugged. "He only mentioned that there was some confusion and misinterpretation of the facts."

"Facts like how much money was available for what kinds of projects?" Mom asked.

"It depends on who saw what reports." I frowned, thinking out loud. "And under what circumstances. If someone just happened onto a piece of a paper without knowing everything, it would be easy to jump to the wrong conclusions."

"OK. Wouldn't the mayor have sat down with the council and explained everything?" Mom kneaded her eyebrows between thumb and forefinger.

"One would think," Adam said. "Remember, they're good people, but have they ever been involved in a project of this magnitude? It isn't easy to understand how everything works when you don't have the experience."

Mom sighed. "So, there may have been opportunity to find out about the money that the mayor wouldn't have divulged directly." She unfolded the chart she'd placed on the coffee table and made a few notes. "Perhaps we can contact the council members and talk to them next week about how they thought grants were to be administered. We'll add another dimension to our 'unknown' person or persons, due to the threat you received tonight. Are you sure you're both all right?"

"Yes, thank you, Mom."

"I'm getting tired." Mom stood. "I think I'll call it a night. I plan to stay through the weekend. Shall I see you again, Adam? Did anyone say when the mayor's funeral would be held?"

Adam stood and squeezed her hand. "We didn't hear. I suppose once Margaret is found, she'll take care of it. It was nice seeing you again. Good night."

Very transparent, Mother. "Good night." I waved her off down the hall. I did not get up, hoping Adam would get the hint and

126

stay. After a moment, he sat again.

Memnet appeared from behind the couch and jumped on the cushion next to him, circling.

"Ah, there you are, pet," I said. "He hasn't decided if he likes leather."

He cautiously approached. Mem held a polite paw over Adam's leg, as if asking before he climbed up. We laughed at his antics and Adam stroked Mem's back while the cat settled in. Not content with Adam's lap, Mem slowly inched his way up Adam's chest, hunched over the vest. He batted lazily at the tied ends of the scarf, pulling it away from Adam's neck. Adam reached out to stop him.

I jumped up and grabbed Memnet. "Mem! Stop!" I scolded. Mem thrust himself out of my grip and crawled back behind the couch. "I'm sorry. I don't understand why he did that," I said.

"That's all right." He pulled the scarf from around his neck and stuffed it in a pocket. "You've been quite polite about it. Most folks can't even stand to look."

I stood still, unsure what to do next.

He patted the cushion beside him on the sofa. "I don't know what Donald told you about me."

I sat where Adam indicated. "Nothing.

127

Donald never talked to me about you. He simply introduced us."

Adam nodded. "That sounds like him. Gossip wasn't his style."

I watched him swallow, the raised skin on the side of his neck taut. I reached my hand toward him, stopping just sort of contact. "Does it hurt?" I let my hand fall to my lap.

"In certain places I'm somewhat sensitive to cold and heat," he said. "The doctors said that would probably always stay that way, and I should be glad to feel anything at all."

"I heard you tell a customer that you'd had an accident six years ago."

"It wasn't me. At least, I wasn't in the accident. I was at work and received a frantic call from my daughter, Elise. My wife's car went off the road, rammed against a utility pole and turned on its side. Elise was in the car. Her door was blocked by the downed pole and power lines and her mother was unconscious."

My blood congealed in my veins when he said "daughter." I could almost guess what he was about to say, and hot tears welled behind my eyelids.

He watched me a moment, then, averting his gaze, took a deep breath. He spoke quickly. "I called the police right away and

128

then of course drove over there as fast as I could. Sparks were flying everywhere from severed wires. I saw Elise slumped against the window. She wasn't moving. The sharp smell of burning rubber and gasoline was something I'll never get out of my head. The smoke was thick. At first I couldn't see flames."

He closed his eyes. "I think I still hear my daughter scream sometimes, in my dreams. I don't think she was conscious, maybe not even — alive — at that point. I don't think I even turned off my truck, just opened the door and jumped out, trying to reach them. Janet's car was so hot. I used my shoulder to try to force the back of the car forward, to right it so that I could get to the door. The rescue workers who arrived first needed to knock me out." He swallowed. "Later, they said Janet, my wife, never woke up. Elise had just turned thirteen."

My lips trembled. Air whooshed from my lungs, but I was afraid to take a fresh breath in case I choked.

"I needed skin grafts on my arm, chest, and neck where the skin burned on contact with the car. I was in the hospital for two months. My sister, Marie, came to help manage the stores. We ran three of them then. At first, when I came home after the hospital, I was so numb I couldn't care about anything. A friend brought me a cat. Isis." Adam reached to take a sip of cold coffee. He leaned his elbows on his knees. "After I was able to start getting out, I took Isis with me a lot. She received so many compliments. Anyway, people kept asking about her until I researched Maus. A couple of years ago I started attending the conventions." He looked at my damp cheeks. "I noticed you, almost right away. I saw you talking to Donald." Adam leaned toward me, carefully cupping my face in his large hands. He wiped at the tears with his thumbs. "I made it my business to get acquainted with Donald, so I could eventually wangle an introduction to you. You're so pretty. So good with your cat. The first to open doors for someone or help them with their bags."

"I'm so sorry about your . . . your . . ." I whispered, choking up. My gaze dropped to his lips and he obligingly kissed me.

"Thank you," he said. "For crying for us. I'll never forget them, but I'm able to move on at last. Coming here has been good for me."

"To get away from the memories?"

He shook his head and kissed me again, his lips tender and determined at the same time. I closed my eyes while my pulse fluttered and tingled all the way through my stomach to my toes.

"They're always with me," he whispered, his breath warm against my face. I didn't open my eyes. He nibbled at my upper lip as he spoke. "But starting new, I mean. To get to know you when we're on equally unfamiliar turf."

I turned to the side to catch my breath and answer him. "Ah. No unfair advantages."

"Mmm." He pulled me close to his chest and simply held me. "I guess I should confess that while Donald may not have gossiped about me, he did drop one little factlet about you."

I snorted a little in exasperation. "I can't imagine. There are so many to choose from." I felt his heartbeat under my ear and took a deep breath, reveling in his scent, a mix of skin-warmed leather and the tension of old memories. Stanley had always smelled like the inside of a used car.

"When I casually asked if he knew if you were, um, involved with anyone, he mentioned that you told him you'd been engaged once."

" 'Once' being the operative word." I did not want to talk about Stanley. Conversations about my former fiancé wasted the time I had with Adam. I heaved a sigh. Uncharitable thoughts came and went. "I dated a guy I thought I would marry. For five years. When we finally set a wedding date for last Christmas, made the arrangements, ordered my dress, and sent the invitations, he backed out. Changed his mind about getting married. I guess thinking you're a potential divorcee is better contemplated beforehand. I hate Christmas."

I could not look at him. After his story, mine seemed so petty. "A few months after I got my share of the down payment for the wedding money back, I jumped at Donald's invitation to start over in this pleasant little community of Apple Grove, where the people are so warm and friendly, and the crime rate is practically non-existent."

Donald. He had made such a big difference in our lives. Now I pulled back, forgetting my tears, to face Adam. "What can we do about Donald and Tut?"

His jaw muscle clenched and released. "I don't know. After the warning we received tonight, someone apparently thinks we're doing too much already. Trust the police, I guess. Do you think your mother's students will figure anything out?"

"They've had some training. To do field work, they have to have taken several courses already. And a fresh look at the situation won't hurt. People who are close to a situation tend to overlook the obvious."

"I agree." He stood, holding my hand and pulling me up. "I'd better go."

We walked toward the back door, Adam's arm across my shoulder. Once there, we stopped. He drew me close to kiss again, a more lingering promise this time. Although there should be a wedding in there somewhere, I preferred to jump ahead and mentally pictured us, an old married couple, enjoying coffee and the paper together at the kitchen table. Something bothered me. "Adam?"

"Yes?"

"You said earlier that you felt responsible for me."

"You're uncomfortable with that," he stated, pulling away.

I touched his jaw to turn his face toward me. "I've always needed to be independent. I guess it has something to do with my mom being widowed so early in life. Even with Stanley, I never felt that I could just . . . give myself up. Maybe that was really the issue all along, and he realized it."

"I'd never ask you to be an extension of

me," he said firmly. "But a relationship does need a sense of trust between the parties involved."

"You want a relationship?"

"Is it too soon for you, after your break up?" His eyes reflected sympathy. "I've waited this long. I'm not going anywhere."

I should ask for that in writing. "It's not too soon," I said. "Breaking up is different, I think, than the way you lost your family. Not as horrible, certainly." I shivered, and Adam rubbed my arms. "I feel unworthy," I mumbled against his shoulder.

"Unworthy of what?"

"Of anyone like you," I told him. "Anyone as won—"

His kiss almost made me cry again. "Shh. I'm the blessed one, here." He cradled me for a couple of minutes, then let me go. "Try to get some sleep. I'll see you tomorrow."

News of business grants, tax grants and an upgraded wastewater treatment plant flashed around Apple Grove, ground into a hybrid fertilizer of gossip and innuendo, and spread liberally around the community. Bob Green was in a prime position as a central hub of information. He heard all kinds of tales from his position between a customer in the barber's chair to the rest of the men

134

waiting a turn to be clipped and shorn.

Marion called me at noon with an update on the collective confusion of Apple Grove citizens, gleaned directly from her husband. "Bob told me when he came home for lunch that he'd never have believed my version of last night's meeting compared to the stories buzzing around now," Marion said.

"What'll happen when the newspaper comes out?" I wondered out loud.

"That depends on the slant Yolanda gives it, doesn't it?"

I glanced at my personal answering machine. The indicator flashed a number four, all calls from curiosity seekers, one distinctly unfriendly and attempted anonymous. That caller must have forgotten about caller ID. Trouble was, anyone could have used Tiny's telephone at the buffet to call my house, threatening to ruin my reputation by exposing me as an extortionist who took personal information and then used it for blackmail.

The anonymous caller claimed he had proof that I had done this in the past. I had never done anything of the sort, of course, but I wondered what "proof" the caller had.

I kept a tape recording of the call and the time it was made but had only the source of the almost public location the caller used. I doubted it would be admissible in court should I need to defend myself the next time I was robbed or threatened. I groaned. Like threatening behavior was becoming a regularly expected occurrence. "So, what are some of the best rumors?" I asked Marion. "I'd better be ready to answer questions."

"They appear to be based on three recurring themes. One is that you, um — sorry — compromised the mayor somehow to get your business set up in Apple Grove. Which is laughable, at best. The second theme is that the mayor scrambled the city books to make it appear as if he'd either had a windfall, or he's been cheating the people long enough to really have a windfall of cash. That's not too popular, because most people liked Donald. Lastly, that you're all criminals involved in some high-stakes money laundering scheme. They like that one."

" 'You all' I assume refers to me and Adam Thompson?"

I could practically hear her squirm over the phone.

"Ivy, we were at that meeting last night. Of course, you're not involved in any kind of crime ring." She didn't have to voice the hesitant "are you?" She had not known us that long.

"A lot of people have been calling city hall. Margaret's gone. She's checked out of the Chicago hotel where she said she'd be. And there's no answer at her house or her mobile phone. She's pulled the disappearing act plenty of times before, but not without Donald making excuses for her. No one knows what to do about the funeral now that the body's been released to the morgue. Rupert Murphy and Georgine Crosby are working together to find out what's going on and both of them are hopping mad. In fact, I have to go now. Rupert says he's my temporary boss and that I should report to work this afternoon."

I was not sure what to make of our two "number two" suspects working together. I had wanted to take Crosby's name off the list after the last council meeting when she obviously had no clue what Donald had been up to. But I wavered. Maybe she and Murphy were just trying to keep an eye on each other.

But, first: "Body released? That sounds cold, Marion. What can you tell me about how he died?"

"I didn't quite catch it," she said. "Something about infections. He was sick."

Oh, no . . . "Nothing contagious, I hope?" My voice squeaked.

"Nah . . . they didn't say that." Her voice was way too cheery.

"You'll call if you hear anything for sure?"

"Of course."

We hung up. Marion's news of the police report relieved me, despite her inability to put a definitive period on the cause of Donald's demise. If no one seemed alarmed that he was carrying the plague, or something, then I shouldn't be, either. Could his death just be some accident?

I didn't like the indignity of Donald getting sick and dying in the men's room. There were just too many problems to believe that — starting with Mom's theory that his body had been moved. And what was that about Murphy signing a "do not clean" order? He moved back up a notch on the suspect list.

I thought of Summersby Building again and wondered if there might be some kind of connection. Perhaps I would casually call the Happy Hearts people in Madison, see if anyone there could say when the move was taking place. Maybe Donald had taken Tut with him, and someone might remember if Donald said anything about taking his cat somewhere else.

Yolanda might want to do a profile on the company for the paper. I could certainly help her with some groundwork. I grinned. Mom would be proud when she heard my latest strategy.

That afternoon when Mom and I stopped in at the library, so I could read through my e-mails, I got the silent treatment from a couple of patrons.

Nancy, who worked behind the counter three afternoons a week, gave me a stern shush before I even said a word.

I was not responsible for raising the taxes or the crime rate in Apple Grove, but it would take work to make them believe that. I felt the fragile friendliness I had worked hard to build in Apple Grove melting. I was not taking anything away from anyone by accepting money that had not been in the city coffers to begin with. Try explaining that in light of the allegations of being a mafia maven.

I signed in to use the internet. Of my business e-mails, one client's term of service expired without his renewal and another one whose website design I had started canceled the second week into his contract, writing that he didn't believe he owed me anything since I could not perform the agreed-upon service because he heard my equipment was out of order.

My equipment was not out of order,

exactly, but suing people for nonpayment was not good business, either.

Only Gina, the high school girl, sent me a note saying she was sorry to hear I had been robbed, and who did I think was responsible and was Memnet all right? She would be happy to take care of Memnet, if I ever needed her. It would be something different than racing after human brats.

I chuckled quietly and typed a quick e-mail back that, yes, we were fine and thanked her for her concern.

When I shut down my inbox, I motioned Mom to come close so that we could check directories for a building company in Chicago called "Summersby." It didn't take long to go through the yellow pages.

"Here!" Mom pointed to the screen. "Got your pen?" she asked in a whisper.

I peeked at the clock, which showed our internet time was nearly up. "Ready. Read it to me."

"Summersby. The only hit I got was the name of a place. The Summersby Building." She rattled off a long string of numbers and names. It was in Chicago. We eyeballed each other. "Do you have time to find the neighborhood on a city map?"

We quickly pulled up a popular map site and plugged in the coordinates. The computer desk guard began to saunter in our direction. "Hurry!"

Mom's fingers flew over the keyboard and we mentally willed the picture to come up quickly on the screen. She hit "print" and we closed the windows.

When we got home I sighed when I saw one more message had been left on my answering machine. I played it anyway. Twice. And was glad I did. Mom and I shared a little jig of joy at welcome news from Marion. Not only had Margaret worked in her chosen career field of pharmacy, she also worked for MerriFoods, a company in which her family owned a large financial stake, according to Bob's aunt.

Mom filled in more information on her chart.

On the last morning of Mom's visit, we attended church where Pastor Belman Gaines preached on the kindness of strangers. "Be careful to be generous to everyone. You never know when you'll entertain angels and not be aware of it."

Right now, the nearest angels in my life were Marion and Bob Green, besides Adam. Bob made a point to be loudly friendly to Adam, who I was glad to see had come to church and squeezed in next to us just as the opening hymn began.

Mom and I stood around the hall with other lingerers after the service.

"You got my message?" Marion asked in a whisper shortly before we left.

"Did I ever! No time wasted on ferreting out that little bit of information, Marion. How on earth did you get anyone to talk about Margaret?"

"With everyone being so upset at Mrs. Conklin's absence during this time of disillusionment, the good folks were ready to complain long and loud. All I did was wonder out loud about what kind of connections Donald and Margaret had to get their hands on that kind of money."

"You were at the buffet?"

"Yeah. Everyone's always known Margaret's family was loaded. Seems her grandfather got his start in the pet food industry and in fact, was a founding partner of MerriFood."

"I thought Margaret was allergic to animals," I said, glancing around to make sure no one was paying undue attention to us. "So why would she want to work with them?"

Marion shrugged. "Maybe she just doesn't like anything that takes attention away from her. Tut was unusual. But she probably went to MerriFood because of her granddad. She was a researcher on the chemical side. Maybe she didn't have to touch them. Who knows?"

"Well, thanks. And thank you for your support today."

"People get the strangest ideas, don't they? Who in their right mind would think you or Adam could kill anyone?" Marion laughed and sauntered off toward her family.

Incredulous, I shook my head as Mom and Adam joined me. After noting his somber expression, I decided not to repeat Marion's last comment, which was a new twist on the whole rumor thing. I wondered who started that one and hated to think that Mom might be on to something, putting Marion's name on the suspect list. A rumor was like dandelion seeds floating on the breeze into people's yards. One like that might just be the thing to take suspicion off of the real killer. On the other hand, at least more people than just me believed Donald's death was no whim of fate.

8

On Monday, I threw myself into setting up the new equipment I bought to replace my stolen and damaged computer setup. I soon became sorry I ever chose this business. My message boxes were jammed with huge files of notes and requests for service that I learned were bogus when I called to confirm. Included were two warnings that terrible things would happen to Memnet and me if we did not leave town. That mystery caller from Tiny's the other week was tame compared to some of this electronic hash. These messages came from anonymous mailboxes, each with a different website and user name that shut down by the time I traced the path.

Both Marion, even though she had been put peripherally on our suspect list, and Adam, came over at different times to help me sort through the mess. The warnings were intermingled with requests to send more information regarding the revitalization of Apple Grove to outside contacts that Donald made before he disappeared. It was difficult to sort through them all to find legitimate ones. Marion was a gem due to her knowledge of the people of Apple Grove who might have a reason to want to understand what was going on. Adam was helpful because . . . he was Adam. I soaked up his warmth and security.

"These threats and fake work orders burn me up," I told Adam when we were alone. I did not like to think of Marion as a suspect, but I wasn't ready to take her into our complete confidence yet, either. I should stop second-guessing myself. "No one's come after you, have they?" I asked him. I would have hoped he would volunteer such information but asking seemed a good way of making conversation.

"I suppose it's only a matter of time." He held up the page he had been reading. "This one's from Yolanda Toynsbee, asking you for an interview."

"Oh?" I reached for the printout.

"When she asked me what I thought about the events at the meeting the other night, I told her I would be happy to talk about my business and things of that nature, but that I hadn't even settled in yet and had no opinion about politics."

"I see. You think she wants to talk about the tax credits?"

"I'm sure she'll let you know." Adam's lips turned upward.

My immediate reaction had been to ask him what he thought I should do. I reminded myself that we weren't even officially dating . . . yet . . . or even if he wanted a relationship. Definitely too early for love. Or was it? "I have some other things I'd like to discuss with Yolanda. I'll call her later," I said.

I watched him for a moment, appreciating the way he held the page and scanned it, before joining in the last of the sorting.

Although I did not think anything would come of it, we would turn in the two messages labeled "detailed threat" to the police. I hesitated to talk about the idea forming in my head. The Summersby building haunted me. Officer Ripple told Mom that the force was spread thin enough already. A field trip, or wild goose chase, to Chicago seemed out of the question for them. Just because I was raised in the western suburbs did not mean that I liked anything to do with driving in downtown Chicago. Alone. To a strange place I most certainly never visited before.

As the days passed I felt Donald's murderer slipping out of our reach — if, indeed, Donald had been murdered. I wished I could guess Adam's reaction if I mentioned my plan to drive into the city and check it out. He might want to come, and this was something I needed to do for myself, for my sense of independence. I held Donald's picture from Marion and wanted to ask everyone there at the building if they had seen him. I also could not forget about Tut . . . poor Tut deserved better. What had happened to him?

I wondered how long they would search for Margaret before holding Donald's funeral. Letty Grimm showed up in town, alone on Wednesday, claiming Margaret had arranged to meet her after some other personal business. When Margaret failed to show by Monday, Letty filed a police report. Another twist. I had been certain they were together.

I made more trips to the library to use their internet system to check the archived files of newspapers in hopes of keeping away from the hackers presently engaged in flooding my system at home. My mind wandered while articles downloaded after my search. Adam and I expected Mom's students on Sunday afternoon. Father's Day. I couldn't honestly say I missed my father terribly since he had been gone most of my life. I wondered how Adam felt, having lost his daughter.

At least I had a few new clues to bring to the table. And here! I was right. Print these pages off . . . there. On my way to pick up my print copies I bumped into Yolanda Toynsbee. We looked at each other a long moment, assessing sides, and the benefits of confiding in each other. I took the first step. "It's Saturday tomorrow. Why don't you and Jenny come over to my house for lunch? She can play with Memnet."

I was not positive about the reason for her hesitation, so I added a sweetener. "I'm expecting some unusual guests this weekend. I thought this might make a good story. My mother teaches criminology at Maplewood Community College. When she was visiting, she thought highly of our local police station and asked if they would allow some of her students to do their fieldwork here. Chief Hackman and Officer Ripple agreed."

Yolanda's raised eyebrow led me to hope.

"Wouldn't that make an interesting article?" I wheedled.

"You're right. It would." Her gaze moved past my left shoulder briefly before returning to me. "We'll be over, then. What time?"

After we made the arrangements I went to pick up my pages from the printer. I noticed they were not in numerical order.

From across the library counter at the front circulation desk, Nancy merely held out her hand for my change to pay for the printouts. I left the library, holding the articles gingerly by their edges, wondering about fingerprints. The prospect of sharing my home with strangers for a week, especially ones who were training to track criminals, set my comfort level on par with fine chocolate.

Yolanda and Jenny arrived on time for our lunch chat the next afternoon. "This is Memnet," I introduced my pet.

"He's here! Did you go home when I told you to? He looks like a cheetah," Jenny squealed when she first saw him.

Memnet's large ears went back. If he could have raised his brow, he would have.

I wondered what she was chattering about but decided to focus on her last comment. "That's very observant, Miss Jenny," I told her. "Not everyone notices that Memnet is so special. His is the only kind of pet cat that has spots like that, instead of patches of colors or stripes."

Memnet closed his eyes and behaved as if

he adored children. He allowed little Jenny to gently poke all of his spots and scrub at his ears. "Moo," Jenny said, plopping down on the floor next to Mem and burying her face in his belly. Adoration time was about over.

His claws came out.

I cleared my throat.

He glared at me, then sheathed them.

"Um, Mem has spots, Jenny, but cats say —"

"She meant 'Mau' didn't you, lovey?" Yolanda broke in. "We talked about that." She set her purse on the floor beside one of the kitchen chairs. "Come here, now. Let's have a nice little chat with Ivy. Then maybe you can make some pictures of him."

The little girl obediently got up. On the way to the table, she noticed that her giraffe picture was on the front of my refrigerator. "I made that! You've got my picture in your house."

"That's right. Remember when we first met? At your grandma's office?"

Jenny nodded.

"You were drawing pictures and you made that giraffe for me."

She nodded again, sending her curls bouncing along the scalloped collar of her striped shirt. I set a plastic cup two-thirds

150

full of lemonade in front of her. I let Yolanda pour her own. Jenny swiped a hand over her mouth after her drink.

I waited. Yolanda tapped her glass with a fingernail, her mouth set in a straight line.

Mem watched us from his supine position in the patch of light on the floor.

"Jenny, dear," Yolanda broke the silence.

I held my breath.

"Yes, Gramma?" The little girl held her cup with both chubby palms.

"You remember last week when Daddy was angry?" Jenny's little brow wrinkled, and she lowered her chin. "Can you tell Ivy why?"

Jenny's voice dropped to a whisper.

Yolanda and I leaned closer, although I was surprised at the wobbly pucker of Yolanda's mouth.

"I went too close to the water," Jenny said. One fat tear squeezed between her eyelids.

"What was at the water?" Yolanda prompted.

"Kitty. I saw a kitty." She turned and pointed. "Him. Like a cheetah. Only lion-colored. I thought he would get drownded and I jus' wanted to save him." Jenny lifted her fists to her eyes.

Even Mem sat up, but licked a paw, as if he wasn't interested in a story that wasn't

151

about him.

Jenny obviously left out some details. Grandma Yolanda tried to make her frown serious. "You know why Daddy was angry, don't you? He was scared."

Jenny nodded, fists covering her eyes.

"All of us love you and we never want you to drown."

"I go to tiny tot swim lessons," Jenny whispered.

"True. But the river is dangerous. Even if you thought you saw a kitty there, what should you have done?"

"Told an adult."

"That's right." Yolanda patted her granddaughter's little shoulder.

Mem's whereabouts were accounted for all week. Of course, any cat could look like Memnet in a little girl's eyes. The sun could have made a cat look light-colored and dappled. Spotty. I took in a breath, about to tell them so.

Yolanda widened her eyes to signal me for what I assumed would be a private chat later.

I mentally switched gears. "How about we have our lunch?" I said instead. I had cut up small squares of cheese and bologna earlier, and now served them on a plate with crackers to Jenny. I was glad I'd had enough lunches with the children of friends to be prepared. Jenny also enjoyed spearing cut grapes and sliced bananas with a toothpick while we ate shrimp salad. Watching Yolanda's granddaughter made me acutely aware of my withering ovaries.

After we finished eating, I set the little girl up with plenty of paper and crayons at a lap desk on the living room carpet. She drew pictures while we spoke in low tones at the kitchen table.

"Memnet wasn't out at all last week," I told Yolanda.

"I suspected as much," she said. "Mr. Thompson's cat is a slightly different color, isn't it?"

"Enough that Jenny wouldn't think it was the same," I said.

"Then that leaves the mayor's cat. Tut."

"Has Jenny ever seen Tut?"

"The mayor has had his cat for a number of years. We did a story about it when Tut was new, but that was before Jenny was born. As you can imagine, the mayor didn't let his cat out much, either. Whenever he came in, or we interviewed him, the cat was with him."

"But could Tut be on the loose now? Perhaps Tut escaped after Donald's . . . death. What day did Jenny see him? And where, exactly?"

"Last Tuesday. On the other side of the big bridge, behind the old theater."

Apple Grove meandered along Founders River, a shallow, weed-choked stream that erupted from a natural spring about four miles away. At one time, I read in a history of the town, it had washed with enough power to operate a gristmill. In the ensuing years, the dam was removed, and the resulting pond filled in. The slope slowly eroded.

"You know," Yolanda told me, "a couple of generations ago, the city council decided to prepare for possible floods. Boy, you think the folks complain now about taxes, you should read some of the stuff we printed when they built that bridge on the south side!"

"I can hear it." I smiled. "Since almost all businesses are on the west side." A number of rundown buildings faced the empty gravel and weed-encrusted banks. The state had helped build a new, ugly cement bridge on the north side. Apple Grove's movie house shut down about twenty years ago and, abandoned, was settling in upon itself behind the hardware store. I heard there was a small pool going about which buildings would collapse when. No wonder Donald felt desperate to revitalize this community.

"Things wash up on the shore," Yolanda said. "Sometimes kids wander along the streambed searching for anything valuable or interesting."

"Hmmm. Sounds like something I might do," I said.

"Can I ask you when you believe Mayor Conklin first —"

"Disappeared?" I shook my head. "That sounds strange. You must have read the first police report. Routine procedure, I know, for the newspaper. Yes, I called in that I thought something was wrong with the mayor soon after he left. He'd planned that business, but I also knew he planned to attend the annual CAT convention and hadn't registered, so I wanted to remind him. He didn't answer my calls. Margaret didn't seem to think anything was unusual. She claimed Tut was fine when I went to see her. But later, her assistant said Donald had his cat with him." I decided against sharing the fact that Adam and I broke and entered Tut's little temple.

"You seem to hold a great deal of affection for Tut," she said.

Yolanda was beginning to believe me about the importance of finding Tut.

"I don't believe Donald would have willingly abandoned him. Yes, I do like Tut and
I want to take care of him. He's familiar
with me. It's all we have left of Donald."

Yolanda put her hand over mine in sympathy. "I understand the police have started
an official investigation into the whereabouts
of Margaret."

I felt ready to take another person into
our tiny sleuthing group's confidence.
"With Tut and Margaret missing, there's no
one else to ask where they might have gone.
And poor Donald . . . waiting all this time
for a funeral."

"I heard that the Baders have hired their
own private people to search for Margaret,"
Yolanda told me. "And I understand that
since Donald has no other family, and Margaret's family won't step in, Rupert Murphy is scheduling a memorial service for
next Wednesday. The autopsy's already been
done and there's no reason to hold the body
any longer."

"He can do that? When will the autopsy
report be available?"

"Somebody should. There's no reason not
to. Donald had already purchased gravesites.
And the autopsy comes back in parts,
depending on what's being tested. That's all
I can say."

"So, you don't know the cause of death?"

"No."

If Yolanda had been a cat, her fur would be raised.

So sad. But Donald would get a proper send-off at least, with or without his not-quite-so-beloved wife, Margaret. But would I call it closure? Would anybody else care that he shouldn't be dead at all? Time to ask another question from the growing list of motives I tossed around. "Yolanda, have you decided to print that article of Margaret welcoming MerriFoods to Apple Grove yet?"

"Funny you should ask." Yolanda pursed her lips. "Only yesterday I received information from officials at Feli-Mix in order to print their side, too. As far as they were concerned, a facilities committee to search location was still scheduled for next month."

"What did they say about MerriFood?"

Yolanda gave me a serious, cocked eyebrow stare over her half-glasses. "That business didn't come up." She leaned back in the kitchen chair and folded her arms. "Now, what about that article you wanted to discuss?"

I smiled, the tension diffusing. "I told you that my mother teaches criminology at Maplewood Community College and that she arranged for three of her students to do some fieldwork in Apple Grove. They'll be here tomorrow, and I thought you, or someone, could shadow them, sort of like learning the ropes of small town law enforcement. With the right treatment" — I ignored her narrowed eyes — "it could be a nice profile for the town. Right?" I found myself adding, with just a touch of pleading.

"I won't guarantee that the article will come out with the angle you're proposing. But I agree that this subject will make an interesting story. Something about examining our town through the eyes of others." She frowned and leaned forward, drumming her fingertips on the table. "Unfortunately, with Jim so ill at the moment, I don't have spare time to follow through. Do you have any suggestions, or any writing skills of your own?"

I grinned, despite the unwelcome news that she had her own personal crisis. Also, I should have suspected that if I proposed an idea, it would come back to nip my heels. "Well, it's not my secret ambition to become a reporter, but I do have a thought. We could ask the students to share their notes about their experience here, maybe do a debriefing every other day. If you could do some photographs in action, if there is any action, that is, that would probably suffice. Then one of us, or even me, or all of them, could do a whole story."

Yolanda nodded. "That's an option. My photographer could follow the students once or twice and give his impressions, as well."

"Of course, you realize the real reason my mother arranged for the fieldwork to take place here, don't you?"

Yolanda nodded soberly. "I expect so. How do you feel about it? Or was this your idea, to bring them here?"

Aware that the editor turned the tables on me, I was quick to deny my involvement. "No, it wasn't my idea. Mother went ahead and arranged it with Officer Ripple and Chief Hackman. She told me what she'd done later."

Yolanda clasped her hands and bowed over them, almost in prayer. She was quiet for a minute, and then she shook her head dazedly and blinked at me. "Sorry. I get lost in thought sometimes."

"That's all right. So do I. I'm sorry to hear about your husband. I didn't realize he was sick."

"Jim's whole family history is plagued by bad hearts. He had his first attack when he was forty. Then another three years ago. I think all that's holding him together sometimes are wires and tape. He's in the hospital for a while, having a pacemaker and medication regulated, and they're having a tough time figuring out the dosage of blood thinner."

"I've heard that can be tricky. Yolanda, I'd like to help you." I waved my hand at the empty equipment boxes I lined up to store in the basement when I was comfortable that I didn't need to return anything. "Business is a bit slow for me right now." I appreciated her sympathetic grimace. "What can I do? I worked at the college newspaper. I can help with layouts, maybe even some stories, if you need that. I understand the day-to-day stuff can be hard when you're constantly being interrupted."

On cue, Memnet sped in like a shadow along the wall, tail twitching, with Jenny in hot pursuit. Memnet stopped at the screen door then put up a paw, indicating he would like to go outside now, please.

"Can we go outside?" Jenny asked, frenetically hopping from foot to foot.

"Why don't you visit the bathroom first, girl? Give Memnet a rest for a minute." Yolanda was kind, but firm.

"But then, after? Can we? Can we, Ivy?"

If you don't hear the answer you want to your question the first time, keep asking until you do. I remembered the saying from somewhere and laughed. "If it's all right with your grandma, Jenny, you and Memnet can go outside. But you have to stay in my yard, all right? It's a rule with Memnet, and he knows the boundaries. Can I trust you?"

The little girl nodded quickly, then made a beeline for my bathroom.

Yolanda shared her light-lipped smile. "No time for the necessary when you're that age."

Memnet sat calmly licking his outstretched toes, the need to go outside apparently not so urgent now that his pursuer was out of sight.

"We can watch them from the window," I remarked. I had a window that overlooked the yard, thanks to a detached garage. "Mem's not too crazy about the neighborhood children — not that they're mean or anything — he's just used to being quiet. So, he knows where to hide. I think they'll be fine."

Yolanda ducked her chin in agreement. "I am acquainted with most of the families around here. Nice folks. They treating you all right?"

Interview time again. "Oh, they're all nice."

Jenny came prancing back into the kitchen, and after reassuring her grandmother that she had indeed washed her hands, she cautiously opened the door for Memnet then followed him outside. He headed for his favorite tree, the weeping willow that grew near the edge of the yard. I enjoyed watching Mem frisk among the long skinny branches as much as he got a kick out of batting them. Jenny danced among them like a sprite from a fairytale in pink shorts and sandals.

"I think the criminology students should read through back issues of the Gazette, see if there's some information we've missed along the way," Yolanda said. "I'm so close to everyone in Apple Grove that sometimes I can't see the forest for the trees. And you've only just arrived. I can't expect you to figure out all of our secrets. I can't put my finger on it, but Jenny's claims of seeing another cat like Memnet down by the river is important. There might be something told once upon a time in the paper that I've forgotten. They can be reviewing police records for trends, as a cover-up."

"That sounds good to me."

"About your help . . . well, I can't really

pay much. Gloria helps on Sunday and Wednesdays to do set up and the main typing. Jim and I do the rest. The photographer, Greg, gets paid by the photo."

"I'm not looking for make-work, Yolanda. I have a small trust from my grandparents that's been well-tended. I'm not rich and I need to earn some money, but I'm not destitute, either. Whatever you want to give me by way of compensation works in my favor. And of course, if you talk up my business, word-of-mouth advertising covers a lot of bases."

Yolanda clasped her hands in front of her. "I suppose you can type. You know how to work with layout software?"

We worked out a flexible deal, where I would come in for a few hours on Thursday evenings to help Yolanda answer phones and write some copy, which she would assign. I'd get free advertising and lunch once in a while. Suited me just fine. I was glad to have a friendly conversation more than anything else. I loved my house and my neighbors so far didn't seem consumed by the gossip yet, though not everyone around Apple Grove had accepted me.

After another half-hour or so of chatting, Yolanda continued to thaw toward me. In a profession that demanded objective observer status to life in a small town, it must have been hard for her to have any friends at all. I told her a little of what it was like for me to grow up with a single parent, and I think she was bracing herself for what would happen to the paper if Jim could no longer continue to run it. Most of their assets were tied up with the business, she let slip. I liked Yolanda Toynsbee.

After she and Jenny left, I took a walk along the river, enjoying the late afternoon sun. I couldn't figure out where a cat would hide. Even the bridge area had no rocks or crevices or bits of garbage to hide under. I stared across the expanse of the stream, thinking about what made a place a home. The 'burbs were comfortable because that was what I knew.

But there was nothing like a real small town, a great place to settle down and raise a family, with a man like Adam Truegood Thompson. I wondered how our cats would do if we ever got the point where we wanted to set up housekeeping together.

9

On Sunday afternoon, as promised, Mom's posse showed up in my driveway, stuffed into a tiny car. As the young people pried themselves out of the little metallic blue automobile, I noted that the driver stood a head taller than the others of the group.

She introduced herself as Sonja Guth, and apparently was also the leader of the pack. She held out a hand immediately upon meeting me and spoke in a no-nonsense manner. Her grip was firm. I glanced up at her. A brown-eyed blonde, she possessed a sharp, nasally voice that made me grit my teeth for the first three sentences. I gradually learned that if I stayed with her long enough and got used to her speaking tone, her operatic laugh made up for it.

Her female counterpart, Lucy Ballentine, was sharp and not inclined to waste words. Deep grooves graced the space between her dark eyebrows and she had an unusual patch of white hair over her left ear. "It's always been like that," she said as soon as she noticed my gaze lingering in that direction. Lucy struck me as someone who could melt into the background, despite the hair, compared to Sonja, who stood out like a Valkyrie.

A copper-headed young man with matching penny freckles and bearing the unlikely name of Elvis Thorson completed the trio. "What can I say?" He shrugged when Sonja introduced him, and he saw my smile at his first name. "My mother was a believer."

It appeared as though he had quickly cased the whole area and relaxed only after he determined there was no hint of danger. Elvis was to stay with Adam while the girls would share my guestroom. I showed them inside, and then I telephoned Adam.

"Can I get you some lemonade or something else to drink?" I asked them.

"Maybe after we settle in," Sonja answered for them all. The girls took their bags to my guestroom while we waited for Adam.

Elvis asked about my business and I pointed him upstairs to my office. He took a keen interest in my equipment. We held a juicy technical discussion regarding connection speeds and methods of storing information. Elvis had a rapid-fire curiosity, which translated into an ability to ferret details I didn't know existed.

"Here's a site," his fingers flew over my keyboard, "that will allow you secure space to save some of your most important files . . ."

The young women joined us, crowding around the largest screen of my computer system.

The doorbell rang.

We all tromped down the steps.

"Ah, sharing trade secrets?" Adam asked as I ushered him in, explaining what we'd been up to. "New methods of taking fingerprints, or detecting falsified voices?"

"Nothing so mundane." Sonja stretched to her full height and reached for his hand. The "interested, available" gleam in her eye took me aback. I hurriedly pulled Lucy forward for her introduction and chided myself at Adam's mock grin at my discomfiture.

Sonja jumped back into the lead. "And this is Elvis, Elvis Thorson. He had a preliminary interview with the FBI last trimester break and was invited for training."

I was impressed. Adam and I congratulated the young man whose face had almost attained the brilliance of his hair.

167

"It's a long-term goal of mine," he said with a shrug. "After graduation."

"Professor Preston filled us in on some of the merits of the case," Sonja said. "But now that you're both here, we'd like to get your side of the story. May we?" She indicated my living room where we adjourned. Lucy held a legal pad and three pens while the other two checked and started an MP3 recorder and a newer model digital personal recorder.

"We talked about the details on the way here," Lucy said. "We'd like to learn about the cat fancier's group you all belong to, how long you've been there and how you got to know each other."

Sounded reasonable to me. Adam and I traded shrugs about who would start. He deferred to me with a head bob.

Memnet wound through my legs and jumped onto my lap.

"That's your cat?" Sonja was goggle-eyed at him. "He really does have spots. And big ears."

"I've had Memnet since I was in college. When I had my own apartment, I was lonely at first, so I decided to adopt a pet. I fell in love with this rare breed called Egyptian Mau and got Memnet. I wanted to learn more about the cats and meet other people,

168

so joining this group, Cat Association Titlists, covered both bases. That's where I first met Donald Conklin. We owned different colored Maus, and sometimes competed against each other. Tut's a bronze. Mem is a silver, only slightly different from Isis, who's a smoke. We became friendly — just casually friendly. He told me about his work and how his wife didn't care for cats, and I told him about . . . me. He was just —" I broke off a second to search Adam's neutral expression — "supportive. Nice. I didn't seek him out other than when we met a few times a year, and he spent time with a lot of different people at the meetings. Murder . . . just seems unreasonable."

Lucy wrote fast in small disjointed squiggles, dashes and lines. She glanced up expectantly when I stopped talking. "Crimes of passion don't usually have much reason behind them."

"Or forewarning," Elvis said.

I felt my chin start to wobble and I didn't trust my voice. These students obviously paid attention to my mother.

Adam told his side briefly about how he got involved with the type of cat and the group. "The Association has, I believe, about five hundred members with six branches that meet regularly in different parts of the country. We have an annual meeting to exchange news and have an overall competition, in different locations. I've only been involved the past two years."

"OK," Sonja said. She checked the volume and jotted the time index on her recorder, while watching Memnet with furtive, longing glances. "How about telling us your impressions of the mayor, Mr. Thompson?"

"Call me Adam. Donald Conklin was a very personable man, just right for his position. Not oily, as some people can be, knowing how to manipulate others to get what they want. You get what I mean?"

I watched Adam as he spoke, but at this, I caught the nods of affirmation from my three other guests out of the corner of my eye.

"How much time overall do you think you spent with him?" Elvis asked.

"Just a couple of hours, if that, at each convention," I answered.

The students looked at each other, eyebrows raised.

"I knew Donald a much shorter period than Ivy," Adam said.

Sonja glanced at the others before looking at me and Memnet. "You realize, of course, that personal impressions can't be used as evidence during a trial."

"Yes, of course. But what about the twelve million dollars in grant money? Controlled by the mayor? And the fact that the mayor's cat, and now his wife, have vanished?"

"Is the money accounted for? Has anyone absconded with it?" Lucy asked.

"I believe the money's in a special trust fund controlled by the mayor's office, according to Marion Green, the mayor's secretary. And I don't know that the money's all accounted for," I answered.

Elvis said, with a touch more sympathy than Lucy displayed, "Our first stop will be the mayor's office to interview the secretary, then. I think we'll be able to sift through the police file as part of our fieldwork."

Adam squeezed my hand.

"Sounds good," I said.

"We thought we should go over our schedule a bit with you both," Sonja said. "The three of us are to report to the police station tomorrow from nine o'clock until noon for a tour, a ride-along, and a lecture on the procedure book. After lunch we're to review old casebooks at both solved and unsolved crimes for a couple of hours."

"The chief said there'd be some hands-on experience in finger printing or investigation procedure or follow-up on tips as they come in to the station," Lucy said. "Although we were warned that Apple Grove tends to be a fairly quiet community."

We all looked at each other.

"We'll do a conference call with Professor Preston," Elvis explained, "in the evening. But that leaves plenty of time to nose around, listen to conversations at the local hang-outs, check out the businesses. We might even have a legitimate claim to interview the town council members in the interest of learning how small communities function and protect themselves."

"That's a good idea," I said. "I haven't been able to follow through on talking to them. There's something else that's come up since yesterday." I explained about the newspaper and its owners. "Yolanda thinks you people might figure out a pattern of events or find clues about the mayor that Adam or I wouldn't recognize, or she thought too trivial."

"Hmmm, there's merit to that idea," Sonja muttered. "We'll fit it in somehow. Was the mayor from Apple Grove originally?"

"Yes," Adam answered.

I felt even worse about how little I had bothered to get acquainted with the man for whom I had uprooted my whole life. Had moving to Apple Grove been worth the risk? I also realized the schedule the students outlined would leave no time for a field trip to Chicago. I decided to delay my adventure until I didn't have to explain anything to anyone.

Sonja and Lucy were considerate housemates.

Memnet allowed Sonja to stroke his back while he chortled and blinked in feline pleasure. Lucy's interest in my pet appeared more historical and scientific, so we discussed the ancestry of the breed, way back to the Pharaohs.

The young women rose early the next morning and got themselves breakfast. Each had brought along a bag of groceries with their particular favorite foods. They cleaned up after themselves and fixed bag lunches. Mom told me the college would be sending a reimbursement for their lodging expenses. With business down at the moment, I didn't protest.

"We'll meet back here after one," Sonja said as she and Lucy left.

"I hope you have a productive morning." Still in a housecoat, I waved them down the drive on their way to pick up Elvis from Adam's apartment before going to the police station.

By 11:00 I had dealt with my business and dressed for a warm and sticky summer day. I had already taken care of a few small household chores in anticipation of my guests, so I thought I would head downtown. Mea Cuppa's first business drawing for free coffee was scheduled at noon and I wanted to be there. Hopefully, Adam could get some positive publicity out of the event.

Adam glanced up at the bell announcing my entry. He stood behind the counter in his long, wine-colored apron with stylized lettering "Mea Cuppa," a steaming coffee cup, and an outline of a stack of books decorating the front. He nodded as if he'd been watching for me, and I felt a little thrill between my shoulder blades.

Several gawking customers stood in a loose semicircle around the counter, waiting. Yolanda's stringer photographer pulled a chair close and stood on its seat above the crowd to get a bird's eye view of the event. Excited babble ceased as Adam announced it was time for the drawing. A shiver of anticipation grew the smile I shared with Bob Green, in his barber's garb, who wandered over from next door.

Adam offered the fishbowl, filled a third of the way with cardboard rectangles, to one of the women. He held it high, nearly out of her reach, so that she could not see the names on the cards she touched. He attracted a fair number of traveling people who stopped for a coffee while passing through Apple Grove, so I hoped that at least this first winner would be local.

The camera flashed as Adam waved the winning card at the crowd.

"Apple Grove Gazette, Jim and Yolanda Toynsbee. The news you need to know," Adam shouted. A few "awws" amidst the claps indicated a general pleasant reaction to the winner. "The Toynsbees and their staff win a cup of coffee delivered daily to the shop for all of this week," Adam said. "Don't forget to try again for next week's drawing."

The group dispersed, some out the door, some forming a queue at the counter and a few roaming toward the shelves.

The photographer got another shot of Adam holding up the fishbowl. The young man grabbed a latte for being on the newspaper office staff, and then he disappeared.

I waited until Adam served his customers and also checked out those who had decided on a book purchase. The shop was nearly empty by the time I approached him. "You had a nice crowd this morning. The drawing is a good idea."

He blinked at the compliment. "Thanks."

"Can I help you take coffee to the newspaper office?"

Adam glanced around his now emptied shop. "Sure. I can close for a couple of minutes. Do you know if there's anyone else with them today?"

I shook my head. "Yolanda's husband is at the hospital. I haven't even met him. The set-up person who helps with layouts only comes in Sunday and Wednesday evenings. I've offered to help, just flexible with some copy and phones, on Thursday nights."

Adam smiled and handed me a small covered cup of his hazelnut brew. "For you, then."

I inhaled through the sip tab. "Thanks."

"Let me call over to the office and find out what Yolanda likes, then I'd be grateful for your company."

While Adam made his call, I went to the front window and peered at Apple Grove's Main Street. Tiny's Buffet was quite full for lunch, judging by the customers visible through the windows and wrought-iron lamp posts in the sidewalk. Drivers motored past. There were few empty parking spaces.

As Adam stacked the paper holder with a lidded takeout cup, I pushed the plastic clock hands on the outside of the door to mark that the shop would reopen in fifteen minutes. He set the lock and pulled the door closed after us.

Walking the few blocks that made up Apple Grove's quaint little downtown made me feel like we were on an old west movie set. The narrow store fronts and old square brick facades that gave false pride shadowed the street like the parapets of a castle wall. A few stores had canvas awnings to roll out for afternoon shade. A hot little breeze whipped along the sidewalk at our backs while waving the long stems of a hanging petunia basket in front of Roberta's flower shop, next door to the newspaper.

As we approached the office of the Gazette, Yolanda came barreling out the front door, waving both arms.

"Oh, look. Yolanda's come out —"

"Back!" she shrieked. "Away!"

The flash of light and wall of smoke billowing from the open door of the newspaper building added to the surrealistic atmosphere.

Adam tossed the coffee aside and grabbed me around the middle, pushing me against Roberta's shop window and shielding me. When nothing further happened, Adam straightened and turned in time to meet Yolanda, breathless, who had run the length of the block. Oozy yellow smoke stirred in the wind.

"What happened!" He grabbed her elbows. "Are you all right? Is anyone else in there?"

"I — I don't know," Yolanda hunched over to gasp in lungfuls of air. "But, no — I — was alone! I just hung up the phone when I heard a metallic click and something bouncing up the hallway from the back door. Then the screen door slammed. We never lock the door back there."

I heard the siren of one of Apple Grove's cruisers approaching. The sulfurous odor made me choke and wheeze. I waved my hand in front of my face to waft away the fumes and blinked my watering eyes.

Across the street, customers and vendors alike lined the sidewalk, mouths open in shock, talking, pointing. The smoke began to clear.

Adam stared down the alley toward the back of the building.

"Don't you dare think of going back there alone, Adam Thompson!" I wasn't usually bossy, but fear made me speak my mind.

He put his hands on his hips as he turned to stare at me with a quizzical expression.

Officer Ripple squealed up, accompanied by Elvis.

"Stay here!" Ripple shouted.

Elvis opened his door. He closed his door but had the window down by then and thrust his head through. "Everyone all right?"

We all indicated yes while Ripple rushed over. "What's going on? I've called for the fire department and backup."

"I think it was some kind of grenade," Yolanda said. "There's no fire. Just smoke and smell."

A small crowd began to converge.

Roberta, a plump brunette, whose age I guessed to be somewhere between Yolanda and me, bustled out of her door. "I heard a sound. Whump. Like a bomb you hear on TV," she contributed. "I'm glad you're OK," she told Yolanda. "At least you didn't have Jenny in there with you today."

Yolanda went white. "I don't know what I would have done."

Apple Grove's volunteer fire fighters jumped off the wailing cherry red pumper truck that pulled up. Two tan and iridescent yellow-suited figures ventured into the now quiet shop.

We all watched for a long five minutes until they reappeared.

I made my way over to Elvis. He hung as much of his skinny person out the window as he could to get a good view of the action.

The crowd blocked his line of sight.

"What's going on? I can't see a thing," he complained as soon as I came in earshot.

I bent to peek through the mass of elbows and guts of my fellow Grovers. "The firefighters are coming out. Thumbs up. They're giving the 'all clear,' " I told Elvis. "Say, what was the call, anyway? Who called this in?"

"A woman's voice shouted, 'they just bombed me out,' or something like that," he replied. "I was at the monitoring station when the operator took the call. I could hear through her headset." His cell phone bleeped. "It's Sonja. I'd better let her know what's going on. We'll be late for our lunch meeting today."

Adam hiked over to us. "I just overheard the captain telling Chief Hackman he thought there was only smoke damage. The grenade was apparently something SWAT teams use when they want to roust out a suspect, like in a hostage situation. He called it an OC grenade. Had that pepper stuff in it that makes your eyes water."

"Must be strong if it affects us from this far away," I said.

Elvis got out of the car. "Oh, yeah! That

was on our list of weapons at the terrorism seminar I went to. Sometimes there's tear gas, too. Or they color the smoke to determine targets. But why would anyone toss one around here?"

"That's what I'd like to know." A grim-faced Yolanda strode up to the group, notebook in hand, graying curls springing angrily as she spoke. With her pen poised she began rapid-fire questioning of me. "You two were just on your way. Did you see anything?"

"No, I'm sorry, Yolanda," I replied.

Adam denied noticing anything out of the ordinary as well.

"I'd chalk this up to some kind of high school prank, if it weren't for —"

"For what, Yolanda?" Chief Hackman silently joined our group. "We're taping off the scene, but anything you could tell us would be helpful."

"Like I told you, Gene, it all happened so fast. I didn't even see what it was before I leaped outta there. But whoever threw it was at the back door. If there's any evidence, you'd find it around back."

"You were saying something else, Yolanda," Hackman prompted.

"Well, I was opening the weekend mail, and I came across —"

A shout from the street interrupted us. "What did I tell you!"

For a Monday at lunchtime, there were a lot of people milling about. The sight of Tiny Alnord clutching a megaphone and standing in the rusty bed of a once-blue pickup truck would have given me the giggles had the message of his impromptu speech not been so vicious.

I caught a glimpse of an unsmiling man leaning against a light pole behind Alnord, with his arms folded. Our friendly neighborhood sewer guy, Jeff Hanley.

"Strangers bring problems," Alnord shouted. "We never had anything like this happen before in our beloved village. We need a mayor to help us in our darkest hour!"

Grim-faced, Hackman waded toward the truck. "Tiny!"

"Oh-oh!" Lucy and Sonja skidded up to us at this point. "Just in time. Looks as if things are getting ugly."

"Where did these upstarts came from? For all we know —"

"Disperse at once!" Hackman called out when he reached the curb. "Before we fine you all for loitering and unlawful assembly." He addressed Tiny next. "Alnord, I oughtta give you a ticket for inciting a riot! What in the world do you think you're up to? Anyone would think you purposefully caused this incident. Where were you half an hour ago, anyway?" Hackman was so outraged, we could hear his shouting from where we stood on the sidewalk.

"I got my rights!" Tiny declared to Hackman. "You can't stop me from speaking. It's my constitutional right."

"I'm not stopping you from making a fool of yourself. I am stopping you from doing it without a permit to hold an assembly, and from blocking traffic, and from inciting a riot."

By now two other officers had arrived, including the parking ticket lady.

"She's really the Community Services Officer. Her name is Rachel," Yolanda whispered to me. "Besides checking the parking meters downtown, she also puts on school safety programs."

The uniformed officers encouraged people to move away from the scene.

On a whim, I asked Yolanda, "How well do you know Jeff Hanley?"

"The bank guy?"

"Banker? He's the one on the town council . . . um, in charge of sewage."

"Yes, that's right. What about him?"

"I didn't realize he was a banker. He was

watching, just a few minutes ago."

"A lot of people were. Ivy, what're you up to?"

"I just wondered, that's all. He seemed to know about the money for Apple Grove."

"He's vice president at State's Bank," Yolanda said. "Donald kept that money somewhere, right?"

"Yeah. What was in the mail that you were about to mention?"

Yolanda's expression closed down. Her mouth narrowed. "Just stupid stuff, and that's all I'll say for now."

I swallowed. "Was the office damaged much?"

"Not sure. If it's just smoke . . . well, I don't know until I get in there."

"I not only type, I clean."

Yolanda smiled. "You sound like a walking advertisement for a Girl Friday. But, thanks. We'd better move on before we get a ticket."

I squeezed her arm and turned.

Adam zeroed in on me and pulled me down an alley.

"Are you sure this is a good idea?" I asked.

"Shhh! The kids have gone back to your house to compare notes, or whatever they said they were doing. I just want to see what's back here."

"Adam! You'll get us in a lot of trouble."

"Shhh. Watch."

One of the police officers worked his way down the weedy embankment toward the river.

"I wonder if our suspect left footprints?" Adam asked. "He or she couldn't have used a boat on that little drainage. But still, the river might be important."

"Um, Adam," I said. "There's something I forgot to tell you — well, all of you." A tingle of cold sweat on my brow accompanied my realization. Jenny's story of seeing the kitty that looked like Memnet might, indeed, be an important clue.

10

"I think I'll just close up early," Adam announced when we reached Mea Cuppa. The streets were deserted, and he wasn't the first shop owner to feel that way. "Closed" signs were up at the Odds 'n Ends shop and the ice cream parlor. Only the barber shop and the drug store, besides Tiny's, defied the stressful events of the morning.

Bob Green lounged next to his striped barber pole.

We stopped to speak to him.

"Bob. Looks as though most everybody went home," I said, trying not to sound morose, but failing.

"Yeah, appears so. Did you see what happened?"

"Just a prank," Adam told him. "Probably some kids with a stink grenade. You can order anything off the internet these days."

Bob and Adam exchanged a wordless dialog.

"That's right," Bob said after a couple of seconds. "I'll make sure my customers understand that. See you around." He waved us off.

Adam unlocked the door and we stepped inside Mea Cuppa. He drew the shade and turned off the orange neon "open" sign.

"Why don't you come over to my place? We can talk this out with the others," I said.

"Sure. Let me turn off the machines and put away the cold stuff." Isis came from the direction of his office, mewing. "Hi, there, sweet thing. Were you all alone?"

"Bring her, too," I said.

He grinned and picked her up. "Are you sure that's safe?"

We took my car back to the house where I parked alongside Sonja's car.

Elvis accosted us in the kitchen. "Did you get Yolanda to tell you what was in her mail?"

"Hello! Well, I asked her," I replied.

Adam's cat grabbed our attention. Isis plopped to the floor, sniffing suspiciously at some scent near the cupboards.

"How beautiful!" Sonja said. "What's your name?"

"Meet Isis," Adam said.

"Female? She looks like Memnet."

"Different color," Elvis said. "Remember,

187

Isis is a smoke." Elvis had obviously made friends with her, for Adam's cat trotted over to him and rubbed her head against his leg. She ignored the girls.

Mem's whiskers and one eye peeked cautiously around the corner from the living room. He blinked when he saw Isis and retreated.

Isis turned her head in the direction of the living room. She sat and licked her paws.

Her act of innocent charm didn't fool me. I'd seen her chase Mem.

We all watched her, as if she were a much-awaited newborn or some exotic creature from another planet.

"Hey!" Lucy shook us out of our communal reverie. "The newspaper publisher's mail?"

"Right. I did talk to her, but she was tight as a pinched nerve. I have something else I need to tell you. I don't know how this slipped my mind."

We sat around the kitchen table.

Adam snagged a padded chair from the living room and straddled it backward with his forearms crossed over the top.

"Last Saturday, the day before you came, Yolanda and her granddaughter —"

"Oh! Wait just a minute! Lemme get the recorder!" Sonja was up in a flash, bounding down the hall to the bedroom to pick up her machine.

Lucy flipped open her notebook and began to scribble.

Sonja returned and curled one foot behind the opposite knee. "OK. Start again."

"Last Saturday, Yolanda Toynsbee and her granddaughter Jenny came over for lunch," I said, clarifying for posterity exactly who and when and where I got the information. "I wanted to trade notes about the Conklins' business and family connections, and also to tell her about you three coming here as a potential story. Oh, nuts. And that reminds me, she can't spare a reporter, but would like to run a story about your visit if you guys, um —"

"Wrote it?" Lucy tapped the tablet, grinning.

I wiggled. "Um, yeah. Sort of. At least, kept some good notes on what happens."

"The photographer snapped pictures of us this morning," Elvis said.

"Good. But that's not what I wanted to say. Yolanda had Jenny tell me about an incident at the river. Jenny knew she wasn't supposed to go near the water, but she saw a kitty down there that looked like Tut, the mayor's cat. She wanted to rescue it, and apparently got close to the water and her father scolded her. I was ready to dismiss it as any stray cat prowling around, but Jenny, who's five, by the way, said the cat had spots like a cheetah."

Lucy was all business. She held her pen poised. "What does this information add to our case?"

"It wasn't your cat, Adam, or yours, Ivy?" Elvis asked.

"No." Adam and I responded in tandem.

"Isis hasn't left the shop except with me," Adam added. "Too much traffic."

"Memnet goes out, but I can usually see him. I've never noticed him gone for the length of time it would take to go all the way downtown and back. I'd panic."

"That's right," Sonja said. "He's had some rough experiences lately, hasn't he?"

Lucy tapped her pen on the pad some more. "So, didn't you say the mayor was courting other owners of Egyptian Maus to settle in Apple Grove, and in fact, pursued other businesses relating to animals? Might there be someone else new in town, or even just visiting, who owns a similar cat?"

"That's a good question, Lucy." Adam shifted restlessly in the chair. "If Donald wasn't here to connect with a visitor, he or she might have just come and gone without any of us noticing."

I rapped the table lightly with my fist, thinking about how to put my next thought. "I just have a funny feeling that the river is important somehow."

The other four shared thoughtful glances. "Sixth sense is nothing to sneer at," Sonja said. "Does anyone know when we can get into the newspaper office? We don't have all that much time, and I hope we actually figure out why the mayor was killed. By the way, wasn't there an autopsy report? How did he die?"

Adam spoke up. "Bob told me that Dr. Bailey was called in by the coroner to confirm Bartonella henselae, which causes CSD."

Elvis translated: "Cat scratch fever. Disease, I guess — CSD."

"Donald died of cat scratch fever?" I squeaked. "Marion said she'd heard some kind of infection."

Elvis gave me the look my mother reserved for unforgivable ignorance. "It is an infection."

I couldn't believe it. "So, that's it? Donald just got sick and died? Case closed?"

Sonja frowned. "Not necessarily. That gives us cause of death. The timing and circumstances are still suspicious, to say the least. I'll have to study up on the disease."

"CSD's generally not that serious," Elvis said. "My sister got it when we were little. It's sort of like the flu, only not contagious, and usually you just get over it. Your mayor must have had something else going on with his immune system."

"Could he have been deliberately infected?" I asked.

"And treatment withheld?" Elvis nodded. "I see where you're going." He flipped through his notebook again. "Professor Preston did note the unusual position of the body, and commented she thought it had been placed in the stall of the restroom after death occurred."

"The doctor's been ordered to examine every pet in town, and all the strays are to be rounded up," Adam said. "She asked to put up a poster in the shop. The city will pay two dollars for each animal without a collar that's brought in. The city ordered cages to keep the animals at the municipal garage."

I decided Memnet would be strictly a housecat for a long time. The word "strays" made me catch my breath. "I bet the license office will be busy." Then another shiver ran along my back. "Do they think Tut — what will happen to him? It'll be like a bounty hunt with everyone rounding up cats. He'll be hurt."

"All the more reason to find him first," Adam said firmly. "Now, how can we use this information?"

"We have to have our field hours relate to specific elements of police procedure." Sonja spoke for the group. "But there's nothing saying how we should spend the rest of our time."

Lucy nodded. "Right. I still think we need to follow up with the newspaper, in between trying to figure out places Tut would hide. I don't know when the Gazette office will reopen, but I do know that once the site has been secured, Detective Reyes from the station can process the scene. Then, finally, decontamination can begin." She shrugged when we all turned our attention on her. "It was in a manual I studied. Anyway, after an attack like this, the cleanup is similar to the smoke damage from an actual fire. They have to scrub everything and test the equipment. I doubt there'll be a paper for a while."

"Which might put a crimp in Dr. Bailey's mission to test all cats," Adam said, "if they can't get word out that fast."

"It seems strange that a pet would be the cause of Donald's death," I said. "He loved cats so much."

"It might not have been," Lucy reminded me. "There are any number of ways to deliberately administer bacterium."

I wondered if I were getting fevered myself, the way I kept shivering. "Lucy, you're scaring me."

"Germ warfare should scare everybody," the dark-haired girl said.

"Luce . . ." Sonja uttered, in an admonishing tone.

"There's another thing I need to mention," I told them hastily, before our — ahem — peaceful discussion turned contentious. "I saw our friendly council member in charge of sewage, Jeff Hanley, looking on during Tiny's speech."

The others gave me "yeah — so?" shrugs.

"I learned that he's also vice president of the Apple Grove branch of the State's Bank. He's taken his turn as council treasurer in the past."

Lucy turned a baleful eye on me. "And?"

I took a deep breath and stifled the urge to shake her.

Elvis answered. "I think I get it. Remember? Adam and Ivy originally noticed that only a few of the council members appeared to know how the twelve million dollars would be distributed. Hanley was one of them. As a banker, that might mean he has access to it somehow, since the city does business through State's."

"Still," Sonja said, "What kind of means and motive would Hanley have to murder the mayor?"

"Wouldn't the real killers be elsewhere if this isn't the scene of the murder?" Adam asked.

"Who actually controls the money?" Elvis asked.

"Wouldn't it revert to the city treasury, or something?" I felt like a gerbil running on one of those exercise wheels, spinning and getting nowhere.

"Losing that much money would be hard to cover up." Sonja's forehead crinkled. "If the mayor was the only person who had control, business records could be cooked."

Elvis got up. "Including the fact that Mrs. Bader-Conklin has ties to the rival pet food company she's personally invited to move to Apple Grove." He spoke over his shoulder as he went to the tap to get more water. "The corporate world understands these things. Trust me."

"Unfortunately, we're not solving anything with speculation," Sonja broke in. "While we're waiting for the newspaper office to reopen so we can check records, we can interview people. We can keep track of all

195

the cats that are rounded up and taken to the vet. I'll ask around to see if back issues of the Gazette are kept elsewhere. Sometimes a library microfilms them, or the historical society, if there is one."

"Why don't we make some calls now?" Lucy was already eyeing my telephone and the small phone book nearby.

Elvis returned to his seat. "Hold on a sec, Lucy. I want to talk to Ivy a little more first, OK?"

I admired their enthusiasm, but they made me feel old. Safer perhaps, than being alone, but wilted like a morning-after prom corsage.

Elvis flipped back a few pages in his notebook. "The first thing I have to say is that I think I figured out what the big deal is about the Summersby connection." He studied the page, then glanced at me. "I checked on all the businesses listed within the building, and one stood out. Merris Corp. It's an offshoot of MerriFood that direct-contracts pet security systems, like alarms, invisible fences, that sort of thing. Does that help?"

"Probably," I replied. I had not said anything about checking it out myself. "But how can we connect a case of usually non-threatening cat-scratch fever to a high-profile company like MerriFood?"

"What about the mayor's call for help?" Sonja said. "It came from the building."

"Unconfirmed," Lucy said.

Elvis apparently decided to move to the next item on his agenda. "But worth remembering. The second thing I want to discuss is that Lucy and I had a chance to briefly glance through the police report, including inventory of evidence being held, regarding your robbery." Elvis continued, "I haven't seen that many files from this jurisdiction, but it seemed pretty thorough. The usual photos, prints, statements, specimens, the burlap bag."

Lucy nodded curtly. "Did you know they interviewed the council members about the meeting you attended? And your neighbors about the robbery?"

"I can understand interviewing the neighbors," I said. "But why the council members?" I swallowed. "All of them?"

"Including Hanley." Lucy's voice was soft. She leaned toward me. "I think you have an unofficial ally in Officer Ripple. His notes mentioned your suspicions regarding the absence of the mayor and the differing reactions from council members. He's spent a number of hours on the case and agreed the circumstances around the death warrant a thorough investigation."

Finally! I thought the cops should have been suspicious by now, especially with the M.E. agreeing the body had been moved.

Elvis twisted his neck as if to loosen taut muscles. "I've been impressed that Officer Ripple's looked at the file almost every day and made a lot of personal notes, especially since the missing persons report was filed for Mrs. Conklin."

Adam spoke up. "What did the report say about Hanley's interview?"

Elvis flipped the pad's cover forward and back with nervous energy. "I only skimmed it. He was surprised the mayor had confided about the tax grants to anyone outside of the council. He claimed the mayor told him that, until he was in a position to begin awarding the money, he wanted to keep it quiet. That's mostly the gist. I think we can safely cross him off the suspect list."

Adam shifted in the chair. "How about Letty Grimm?"

Elvis shook his head. "Our time was up for that area of the station. I really didn't study the file as much as I would have liked. Not long after, the call came through about trouble at the newspaper office. Ripple let me come as long as I stayed out of the way."

"We were turned out," Sonja said. She

checked her machine. "You know, this makes me wonder just when Margaret Bader-Conklin figured out what her husband was doing about these grants. The mayor appeared to be able to keep his business and personal life separate, up to a point."

"Until he started mixing the two." Lucy raised a brow.

"What do you mean?" I asked.

Elvis snorted. "Look who he invited to share the wealth."

Lucy wrinkled her nose. "Cat lovers. From the personal side of his life."

"From which his wife was cut off." Elvis smacked his notebook on the edge of the table.

Sonja enunciated the words directly into her tape recorder. "By her allergies."

I watched the students, fascinated with their logic. It made sense. She was a pharmacist, after all. And she was missing. I could go there. I grinned.

Sonja turned off the recorder. "Maybe we should write up a report of the day so far and figure out what we'll say at our teleconference with Professor Preston."

"I should get back to my place," Adam said. As he stood, Isis leapt into his arms.

Memnet slunk into the kitchen.

Surprisingly, both cats ignored each other instead of yowling.

Mem headed for Sonja.

I walked Adam outside. Pulling abreast of my car, I asked, "Would you like a ride?"

"It's nice enough, even if it's a little warm. We'll walk, thanks. I could use the exercise."

I glanced at his firm middle and flexing arm muscles and doubted that very much. "I'll walk with you a little, if that's OK."

"More than OK." Isis perched on his shoulder and he grabbed my hand, swinging it as we turned out of the driveway to walk down the block.

At the intersection, Adam stopped. "I'd like you to consider boarding Elvis here with you."

My steps faltered. I'd expected something like that. The request wasn't unwelcome after words like bioterrorism had been bandied about. "What about you? You shouldn't be alone in your place."

He gave me a wry smile. "Much as I'd like to pretend to be able to take care of myself, I have to agree with you. I have some ideas I'm mulling over. Unfortunately, I don't know who to trust. I thought about calling Jim and Yolanda, but they have enough worries."

"Maybe you should stay with us, too."

200

"Now that could damage your reputation." He squeezed my knuckles. "Your house isn't that big. But I appreciate the offer."

We walked quietly for the next half block.

"How do you feel about Apple Grove, now that we've been here a while?"

Hearing Adam say "we" made my heart twitter. But the tone of his question, the whole idea of it, had me worried. Mostly because I didn't know how to answer.

11

How did I feel about Apple Grove?

In bed that night I thumped my pillow
into moguls and pulled the blankets right
out of their tucks.

The girls and Elvis murmured in the
kitchen. He had declared my sofa perfectly
comfortable and rolled out a sleeping bag.

They were trying to be quiet, but I was
used to being alone in my house, so any
sounds stood out. I rolled again, dragging
the sheet with me.

Memnet leapt down. Apparently, he
couldn't tolerate my restlessness, either.

I wanted to love Apple Grove, my new
home. I had prayed about it and felt calm
and comfortable after the torment of Stanley and our broken engagement.

I flopped onto my back. I loved this house.
My own little house. And I realized I was
falling for Adam Thompson in a way that
made me realize that Stanley had merely

been a crutch — the right kind of guy at the preordained right time to be married in my life. "He respects me" had been my most common description of our relationship. I couldn't even remember the last time we'd said, "I love you" to each other during our years together. We never talked about matters of faith, and my mother had been disappointed to find I had stopped going to church. I'd missed it and enjoyed New Horizons and my new friends.

I turned on my side and stared out the window at the moonlight. I could see the neighbor's clothesline topping the back fence. Taylor Robbins had left her pink pedal power tricycle outside again. These were nice people. They weren't the ones spreading rumors and lies about me. Just because someone robbed me, hurt my pet, threatened Yolanda by vandalizing her business, and maybe even caused the death of the mayor —

I sat up. OK, so Apple Grove had its downside. Didn't every town?

I tossed Grandma Trudy's rose garden quilt aside and got to my feet. "Not like this!" I reached for my robe and clopped down the hall to the kitchen.

"I'm sorry. Did we wake you?" Sonja whispered.

"No, of course not." I spoke in a normal voice.

Sonja flushed.

"I just have a lot to think about." The kettle was already warm, and I set a bag of mint tea to steep in a plain mug.

The light over the stove illuminated the room, setting an intimate atmosphere.

With a foot still in a sock, Lucy pushed a chair out.

They waited for me to speak.

"What's the worst thing that ever happened to you?" I asked.

"Not getting into the university I'd wanted," Lucy said promptly, naming a well-known private school.

Sonja was slower to reply. "Seeing my cousin break her neck in a diving accident."

Elvis balanced his spoon on the rim of his mug. "Not getting an immediate invitation to join the FBI."

"How about you?" Lucy asked me. She took a swig of her drink.

Sometimes the best conversations were held amongst virtual strangers at 1:00 AM.

I studied the bag floating in steaming water in front of me as I cradled the cup with both hands. "Until lately, the worst thing that happened in my life, after the death of my father of course, was my boyfriend leaving me, right before the wedding. I went to the college I wanted, started the business that I wanted. Even my father died when I was just a little girl, so I don't really remember him." I took a sip of fragrant tea. "As we discussed this case, I realized that I didn't know Donald as well as I thought, and I wondered why I shouldn't just leave Apple Grove. The situation is potentially dangerous, and I worry about all of us."

The three students glanced at each other.

Lucy spoke first. "There's a lot to be said for friendship. The mayor, even if you didn't know him very well, was obviously important to you."

I tried not to shudder.

Sonja raised an eyebrow. "And then there's Mr. Thompson."

Yeah, Adam. The one who had asked me how I felt about lovely little Apple Grove, now that we were both settled here. "He's gone to a lot of effort and expense to establish his business," I said, deliberately refusing to discuss any personal relationship. "He has more to lose than I do, especially financially, if we pull up and leave."

Lucy narrowed her eyes and raised her chin. "Not according to Elvis."

"Oh?" I glanced at Elvis who pushed his

mug around the table and drew his mouth tight.

Lucy filled in the blanks for him, talking as if he weren't in the same room. "He says Adam Thompson actually made big bucks by putting a coffee joint in Apple Grove. He has three partners behind the business and the building lease." She held up three fingers, bending them as she spoke. "One is your former mayor; the others are Mr. Jeff Hanley and a Mr. Cal Stewart."

My heart stopped beating and the cup slipped from my nerveless hands.

Lucy ran for a dish towel to mop hot tea.

I sat like stone. I would definitely be tired tomorrow.

Sonja plodded into the house the next afternoon and tossed her notebook onto the kitchen table. "We just had a discussion with Ms. Crosby about the engineering needs of a smaller city. She was polite enough." Sonja's voice trailed off. She flopped onto a seat.

I pushed the plate of peanut butter cookies in front of her.

"Thanks."

Memnet jumped onto her lap, circled and made himself at home, blinking and yawning.

"Did you get around to what she knew about the money or what she might have had against Donald?"

"I thought I was being subtle, but I think she caught on to me sooner than I wanted her to. She just out and out said that the mayor should have included everyone in the grant information. She'd applied for grants herself on behalf of the city in the past and this was the way it had always been done." Sonja consulted the notebook. "Ms. Crosby has quite a way with words. Quote. 'I can't imagine why the mayor would shirk his responsibilities in such an ill-conceived and poorly-mastered plot to deny the city its needed new treatment plant. I have never been involved in such a reprehensible, deceitful act and you can be sure that I will report this activity to the proper state authorities. And obviously owning a cat was a big mistake.' End quote."

I couldn't stop a grin at her rendition of Crosby's assumed huff.

Sonja nibbled at her cookie. "I didn't want her to be guilty. Just to shed some light on the situation."

I patted her hand. "That's all right."

"Elvis got stuck with the mayor's wife's assistant. I can't wait to hear how he did."

Elvis pulled open the kitchen screen door.

"You don't have to." He scrubbed at his curls and heaved a sigh. "Ms. Grimm didn't even open the door. Told me she'd been instructed to call the police should anyone attempt to trespass while Mrs. Conklin was away. I could hear sirens in the background, but I'm pretty sure they were a recording from the house. I didn't stick around to find out."

Sonja bit her lip.

Elvis set my keys in front of me. "Thanks for the use of your car, Ivy."

"You're welcome. Help yourself to something to drink."

Elvis found his favorite computer geek mug in the cupboard and poured milk from the fridge. "How'd it go with you, Sonja?"

"Better than yours, apparently." She smiled. "Sorry you had such a rough time. Crosby was sincerely outraged by everything that's been going on behind her back."

"Is Lucy at the mayor's office now?" I asked them.

"Yes," they replied in unison.

"I think she'll be a while, then. Rupert Murphy likes to gripe in volumes. I can't wait to hear what he had to say about ordering the fourth-floor restroom closed." Although I'd offered to help with the interviews, the students had wanted to handle all the people on the list themselves.

Lucy was supposed to talk to Marion as well as the acting mayor, Rupert Murphy. Margaret Bader-Conklin was currently unavailable, so that left the banker and the vet.

Sonja planned to take Mem in for a little checkup as an excuse to talk to Dr. Bailey, and also get the latest intel on the great stray feline hunt.

I didn't know how they planned to handle Hanley.

Donald's memorial service was held on Wednesday morning, just as Yolanda predicted. It was decorous, sober and completely unremarkable. The justice of the peace, Bill Compton, led the pledge of allegiance. Rupert read a ten-minute eulogy that sounded more like a high school biography, and Pastor Belman prayed right out of his little black book. That was it. The funeral home was decked out like Independence Day.

People came in for the service and left. There had been no receiving line, as there was no one to comfort but ourselves. Margaret's family did not attend. Very bizarre. Definitely no closure for me. I sat next to Adam the whole time, hugging my elbows and trying not to cry.

Nobody lingered.

He went back to work afterward.

I couldn't bring myself to mention that I was aware of his silent partners and wondered if I needed to add him to the suspect list. Mom would have been heart-broken to learn of his deception.

In the late afternoon, I decided to see what was happening downtown. I parked in the municipal lot and hiked up the several blocks to the newspaper office. A little humid breeze from the river swirled through the alleys.

Yolanda stood on the sidewalk in front of the open Gazette door, thin in dark shorts and a white tank top, brandishing a mop at someone inside. She pointed to her front window with her free hand. From my angle I could see just the middle of another person on a ladder inside, vigorously shaking his hips as a white cloth was applied to the glass.

"There! Right top — center — you got it. Hi, Ivy," she called to me. "This is it! The cleaning crew is nearly done, and we can get back to business. We only needed to borrow PrintCraft's shop for one edition." She named a private specialty printing chain, which had a branch in Colby.

"Congratulations. I knew nothing much would keep the presses down. What can I do to help?"

"Oh, if you want to stop in tomorrow, after lunch, you can work on some ads. Jenny will be coming and she's quite the little interrupter."

"I'll do that. About one?" Everything sparkled, and the smell of bleach overrode the faint underlying hints of sulfur. "I think the kids will be in soon then to sort through your back issues."

"Fine. You can all come together."

On to my next stop. I crossed the street to walk down the other side. I stuck my hands in the pockets of my jeans as I sauntered along Main Street, casually glancing down the various narrow alleys between the soft red brick buildings. The smell of fried potatoes and onions wafted from Tiny's across the width of the street.

The drug store door opened for an elderly woman who was dressed in a rumpled raincoat and carried a cane. She wore a plastic rain hood tied under her chin.

I waited until she hobbled out of my path.

Visible through the big window of the barber shop, Bob had a customer in the chair. He waved his scissors.

I waved back. I halted when I reached the

junction of the next building. Adam's sandwich board sign proclaimed that chocolate truffle was the flavor of the day and he had just gotten in the newest Café murder mystery. A popular line of mysteries out over the past eight years, I mentioned that I was eager to read the next installment myself. I hoped no one in town would take the subject matter as a suggested course of action or a sign of things to come.

As I hesitated on the sidewalk, a solid presence thunked into me.

"Sorry," the man called over his shoulder. He never stopped, and I didn't get a good look at him. Just an anonymous stranger with a black businessman's satchel slung over his shoulder.

A trio of ladies exited Tiny's and stood under the green striped awning, fussing with their purses and scarves.

I recognized them from church and raised my hand and smiled. I could only remember Mrs. Engelbrecht's name. "Hello!" I called.

Mrs. Engelbrecht looked across at me. She assumed an expression of having just tasted a spoonful of revolting medicine. She elbowed her partner.

The other woman hollered in a loud voice. "You ought to be ashamed, young lady! Coming to our nice village and carrying on like you do!"

Mrs. Engelbrecht pulled on a pale leather driving glove. "We don't want your kind here."

The three of them took each other's elbows, stuck their noses in the air and strode away.

I lowered my hand and closed my mouth, swallowing against acid reflux. Not yet ready to confront Adam about his backers, I slumped against the bricks, thinking. What could those ladies have meant? They had been polite but distant in church last Sunday, and of course they'd been to the funeral that morning, although no one said much of anything to anyone else. It was almost as if Donald's last public appearance had been a shameful one.

I shook my head, gathered in a deep breath and straightened.

Letty Grimm was staring at me from the window of Tiny's. She immediately turned away and chatted with her companions, whom I could not see clearly.

Marion Green had told me that Margaret's assistant was up to no good. Letty had already passed around town that Adam's family had been killed while he watched. Oh, and something or other about us trying to take over the city. According to her, that's why we attended that council meeting: to test the strength of the board members and see who could potentially be turned to the dark side. He and I obviously were behind the plot to assassinate the mayor and that was why Margaret needed to hide out. She was next. I had thought Marion was joking when she'd hesitatingly brought the story to my attention yesterday on the phone.

Now I was in a melancholy mood. If I were being accused of something wicked, the thought of actually doing it cheered me up. Yeah, right. I couldn't think of anything remotely evil to do. Besides I was the one who always got caught. People could be speeding around me on the highway, but if I went five miles over, flashers appeared from nowhere in my rearview mirror. I stared after the church ladies, who disappeared around the corner.

Once again, I breathed in and bowed my head. "Sorry, Lord." I had once been active in the church my mother and I attended all the while I lived at home. Stanley held a profoundly indifferent faith, and I fell out of regular prayer and worship. Even if Apple Grove had not put out the proverbial welcome mat for me, I was determined to go back to a habitual church life. The thought of seeing those ladies at New Horizons next week made me squirm, but I liked the Gainses.

I entered Adam's empty shop, rejoicing in the air-conditioning. Stacks of new books sat in an enticing array on the coffee table between blue wing chairs. The smell of chocolate made my stomach rumble. I had not had much of an appetite since yesterday. Adam's voice floated out from his office. As I passed the coffee counter I noticed a dish of complimentary cubes of chocolate candy. I snagged a piece, unwrapped it and put it in my mouth as I meandered toward the magazine racks.

Adam came out. "Ivy. I'm glad you stopped in." He shook his head. "I can't imagine what Donald would have thought of that funeral."

I swallowed, unable to make words come out yet. I nodded, hoping he would accept that. His eyes were dark with a fatigue that matched mine, his features wary. I felt sorry for him, even in my present distress.

"I wondered if I'd get many traveling sales reps in Apple Grove," he said. "How do you like that candy? A salesman stopped in here earlier. Once I tasted it, I thought it wouldn't hurt to try. He said they just started a new coffee line, too. That's what's on special today."

It wasn't like Adam to prattle. Maybe he'd had a caffeine overload.

Chocolate worked better on me when I was upset. "My former fiancé worked in sales for a chocolate company. Not this one, though. This is good — nice and fudgy."

He cleared his throat. "Would you like a cup of coffee?"

"Sure." We moved over to the counter and he worked the machine.

I reached for the coin purse I carried with me in my right pocket when I didn't want to lug a purse around. My pocket was empty. Out of my left pocket I pulled a tissue and my cell phone and a piece of lint. No coin purse. I felt the prickle of sweat around my hairline.

Adam set the paper cup in front of me. "What's the matter, Ivy? It's on the house."

"Thanks, but I think I — oh, no."

"What?"

"I think I've been pick-pocketed."

"Are you sure? When?"

"I'm sure I had my coin purse with me. I put the car key, my license and some change in it. It had to have been that guy."

"What guy?"

I explained about the man who bumped into me on the sidewalk. "Right before Mrs.

Engelbrecht and her friends shouted at me."

Adam came around the counter to put a soothing hand on my shoulder. "You've got me more than a little concerned here. What's this about Mrs. Engelbrecht? But wait, we should call the police first."

"Not again!" I wilted into a deep cushioned chair with my chocolate coffee and another candy from the dish.

He went to call the station. He also turned off the background recording of Carmen. "Officer Ripple's on his way. I think I heard him call for Lucy as he hung up."

"Great. Thanks. This candy is pretty good," I repeated.

Adam sat on the arm of the oversize chair, leaning forward with his elbows on his lap. "You didn't seem very happy when you came in. More than sad from the funeral. Is there something you want to talk about? What did the Engelbrecht woman say?"

"I'm certainly not happy about that, and I can't imagine what she meant when she accused me of 'carrying on.' " I shook my head and took a sip of the coffee. "I saw Letty Grimm and company in the window of the buffet, so I can guess how the gossip is being churned. Marion told me yesterday about some fantastic tale going around how you and I are in cahoots to take over Apple

Grove." I bit the insides of my lips and risked a glance at his amused expression. "But, no, I wanted to ask you, ask you —"

Adam's door chime sounded as my favorite policeman and his current sidekick arrived.

"Officer Ripple, Lucy. Thanks for coming," I interrupted myself, heaving a sigh of relief.

Adam narrowed his eyes and stood.

I gave my statement as Ripple took the opportunity to explain things in detail to Lucy. We even walked outside so I could show them the spot where the presumed theft occurred. We all searched the sidewalk and gutter carefully to make sure I had not simply dropped my purse.

"All righty, then," Ripple said. "We'll be in touch." He and Lucy took off.

Adam stood in the door of Mea Cuppa waiting for me.

Since I kept a spare key hidden by the gas tank, I could at least drive my car home.

"I can take you tomorrow afternoon to get a new driver's license," he said, when we reentered the shop. "With school out, Colleen will come in the afternoons."

"Thank you. That would be great."

"Business seems pretty slow today."

He shrugged. "That happens. Things go

in cycles. When we have the official grand opening, I expect it'll pick up again."

He didn't seem eager to resume our interrupted conversation, and I didn't press for it, since three bad things had already happened today. I finished the coffee and tossed my cup in the waste basket. I grabbed another chocolate hoping it would give me an endorphin rush. "I guess I'll get going. See you later."

The next day the students and I crowded around Yolanda's work table to eat a late lunch.

"You do seem to be the target of an unusual amount of crime," Sonja noted soberly over her roast beef sandwich.

I'd brought one for Yolanda, too, as well as a snack for Jenny.

The munchkin hopped onto Elvis's lap as soon as he sat down.

Elvis waved a hand at Yolanda's sharp retort to her granddaughter. "No worries. I have oodles of nieces and nephews. I like kids."

Lucy finished first. "Let's get to work." She encouraged us to take a last bite or swallow, and then passed around a waste basket.

Yolanda had shown me the ad files earlier

and I sat down now at the computer to begin some updates.

She led the others to a storage room tucked behind the office. Ten minutes later they paraded back, Elvis carrying bound issues. Yolanda, red-faced, sputtered.

Jenny took the rear flank, galloping on an imaginary pony.

I heard Sonja's voice from behind a large file. "We figured out why someone threw the stink grenade — to cover up a theft." She dumped her stack on a table. "The files from the years the mayor was in high school and college are missing."

Elvis set the more recent files he carried next to hers. "Sonja and I can start with these."

Yolanda's sour expression returned. "I told them that we'd recently allowed the historical society to pick up our multiples. That makes more storage room for us. I'll call the police. Lucy will check at the society headquarters for the missing issues. Mrs. Green, Bob's mother, is president of the society."

"They must be important if someone stole them," Lucy declared. She took Sonja's car for the drive to the Old Birch House museum, the home of Solomon Birch, one of Apple Grove's most prominent citizens of the nineteenth century.

I had yet to visit the place myself, but I heard they put on a wonderful Christmas open house. Now I wondered if I would be in Apple Grove that long.

Sonja and Elvis methodically worked their way through recent issues, searching for articles pertaining to city government and the mayor personally. I could hear them, pointing out facts and showing each other columns of interest.

Jenny perched on a chair, drawing more fantastic pictures.

Ripple came.

I tried to make myself invisible while he talked to Yolanda and, other than a sharp glance in my direction, he said nothing to me before he left.

An hour later, Lucy strode in with a box of past issues of the years in question. "They were in the attic," Lucy said. "But they have a great system for keeping track of items. Some computer program called Past Perfect. She said we could keep them as long as we need." She set the box on the floor near the work table. "Let's all look at these together, since someone thought they were important."

Yolanda came out of her office.

I saved my work on the computer and

then bent over the yellowing pages.

"My," Yolanda repeated with each new paragraph. "Jim had just started working with his folks here at the Gazette. Even then he had an eye for a story."

I turned another page. "How are things going with his treatment?"

"I spoke with the doctor a while ago," Yolanda replied. "I could take him home today." Her eyes lit on her granddaughter. "Except for the bundle of energy we have to deal with. He could never stand that. I needed to ask for another day's extension." Her voice dropped to a whisper. "Jenny's daddy will pick her up tomorrow. Then I can get Jim."

I lowered my voice too. "Why don't you let me take her tonight? She can have a slumber party with all of us. I have a little trundle bed in my room she could use."

"Oh, that's too much — would you?"

The tired lines around Yolanda's eyes worried me. "Unless you're too tired yourself to take care of Jim."

"I think that would be great fun," Sonja said, making it clear she'd overheard. "Why don't we take her with us when we leave? We'll go pick up her bag from your place and get a hamburger, since Ivy has to go get a replacement driver's license."

We finalized the plans in hushed tones until Jenny glared at us. Being tossed around from father to mother to grandparent must be unsettling to the five-year-old.

Yolanda took the little girl on her lap. "How would you like to go stay at Ivy's house tonight? With Sonja and Lucy?"

Jenny wasn't sure. She pouted and crossed her little arms. "And Memnet?"

"Yes," the little girl's grandma assured her. "Just for tonight. So I can get Grandpa home."

"OK. What will we play?"

Once Jenny's question was satisfied by the girls, we went back to work.

Sonja noticed the photograph first. "Hey, everyone. Look at this." We gathered around to peer at a grainy black and white pose of the high school debate team.

Yolanda squinted at the page. "Apple Grove and Westward High joined forces, as neither of them had enough kids to make a good team."

Sonja pointed to a figure. "The kid standing next to Donald appears an awful lot like him. Are they related, do you think?"

Yolanda stared at the caption. "Of course. Donald's aunt, his mother's sister, lives in Colby, where Westward is. Her maiden name was —"

"Grimm," Elvis read.

"Yes," Yolanda said. "Abigail Grimm. So, Ronny there is Donald's cousin. His mother never married, so the whole situation was kept hushed."

"That wouldn't happen to be the same as Letty Grimm, would it?" I asked.

"Ronald is, or was, married to Letty," Yolanda told us.

"The same woman who is the mayor's wife's assistant?" Elvis asked.

"Oh, boy," Sonja said.

Not just any "oh, boy." That must have been the guy at Donald's house that day Adam and I visited . . . before we found . . . him.

Lucy held up another later issue. "That's not all. That picture was high school. This is not." She held the society section from summertime, six years later. "Get a load of the mayor's wedding picture."

"Um, folks," Elvis said, after an intense study. "Check out the best man."

In twenty-odd years, Jeff Hanley had not changed all that much.

12

Jeff Hanley, the vice president of the State's Bank branch in Apple Grove where the city government did business, had been Donald's best man at his wedding. Donald's cousin's wife was Margaret's assistant. Adam thought Donald had no living family. What happened to Letty's husband? Had he been the man at the window of Donald's house? The information flickered like lightning across my neurons. What had Donald been up to? I decided not to say anything yet, until I'd spoken to Adam. "Yolanda," I asked, "Did Ronny Grimm pass away?"

"I don't recall," she replied, frowning.

"So, where do we go from here?" Lucy asked. "How do all these bits fit into our puzzle?"

"Hanley's on the city council." Elvis got up to pace across the floor in front of the counter. "He's one of few people who knew about, and presumably could access, the grant money."

Besides being one of the partners backing Adam Thompson. That must mean Hanley had money to invest. But was it his own, or did he use some of the grant money? Elvis knew about Adam's business deal.

"Elvis?" I hated to ask. "Please tell me what, exactly, you know about Mea Cuppa's Apple Grove store. And the partners."

Elvis sneaked a peek at Sonja.

Sonja shrugged permission.

He regained his seat at the work table. "I happened to run across some papers in Adam's office to indicate that he had partners."

I felt a temper tantrum coming on. "I heard Lucy say 'Hanley, Stewart, and the mayor' the other night. Where do you think they got the money?"

Yolanda snorted. That was not a good sign.

My shoulder muscles tensed.

"I think it was a personal business arrangement." Elvis leaned his arm backward over his chair. He twisted his head to stare out the clean front window through the large red, backward lettering proclaiming "ettezaG."

"What *else* did you notice about the papers in Adam's *private* office?"

226

He flinched at my tone.

Sonja began to rattle the books in front of her.

Yolanda hustled to the counter to pull out a notebook and pen. "Taxes, taxes . . ." she mumbled.

Elvis stared at me. "Why don't you talk to Adam about this?" When I didn't reply, he resignedly said, "What I understood about the agreement was that, if the business earned a net profit of at least fifteen percent of the investment and Mr. Thompson wanted to pull out after a year, he'd take the profits and the others would take over the business."

"Thank you." I stood.

Yolanda, in full reporter mode, flipped open her ever-ready notebook.

"I have some things to take care of," I told them. "Yolanda, I'll be back later to finish the page I was on."

She barely acknowledged me before beginning a question and answer session with the students.

It was time to meet Adam, so he could take me to get a replacement driver's license. For the first time since laying my eyes on the handsome but scarred man at the CAT convention, I was apprehensive about being with him. I did not like feeling that way at all. I checked my watch. I had a few minutes, so I decided to call the one person I was sure I could trust. "Mom?"

"Yes, dear." Her tinny voice came through the miniscule receiver I tucked against my ear. "I'm walking through the quad to my next class. What's up?"

I squeezed the tears to the back of my eyeballs. "We have some new information. Donald had a cousin whose wife is Margaret's assistant. Then the students found a photograph that showed Donald's best man was the vice president of the bank. And my purse was stolen." *And I'm so naïve. And the love of my life is a liar.*

"Oh, darling. I'm so sorry. Do you need me to come up this weekend? Do you need any money?"

I choked back a gurgly laugh. "No, Mom. Everything's all right. It was just my little coin purse. I'm sure you'll have a good conversation with the students this evening."

"Yes." She sounded a bit breathless as she walked. She must be in a hurry. "They've been amassing some good field experience. Placing them in Apple Grove is turning out to be a suitable work site. I might have to set up a regular program. But did you make out a police report for your purse? Or did they catch the thief?"

"Yes and no. You're busy. I won't keep you," I said.

"That's all right, dear. I'm sure you can rely on your friends and Adam for support."

"Um, right. Thanks, Mom. I'll talk to you soon."

Big breath in. Out. That's it. Adam and Colleen greeted me when I reached Mea Cuppa. I made myself smile at them before I followed Adam out back where he kept his truck.

"Did you uncover any huge secrets at the Gazette?" he asked once we were underway.

"As a matter of fact, we did." I tried to act naturally while I told him about the photographs and Letty's relationship to the Conklins. And about the look-alike cousin. "That must have been him at the window that first day we went to visit the house and Letty answered the door." My lips ranneth over.

"Makes sense. I wonder why Donald didn't mention his cousin? So, does anyone know if Letty's husband is alive and where he might be now?"

"Yolanda says she never kept track what happened to him, or if he's alive or not."

"Let's assume he is, then. If Margaret and Letty had some kind of plot going on, it would make sense to keep him out of sight."

"Until they want to use him," I said. I wanted to believe Adam knew nothing about Ronald Grimm. I could be convinced that meant he wasn't in on the plot with Hanley.

"Use him? It's not any of our business who his wife hires as her personal assistant."

"You're right. Unless he was the guy who threatened us that night outside of city hall after the meeting. Or the guy who's been in my house and hurt my cat."

"We don't have any proof of that," he said.

Why would Adam defend the bad guys all of a sudden? I decided I didn't want to go down that road.

He pulled into the parking lot of the Department of Motor Vehicles office, narrowly avoiding a grinning teenager with a dazed-looking passenger who peeled out of his spot, radio blasting. "Must be Mom next to him." Adam laughed. "Do you want me to come in with you?"

The lot was full, and I figured it could be a long wait. I wouldn't bring up the questions I needed to ask him in a public place. "It's crowded. I might have to wait in line."

He nodded. I left him sitting there, legs stretched out and catalog in hand.

A half-hour later, when I returned, Adam hadn't even changed position. I had done some soul searching while I stood in line. I admitted an over-active and ultra-sensitive personality. He could not possibly have had anything to do with Donald's death. Donald had respected Adam enough to invite him to Apple Grove. If nothing else, Donald's endorsement was all I needed. I forgave Adam for my delusions. "Hi, there. That wasn't so bad. Thanks so much for bringing me. I owe you lunch."

He waited while I buckled up. "Sounds good. Show me your picture."

I groaned but held up my new license. He didn't laugh. "You take a pretty picture, Miss Preston."

Drat. I had just worked up the courage to ask about his business arrangement.

"Do you have a little time?" Adam asked me now. "I've never been down to that little park we passed. Have you?"

"No."

He turned off the road to drive down a steeply pitched entrance to a small county park along the Founders River. A bubbly gurgle of water splashed along the shallow riverbed a couple of miles out of town. Rusty oak leaves framed a brilliant sky. A crop of dandelion wisps floated lazily over the sparkly water, creating a scene from one of those vintage Americana paintings.

We stood at the edge of the bank, watching ripples form across a wide mossy rock.

He skipped a stone across the narrow expanse and it landed on the other side. "I suspect you wanted to ask me something," Adam said, his back to me. "Something about Mea Cuppa, I believe?"

He couldn't have caught my muse more neatly than if he'd cast with a baited hook and line. I paced a few steps to perch on a faded green picnic table. I folded my hands between my knees. Might as well get it all out now. "Elvis said that you had backers. That you were offered incentives to establish a coffee shop in Apple Grove."

Adam tossed another stone directly to the other side of the river before coming to stand next to me. "Weren't you?"

"What do you mean?"

"Come on, Ivy. Donald helped you get your house and paid for the multiple utility feeds coming in. He even hustled through a zoning code exception, so you could run your business in a residential area."

He had a point.

"What about your partners?" I asked. "Where did the money come from? Did they dig into the money Donald was awarded? Is that why you know so much about it?"

Adam sat next to me and thumped the wooden seat. "Ivy! Is that what you think? I'm 'in' on this big plot to take over Apple Grove?"

I could not look at him. I stared at an ant carrying a huge crumb across the width of the table. I wiped a tear and blew my nose. And I was glad to bury my face in Adam's shirtfront when he pulled me roughly into his embrace.

"Ivy, Ivy. Everything will be all right."

"What's going on? I don't understand any of this. Why would anyone hate us without even getting to know us?"

"It's called prejudice, honey. And it's caused every day by people who have shame, secrets, greed, and fear."

"I'm so afraid." I cried harder, shaking.

"So'm I. That's why I asked you how you felt about living here."

"El-Elvis sa-said you were supposed to stay a year."

Adam laughed. "Where'd he hear that?"

"He saw it on the same paperwork with your partner's names."

"Look, Ivy. Donald knew I owned a successful book and coffeehouse franchise already started in the city. He approached me about setting up another shop in Apple Grove. Apple Grove is small, a potentially unprofitable market for me. I never would have considered it but for Donald contracting with me so that I wouldn't lose money on the deal. He had this prime downtown space already, as well as investors for the equipment and stock." Adam drew back to meet my eyes before speaking again.

How could I not trust him?

"Donald drew up the contract," he said. "I had my lawyer go over it. The names of the partners were in there, but they didn't mean anything to me at the time. It was a good, private deal. The space was owned by the city and Donald explained to me about the business grants that covered it." He rubbed my shoulders. "There was nothing even remotely illegal about it. The partners could operate the business or shut it down after a year if I optioned out of the contract." His voice deepened. "I had nothing to lose. I was ready for a change of pace, even if it was just a year." His hands wandered down my arms and across my back. I watched his lips come closer. "And there was you."

So, I'm weak. Naïve and weak. The man feeds me coffee and chocolate and kisses me senseless. He also loves cats and children. "Um, Adam?"

"Yes?"

"I volunteered to keep Yolanda's grand-daughter tonight. I'd better get back."

"Do you want some company?"

Perfect answer. "Yes, please."

I was amazed at how tolerant Memnet acted with our little visitor that evening. My pet was extraordinarily attentive to Jenny, whom he'd been wary of at their first meeting. She followed him everywhere, and even watched, fascinated, while he used the litter box. They played a sort of jumping contest and also a chase game, which Mem won. He even tugged on a yarn ball for her.

Adam had been Jenny's second favorite play thing and I think it did him good. He'd been patient and lenient to the little girl's demands to both romp and read, but never let her get out of control with all the attention she received.

When he was ready to leave we had to pry Jenny out of his arms. She made a huge show of not wanting to let him go, then performed a touching gesture. She leaned forward and put her lips against the scar on his neck.

I walked him out to his truck. "I didn't think about how you might feel until I watched you with Jenny. Was it hard for you?"

He shook his head, a faintly wistful smile flashing across his face. "No." He turned his profile to me before I heard him say, "Did you ever think about having children?"

I wasn't having a conversation like this to his back, so I waited until he faced me, looking as if he wished I hadn't heard. "Yes."

We stared into each other's eyes. I wasn't sure who blinked first, but it was a good time to change the subject. We talked briefly about alternative plans after the students left and we would each be alone again. He had decided to check into the recently finished convention center hotel, aptly called The Prairie Center, out near the highway for a few nights. Since Elvis came to stay with us to provide another number for our safety, not even Adam wanted to be alone in his downtown apartment.

With the rumor mill spewing, I didn't think it mattered much if Adam stayed at my house unchaperoned, but he didn't like the idea.

"It doesn't matter really, what they think of us, except that we know what's right and what's wrong, and we can't afford to alienate future business," he reasonably pointed out. "Besides," he said with a wolfish grin, "I don't trust you to keep your hands off me."

A few minutes later I walked back into my house, fingers on my kiss-swollen lips and arms achingly empty. He had just cause not to trust me.

Friday was already monumental for being the last day the Maplewood students would be with us. Any more excitement and I would change my name to Alice. As in Wonderland.

At 10:15 in the morning, Marion got through to me on my personal line.

"Ivy! You're not gonna believe this!" Marion said in her breathless excited manner. "I'm on my break, so I just have a couple of minutes. You know how Rupert Murphy's been the acting mayor, right? And acting like a king idiot, I might add?"

"Uh-huh," I mumbled, chasing a quarter that rolled close to the refrigerator. I had upended the contents of my purse on the kitchen table to do a periodic cleaning and didn't want to lose anything.

"Guess who showed up on the throne this morning! Guess!" she commanded.

"Um, I don't know, Marion. King Arthur with Excalibur in his hand?"

"Huh? No. Come on, Ivy!"

"Marion, I'm not good with guessing games. Just tell me."

"Margaret Bader-Conklin, big as life. And the VP of MerriFoods in her train. They're in a meeting right now. Kicked Murphy out of the mayor's office. He threatened to sue. Oh-oh."

"What? What?" I wished I was with her now.

"Hackman's just showed up, trailing Ripple and Larken, and I believe — yes, your Elvis."

"What can the cops do?"

"Gotta go! I'll call you later."

"Marion! Wait!" The line went to the buzz of a hang-up. Now that was news. And I was too far away to do anything about it. I called Yolanda's number to make sure she'd heard, but all I got was a busy signal. I tried Mea Cuppa: same thing.

I didn't dare try to interrupt Lucy or Sonja on her cell. Hmmm . . . what to do. I realized that I had an urge for a cup of Adam's coffee. The shop was probably the closest I would be able to get to city hall. The street parking spaces were full, so I drove behind the bookstore and parked next to Adam's truck and went in the back way.

Unlike the previous few days, several customers wandered the store. Most of them stood in the front window where, I discovered, they had a good view of Yolanda interviewing Rupert Murphy who stood on the sidewalk across the street, a disgruntled and impatient television news crew from Springfield hovering nearby.

"I was wondering when you'd get here," Adam said, as I approached the counter. He was idle for the moment.

"Tell me everything you know," I demanded.

"I think I've forgotten more than I remember over the course of my long life," he teased. "How about just what's going on this morning?" He set a six-ounce size paper cup with Mea Cuppa lettered on the side in front of me, full of coffee. "I ordered them for the official grand opening. So, we're just starting the celebration a little early."

I stirred the contents impatiently.

Adam's eyes crinkled. "OK, OK." He laughed. "It all started an hour and a half ago when Bob stuck his head in the door. Hope Julius, the city hall receptionist, was here picking up a special order, and that's all it took. Marion had just called him about Margaret's impromptu appearance and you should have seen the look on Hope's face. She lit outta here." Adam chuckled again. "Anyway, Bob told me that Rupert blew a gasket when Margaret told him he was no longer needed. He called the police. We both tried to get in touch with you, but your lines were busy. More junk mail?"

I shook my head. "No. Legitimate business. A few loose ends and some research," I told him. "Marion just got through. What do you suppose the police can do?"

"The missing persons report was filed, remember? If a missing person shows up, the least they can do is ask a lot of questions."

Rupert Murphy strode up and down in front of the drug store, waving his arms, yelling.

"He'll have a stroke if he keeps up like that," I said.

"And he's got high blood pressure now," someone murmured near my left ear. I turned.

Roberta from the flower shop smiled. "He's my second cousin," she whispered.

I swallowed back the laugh I felt coming on. "Oh. He must be pretty upset."

"That's not the half of it. He was all ready to announce a new emergency election for mayor. He had his acceptance speech nearly finished. His wife, Lannah, is my bridge partner."

"I see. So, what do you think will happen now that Margaret's back?"

"That one'll hijack the mayor's office,

mark my words." Roberta's plump little cheeks wiggled when she puckered her mouth. She shook her strangely-highlighted chestnut pouf of hair for emphasis and moved off to join her cronies at the window.

"Does this mean we're off the hook for the takeover plot?" Adam stage-whispered in my other ear. I barely got a napkin to my mouth in time as I choked on the sip of coffee I had taken.

Adam thumped me between my shoulder blades. "Sorry."

Yolanda let the television people have their turn with Rupert. She came across to interview bystanders. "How do you feel about Mrs. Conklin's sudden return?" she asked everyone.

Elvis appeared beside me. "Hi. I sneaked in the back. The girls are meeting me here." He surveyed the chaotic scene as the crowd continued to grow along the street. "You should see the scene at city hall. Man, I hate to leave, just when things are getting exciting."

I would be sorry to see them leave, too. "Maybe you could hang around an extra day," I said, even though he and Lucy had weekend family obligations lined up.

Hanley refused to make himself available for the students to interview, claiming to be too busy whenever they called. Lucy reported that she agreed with me about Marion Green. Marion seemed too nice to hold a grudge and didn't seem to have any beef with her former boss, the late mayor. Sure, she knew about the money. She typed up the forms, happy to help Apple Grove prosper so her kids would have a reason to stay.

In Lucy's opinion, Murphy acted either too clever or hid the cleverness too well behind an exterior of bumbling good-hearted passion — such as he was displaying outside right now. He was still on our suspect list, but no longer high priority.

Dr. Bailey canceled Memnet's appointment due to an emergency, so Sonja couldn't get her interview or the current stray cat inventory.

I rescheduled for next week. I would talk to her myself then let the others know what she said.

Elvis folded his arms. "I heard Mrs. Conklin say she was upset that Mr. Murphy took it upon himself to schedule a tasteless little service while she was absent. She's planning a big memorial later. And she's stepping into the mayor's office as her constitutional right."

"Where did she come up with that idea,"

I sputtered. "Anyway, did you hear her say where she'd been? Why couldn't she get in touch with her assistant or her family? Something is really wrong."

Adam went behind the counter to serve customers.

Elvis grabbed one of the few remaining squares of Featherlight Confections chocolate fudge candy samples. "Hey! This is pretty good. I wonder where he gets 'em?"

"Salesman. You'd have to ask Adam if they retail anywhere else. Oh, hi, Lucy, Sonja. Some excitement."

The girls entered. "We stopped at your place and packed up our bags," Sonja said. "Here's your spare key." She handed me the little cat keychain which I had given her last Sunday.

"Thank you. I'll miss all of you. It's been a pleasure. You've been great houseguests," I told them. "Can I take you out for lunch before you leave?"

Sonja said no, quickly echoed by the others. "I wish we could have figured out what happened to Tut." She glanced around. "Among other things. We realized there wasn't much chance with so little time on the case, but maybe now with Mr. Conklin's wife here, the truth will come out."

"Before we came inside we heard the

woman say she didn't know anything about her husband's murderer," Lucy said. "But I get the feeling she does. Oh, and by the way, I have one more tidbit of information for all of you." She waved us to the back hallway of the bookstore, behind the restrooms. "Here. I think this must be — aha! Do we have time for a little more mystery?"

Elvis's brow wrinkled. "What?"

"See?" Lucy opened a door to what I assumed was a closet. I could see steps leading to a lower level. Cool air billowed up at us. "Did you know about this?"

Sonja tapped her foot. "It's just a basement, Lucy." I think she was impatient to get on the road to Chicago.

"Not 'just'," Lucy said. "If you'd been paying attention to Mrs. Green at the historical society — that's Bob next door's mother, remember — instead of her charming, single granddaughter, Amy, who operates the wedding venue, you'd have heard her tell me that there was a central access point to the tunnels below the city. She showed me pictures of the digging and some old-fashioned people kind of stooped down when I took her newspapers back. The ladies wore long skirts and the men straw hats, like around 1900 or something. There were three entrances. One at either end of the street, and this one in the middle. It runs all along the river."

Call me Alice.

13

That got Elvis' attention. "Tunnels? No way! Let's see!"

"Mrs. Green said the tunnels are blocked up," Lucy replied.

Sonja stopped her impatient foot-tapping. "What were they for?"

I glanced back at Adam, who eyed us from his place behind the counter. I jerked my head toward the stairs.

He nodded permission for us to go down, his expression puzzled.

I grabbed a flashlight from the shelves of supplies in the janitor closet nearby then led the way down, while Lucy answered Sonja's question.

"I assumed Mrs. Green would tell me they were some early sewer system, but apparently, when news of World War I spread panic, several communities dug underground storage and hideout places, or tunnels, as they did here in Apple Grove.

Sometimes it was just a series of shelters with doors, like humungous storm cellars. I guess what type of storage space depended on how much manpower and resources the city had."

We creaked our way down the painted wooden staircase. The walls were thickly coated with cement. Here and there field-stone poked through.

I trained the flashlight along an ancient boiler. A cistern took up one side of the room, and we could see a boarded-up spot street side, which I assumed was the former coal chute. Three wooden doors hung crazily from rusty hinges along an otherwise empty wall. My nose twitched with the musty smell, but I expected that. The floor had been swept. Newly built spider webs drifted along the rafters supporting the staircase but, other than that, the space was surprisingly clear of rubble.

"People could hide food and other kinds of supplies, and of course, themselves, in case of an attack."

I could hear Lucy's voice drifting as we wandered around the large room. I was fascinated by the vaulted brick ceiling. I swung the flashlight across it. "Look at the craftsmanship." I oohed.

The others were standing in front of the

three doors, waiting for me.

"Oops, sorry. I bet you wonder what's behind those doors."

Ever-practical Sonja said, "Probably not much."

I held the light on one of the latches and she pushed against it gingerly. The little door creaked and gained momentum as it slammed inward with a cloud of dust. I handed her the light, which illuminated shafts of floating particles.

She peered through the entrance, bending at the waist to thrust her head and shoulders forward. "Right. Not much!" She withdrew. "Just a small empty room. No other entrance or exit," she reported.

Lucy was next. She took the light from Sonja and poked at the latch of the middle door. Lucy pushed at the door and stumbled on the threshold, which had an unexpected dip. "This must be it!" she exclaimed.

I hugged myself in excitement.

"There's a trapdoor here, into the wall. I think. Elvis —"

"Coming!" He plunged into the second room. Sonja and I moved closer to each other as we were left in relative darkness.

Lucy's and Elvis's voices echoed. "This has to be it! It's shut."

Sonja shivered and rubbed her upper

arms. "Can we come in?"

"Nah. It's too small," Elvis replied.

Sonja didn't give up. "Well, at least tell us what you see."

"It's like a doggy door," Lucy called out. "It's closed tight. Nailed. I think. Wait! Elvis —"

We heard a long screech and groan of metal, followed by a sharp crack and human cry.

Thump!

"I can't stand it!" Sonja pushed her way through the entrance. "Are you all right? Here, let me help you up. It's all right, Ivy. Elvis just pried open the door. And it looks as if it was latched from the inside, not nailed shut. Wait! Elvis, you can't — hey!"

Adam's voice came from the stairwell. "Is everything all right down there?"

I stepped back to look up at where he stood at the head of the steps, holding a lantern aloft. "I don't know. Lucy told us some story about an old tunnel system. I think they found the entrance."

He came down. "Colleen just got here. She's manning the counter. What's going on? Where's the tunnel? I've never seen one." He held the lantern near the open doorway. "I looked in here when I first moved. The rooms were empty. In fact," he indicated the third doorway, "this door doesn't lead to a room at all. It's just a set of shelves." He rounded on me. "The kids went in there?"

Elvis came out of the room, holding his hand up to shield his eyes from the light.

Adam lowered the lantern. "Sorry."

Lucy and Sonja followed, dusting their hands and elbows. Sonja brushed at her hair.

"So?" I said.

Elvis shrugged. "I crawled in about ten yards. There were some rocks and other junk blocking the way, so I came out."

"I tried to tell you," Lucy said impatiently. "The tunnels were blocked up. Sometime, like in the 1950s or something, a little kid got hurt. There used to be all kinds of parties, and of course, rats, and you name it. So even before the Cold War really got underway, the entrances were blocked so no one could just go in and hang out."

"But not permanently? People still know about them. What if a nuke went off or something?" Elvis, the practical modern theoreticist.

I shuddered.

"I got in fine," Elvis said. "It was blocked later on. And remember — the door was boarded from the inside."

"What are you talking about?" Adam asked, shining the lantern in the direction of the room.

"That's right," I said. "You weren't here. We checked out the doors when Lucy told us about this shop being the midway point. A tunnel system goes along the river. She learned about it from Mrs. Green at the museum."

"Related to Bob?" he asked me.

"His mother. She'd know — she was born and raised in Apple Grove. Bob's family goes way back, Marion said."

Adam went up to the door to peer inside the room. "Well, that makes sense, I suppose. How'd you get in?"

"We pulled," Lucy said.

Elvis brushed at his hair again. "And I'm afraid the door's broken. I thought it was just rusty. Turns out it was braced from the other side."

Adam traded the lantern for the flashlight and ducked into the room. "That's odd."

I followed.

Adam leaned over, as the slope of the ceiling couldn't have been more than six feet high. There were no windows, nothing of note in the concrete and stone room. It could not have measured more than six by six feet, either. I shuddered. Like a tomb. A gaping hole about three feet square took up a good deal of space on the outer wall. Pieces of dried brittle board cast eerie shadows in the glow of the lantern.

"This is a day of surprises." Adam beckoned with the torch for me to precede him into the main room of the basement. I expected him to show more curiosity. We were a sober group as we stood there, knowing farewells were imminent. "So, you said you crawled maybe ten yards, Elvis?"

"That's right."

"Timing can certainly make or break our best-laid plans, can't they?" Adam commented. "We all wish we could have found this earlier, I suspect. I'd welcome you back whenever you would be able to come."

I was glad we could have this time together as a group to say our good-byes. I could hear the creak of the floorboards upstairs as people walked around in the store. I shivered again in the cool dampness. The back of my neck felt prickly, which was a familiar sign to me that something wasn't quite what it seemed. A blocked-up tunnel with a door closed from the inside. That made no sense.

Lucy's gaze slid toward the gaping tunnel room. "What will you do next?"

Adam looked at me. "We still don't know why Donald was killed or what happened to

Tut. Perhaps we'll learn more from his wife. However, you three did uncover some valuable information regarding his family. We'll watch what happens with the grant money. That's our best lead for now." He put his arm around me. "And, of course, we hope that you learned something about police procedure." He waved the flashlight at the steps. "Lead on." Adam followed and pulled the basement door shut.

"Say good-bye to Memnet for me," Sonja said as we gathered about her little car.

"I will." We shared affectionate hugs and handshakes.

"I'll call if I find time to come and poke around some more," Elvis said to both of us. "I like Apple Grove."

"And a certain granddaughter of a certain historical society matron," Lucy chided.

Elvis blushed.

I obviously missed something. "I look forward to seeing you again any time," I told him.

They stuffed themselves into Sonja's car and we waved them off. We walked arm in arm back into his shop. "Are you sorry to see them go?" he asked me.

"Yes. I'm used to being alone, so sharing the house took some getting used to. But they were all so nice and tidy." We halted in front of the door to the basement. I tilted my head to the side. "I thought you closed this door."

Adam dropped his arm from my shoulders and frowned. "I thought I did, too." He examined the latch, twisting the little knob. "I suppose it didn't catch."

14

Only two customers remained, chatting in front of the big window.

The crowd outside on Main Street had dispersed.

Colleen had come today instead of her usual Saturday duty. She paged through a catalog while she stood at the counter, ready to serve.

"Everything go all right?" Adam asked his young assistant.

She beamed. "Just fine, Mr. Thompson. Most of them were gone anyway." She grabbed the last piece of candy from the dish in front of her. "This sure is good chocolate. Are we stocking it? A lot of kids would love it."

"I'm thinking about it."

Dr. Bailey came in. "So, I have to come book shopping if I want to see my daughter anymore." Her smile belied any sense of accusation.

Colleen's cheeks blossomed pink. "So true. But you also see me at summer swim," she reminded her mother.

"You must have been busy with all that excitement. I just heard the news from Bessie Wilberforce and came on over."

"Bessie's our neighbor," Colleen said to us. "She has this ancient Chihuahua named Tiger that she brings in to see Mom, like every other week."

"Mostly for company," Dr. Bailey said. "I don't mind, if I'm not busy." She looked at me. "As I was earlier in the week. I do apologize for having to miss your appointment. You said Memnet seemed better."

"That's all right. My young friend Sonja planned to bring Mem in. She really wanted an excuse to spend more time with my cat, I think. We also wanted to know how many stray cats had been rounded up, and if any of them were sick."

Isis whizzed past our ankles in a blur. Dr. Bailey's head swiveled to watch her. "What's gotten into her? We've had a couple dozen dropped off by various people. I got two very mild positives so far. The round up will go on for the rest of the year, though."

I followed Isis's flight back toward the basement stairway, where once again, the door stood ajar. I opened my mouth to say how odd that was since we'd just closed it.

"She's in an excitable mood right now, with all the activity of the morning," Adam said, shaking his head faintly in my direction.

I closed my mouth.

Dr. Bailey's eyes narrowed briefly as she glanced between Adam, me, and her daughter. "Well, then. Colleen, you're on duty until 6:00 tonight, is that right? Friday's the night the store's open a little later? How would it be if I came back here then and took you out to eat?"

"Sure, Mom, as long as it's not Tiny's. His food makes me sink in the pool."

"I think I'll go home, check on my messages," I said.

"Would this be a good time to check in on your cat now, Miss Preston? I won't charge extra for a house call."

I wanted to speak to her anyway. "Sure," I replied. "If you'll give me a fifteen-minute head start, I'll just get my business out of the way. You have my address?"

"Yes, I do. I remember Mark and Lee Pagner, who used to own your house. They were expecting their first baby when he got transferred and needed to move. Nice couple. Nice little Yorkie named Scotty. Sure, that sounds fine. I have an errand to run, myself, so it might be a little more than fifteen minutes."

"Good. I'll expect you. See you later." I waved to Adam and Colleen then walked past the wooden door to the basement one more time on my way out the back to get in my car.

I confess I was nervous to host the veterinarian alone in my home. "You'll protect me, though, won't you Mem?" I stroked his ears and he obligingly chortled his happy noises for me.

When I let Dr. Bailey in, she walked right up to Memnet and picked him up.

I would normally have taken affront at this bold behavior if this had not been a professional house call.

More surprisingly, Mem allowed it.

I ushered her into the living room where she gracefully perched on the sofa, Memnet still in her arms. He seemed to be bemused by the doctor, if I read my friend correctly. After being together nearly twelve years, Memnet and I understood each other quite well.

She fussed over my spotted pet. She looked in his eyes and tried to check his sensitive ears and felt all along his underside.

My Mau suffered this examination with

the barest of patience, leaping down from her lap when he had enough.

Dr. Bailey laughed. "Oh, he's all right," she said. She sat back and crossed her long legs. I guessed she was not in any hurry.

"Thank you, Doctor. Can I get you something to drink?"

"Call me Addy. Yes, that would be nice. Water is fine with me."

"I'll be right back." I spent a frantic minute in the kitchen putting ice in tall glasses and trying to come up with questions to ask the doctor — Addy. Our scheduled appointment wasn't until next week, so I hadn't put much time into thinking about it yet. I tried to recall why she was a suspect in the first place. I'd been very upset after my house had been robbed while Mom and I were out, and my beloved Memnet drugged. At least he had not been killed. And that was the problem with the scenario. Only some weirdo cat lover would not have taken out the attack cat that foiled his or her earlier plot. I grabbed our glasses of ice water, took a deep breath, then hiked back into my living room.

"I think you should know that I have stock in Better Pet Food, whose parent company is MerriFood," Addy said.

I deposited her glass on the square trunk I

used for a coffee table. I dropped into one of the chairs across from the sofa, not sure why she was using my house as a confessional. With a shaking hand I gulped from my glass.

"Margaret's family helped put me through graduate school," she said, watching me. She dressed somewhat formally for her profession, I thought, in a beige silk skirt and jacket with a white shell underneath. She blended well with the furniture. "We weren't that close as far as I was concerned, but I was one of the few people Margaret could count as a friend while we were at school. I bought stock in MerriFood as I could afford it based on her recommendations."

I cleared my throat, thinking that the TV killers usually made this kind of tell-all commentary right before they . . . you know. "Oh?"

"May I call you Ivy?"

"Of course." I tried to appear casual as I glanced around for anything I could use to defend myself.

"Ivy, I know you're aware of Margaret Bader-Conklin's sudden appearance in Apple Grove today after a lengthy, mysterious absence."

I bit my lips. "She has a right to grieve in

her own way."

"Huh. Donald contracted with Feli-Mix, the cat food company, to build a factory in Apple Grove. He invited some of his friends to move here to help build up a dying city that he loved. When Margaret found out about this, she hit the roof. So to speak. Her family's a founder of MerriFood. You probably knew that, too."

"But —"

Addy held up her hand to stop me. "I have even advised MerriFood on some of their nutritional value mixes. They paid me. That's a matter of public record. I will also tell you that Margaret — who is a benefactress of my clinic — asked me about tranquilizing small animals. She said Donald's cat had been acting anxious without him and she wondered if we could safely dose Tut with something to calm him. At the time I didn't realize Tut was absent, along with Donald. I told her what I could do for him. I'm telling you this because I realize you might think I drugged Memnet the day you were robbed." She turned to stare out of the picture window facing the street.

I took another deep breath. And let it out. Now what?

We sipped our water, both of us edgy, waiting for the other to speak.

I cracked first. "Donald usually took Tut with him on trips. Addy, what would happen if we took this information to the police?"

She shook head, her cascade of dishwater blonde hair rippling. "I don't know."

"I can't understand why the thieves didn't just kill Memnet."

"Doing something like that always leaves some kind of evidence. A drug might be identified, traced to its maker and distribution records. A weapon leaves traceable marks. And it's messy." She smiled at me. "Sorry to sound so cold. I don't like this business one little bit. And I'm tired of catering to Margaret's whims. I'm also worried about Tut."

"No one's found a Mau to turn in, then. Yolanda Toynsbee's granddaughter chased a cat down by the river a couple weeks ago. She described it to me. I would say she saw Tut."

"Maybe," Addy said.

"What do you mean? I checked around down there but didn't see any place a cat could hide."

"I could get in a lot of trouble for saying this. My business, my reputation . . . I have a daughter who's about to go to an expensive college. If not for Colleen, I wouldn't care. MerriFood has long arms and the Baders have power behind their money."

Breathe, breathe, I reminded myself. I got light-headed anyway. "Wait, Addy —"

"No, Ivy. I just have to tell you this. Please, let me tell you my side of the story. After, I'll — I'll trust you to do the right thing."

I sank back into the wings of the chair and closed my eyes briefly, then focused on the agitated woman in front of me. "Go ahead."

"To pay some of my expenses in school, I worked in an animal shelter, euthanizing unclaimed strays." She made it sound horrible.

I guess it was. "So? Someone had to do it."

"Sometimes there were mistakes in the records. Not all of the animals were unclaimed. They were mislabeled and euthanized."

"Accidents happen. Everyone understands that."

"The shelter owner was a drug addict."

I waited, hoping my suspicions wouldn't ring true.

"The main reason for the huge amount of mistakes in record-keeping — Doug's hazed state of mind. One evening he showed me his list of druggie friends. They included some of the top VIPs of the area around the university, government, too. If I helped him, just made a few drops, he'd pay me well. We used the excuse of doing work for the shelter as a cover. I did this for eight months."

"What made you stop?"

"I got pregnant."

I've heard that plenty of times. As if getting pregnant was something people could just buy or something one could catch, like a cold. Nothing would make me ask her any of the details. It wasn't my business. I just let her go on.

"When I found out I was expecting Colleen, I realized that I couldn't act that way, not for me or the sake of my child. But I didn't turn my boss in, either. In a weak moment, I told my friend Margaret my secrets." Addy dabbed at her eyes.

I got up to find her a tissue. When I returned, she had regained her composure. I said, "I take it your friend said she'd keep your secrets and help pay the bills, as long as you'd do her future favors."

Addy nodded.

"So, you settled in Apple Grove to be near your dear friend, who invested heavily in your veterinarian business. I thought Mrs. Bader-Conklin was pretty smart, herself.

She's got a degree in pharmacology. Why would she need your help to figure out how to drug my cat?"

The veterinarian's expression closed tight. "You're assuming she had anything to do with the robbery."

"What? You just said —"

"I have to go." Addy leapt to her feet and charged through the kitchen, moving as fast and hard as her high-heeled patent pumps would allow.

"Good-bye," I called, trying to follow her. "Can I . . ."

She was gone. She must have seen my next visitor coming up the sidewalk.

"Hi, Ivy. Was that Dr. Bailey? She must have had an emergency."

"Hi, Marion. Come on in. Um, yeah, I think so."

"You look shell-shocked. Is everything all right? Memnet's OK, isn't he?" She walked into my kitchen and turned to talk to me as I stood on the stoop outside. I followed her and watched as she made herself welcome, settling her purse and jacket on a chair and opening the cupboard for a cup. "Got any new tea? I just tried — Hey, Ivy? You all right? Wait until I tell you what's been going on downtown."

I pulled out a chair. "Yes, tell me everything." For the moment, I catalogued my conversation with Addy Bailey into a neat little slot in my mind, so I could write on Mom's chart later. I focused on the mayor's secretary.

"You probably saw Rupert," she began. The microwave dinged. Marion went to retrieve our cups of hot water then plunked mine down in front of me, adding a bag of ginger mint. "He really made a stink, but Gene told him there was nothing the police could do in this situation." She sipped, scrunched her nose. "Too hot. Anyway, he called the television people and the state paper. Honestly. 'What about the missing person report,' he asks Gene. 'She was reported missing,' Gene replies. 'By her assistant, Mrs. Grimm, who's standing right behind you.' " Marion had a gift for putting a different voice with her quoted characters.

I smiled and toasted her with my cup. "So, what about the missing persons report?"

"Gene says, 'She's no longer missing. End of report.' 'What about me?' Rupert asks." Marion giggled. " 'Didn't know you was missin,' Gene says. You shoulda seen Margaret's face."

"I bet it was a picture."

"Yup. Made me wish I owned a camera. Anyhow, she's waving this paper with a

266

signature on it, claiming Donald said she should act as deputy mayor in his absence. None of it's legal, or anything, but the police don't have any precedent to act on. Margaret says Letty will help her, and I should go home. I followed Rupert for a while, but he acted crazy. Walked in circles, waving his arms. Took off his jacket, threw it on the ground and stomped on it. His wife's not gonna be too pleased with that. Then he went to the bank, of all places. Why the bank?"

"What did the others in the office do? Georgine Crosby, for instance? Or any of the other council members? Were any of them there?" I set my chin atop my crossed wrists on the table.

"Oh, there wasn't anyone there, really. On a Friday? Georgine already had the day off. She's out of town at her brother's kid's wedding. The other council members don't actually work at the hall. You know that, Ivy." Marion sipped again at her cooling tea. "Ah, mint and ginger. That's better. So, how're you?"

"Back up, Marion. What's happening next? Margaret wants to have a big, proper send-off for her dearly departed husband, sans tears, while she steps right into his office?"

She shrugged and then wriggled to get more comfortable in the chair. "I think she's made of ice. Lives on her own planet, at any rate. Rupert's spouting off about looking through city ordinances which, believe you me, go back about a hundred years. No one's touched 'em. And Margaret's saying something about an emergency election. She also ordered the zoning commissioner to push through a change from ag to commercial. Half the piece she's selling sits in the rural township, so she's threatening to sue if MerriFood backs out of the deal to build. Apparently, Fred Alnord, Tiny's uncle who farms out that way, you know, saw bulldozers lined up. Got any cookies?"

I put the tips of my fingers against my throbbing temples. "Aren't your kids home?"

"Bob's taking care of them this afternoon. It's his half day off from the shop. The boys are helping with junior football league. Claire's on the summer rec dance team. Practice goes on for a while. Are you OK? I was gonna ask if you want to go to Lo Mah's. We can order in, too. Say, didn't those college kids go home? Those crime kids? They sure were nice. That Elvis of yours — a real cutie. He spent a lot of time hanging around, asking questions. Real smart one, he is. Wanted to know all sorts of stuff about how the mayor's office runs, who does what job, how the council works, how the government connects with the police department. I learned all kinds of stuff. So, what was Dr. Bailey doing here?"

I hoped my head wouldn't spin off with the effort of trying to keep up with Marion. "She offered to check out Memnet for me since she had an emergency when Sonja planned to take him."

"We don't have any time for pets at our house, so I've never spent much time with her. She comes to church, but always leaves right away. Never been involved with the Altar Guild or Women's Servant Team, or anything. Did something with confirmation class, I think, when her daughter was in it. She's always running somewhere, like today. She must be really busy. What's she like?"

"You're right. Busy." I glanced up at Marion. "Let's go get some food."

I was still having trouble getting over Margaret's sudden appearance, apparently unconcerned about her husband's murder. How could the woman be so cold?

"So, what can you tell me about the tunnels under Apple Grove?" I asked as we headed into the summer twilight.

"Oh? Those things? They were all filled in years ago according to the old timers."

15

APPLE GROVE GAZETTE

Apple Grove, Illinois

Tuesday

Margaret Bader-Conklin Returns, Announces News

by Yolanda Toynsbee, Editor

Last Friday, the good citizens of Apple Grove had a surprise when a formerly missing person showed up alive and well at City Hall after an absence of 19 days. When asked where she had been, Mrs. Bader-Conklin replied, "I was in mourning. On a cruise, if that's any of your business. To Cyprus and Italy. It was lovely this time of year."

This reporter questioned Mrs. Bader-Conklin on why her personal assistant, Mrs. Letty Grimm, who is also related to her by marriage, did not know her itinerary. Neither did Mrs. Bader-Conklin's parents, according to Mrs. Grimm, who then felt it necessary to file a missing person report with the local police.

"It was all a misunderstanding," Mrs. Bader-Conklin said. "My assistant was confused. I assure you it will not happen again. I apologize to all the good little people out there in Apple Grove for your confusion. I beg you to forgive my assistant for your fears on our behalf. I am fine. I was shocked about my husband, let me tell you. I just couldn't face the world, and had to take treatment.

"Let me assure you that I will host a wake in the mayor's honor at my earliest convenience. I couldn't face it before. That is why I needed to go on a cruise," she said. "I needed to make some decisions. Being near water helps."

When asked how she felt about replacing her husband, Donald Conklin, Apple Grove's own mayor, Mrs. Bader-Conklin declared that she was ready to serve.

"The mayor trusted me. I miss him dreadfully."

This reporter asked what caused her to leave home so abruptly and what prompted her return.

"Most people are not aware of this, but the mayor was unstable for quite some time. I've tried to keep this quiet, but I can no longer do so. The fact is, the mayor hoarded a large sum of money under suspicious circumstances. He made overtures to business people under false pretenses. I'm just glad he was stopped. Not that I'm glad he was stopped so ignominiously, of course.

"But I hurried back as soon as I could to make sure the people of this city know I'm going to do all I can to make things right."

What will Mrs. Bader-Conklin do to stop her husband's plans? This reporter asked.

"I have my own plans," Mrs. Bader-Conklin replied.

When asked what kind of plans, Mrs. Bader-Conklin responded, "No comment."

When asked if she would seek training or other legal counsel to help her in the role of mayor, Mrs. Bader Conklin replied, "I plan to serve all the good people of Apple Grove as long as I can.

"The former mayor wanted to update the poorly maintained utilities. I will make sure we get the newest, most modern water works money can buy.

"The former mayor wanted to provide business opportunities. I will bring better ones.

"Everyone will work. In fact, let me tell all the people the marvelous good news now about the wonderful good fortune for all of you out there. MerriFood Corporation, an international conglomerate of food products of all kinds, has agreed to open a branch of their pet food packaging and distribution division in Apple Grove."

MerriFood is a sixty-seven-year-old company, founded by four partners, including the grandparents of Margaret Bader-Conklin. The Bader family owns substantial stock and Mrs. Bader-Conklin once held the position of research assistant at Merri-Food until her marriage and subsequent settlement in Apple Grove.

Vice President of Marketing for Merri-Food, Van Gerke, had this to say: "Merri-Food is pleased to bring our Better Pet brand packaging division to America's heartland. Our base in Apple Grove is a good business move for MerriFood, a move that will benefit both the company and the local populace.

"The environmental impact studies will be completed soon and, I'm told, already looks favorable. The new rail line extension plans, and storage facility blueprints are already finished.

"We will begin hiring approximately one hundred employees beginning early next year. Details and contact information will be forthcoming."

Mrs. Bader-Conklin plans to implement an ordinance from the annals of Apple Grove which state that a deputized member of the current mayor's family may step in as acting mayor in an emergency situation.

The question remains. Has Mrs. Bader-Conklin ever been deputized? She claims the distinction and the proof. Apparently eleven years ago when the mayor underwent a tonsillectomy, he deputized Mrs. Bader-Conklin to meet visiting dignitaries from our sister city in Mexico, Cabo San Isidro Bueno, for the afternoon.

City Council President, Rupert Murphy, is filing a protest on behalf of Apple Grove with the National Association of Mayors, or NAM.

"NAM will declare that woman's claims invalid," stated Mr. Murphy in an exclusive interview over the weekend.

"You mark my words. Apple Grove will have an election to fill the mayor's term. I will be the winner, fair and square. I don't need to resort to mothballed tactics to win. The good people of this city expect me to serve them with dignity and honor. I will not disappear for weeks on end, or spend our money ill-advisedly."

Chief Gene Hackman for the Apple Grove Police Department stated that the force was doing "everything in our power to apprehend the criminals who were responsible for the death of our mayor."

When asked about the measures being undertaken to locate the perpetrators, the chief had this to say: "All I can tell you is that we're doing our best. We are following numerous leads, continuing from the mayor's last known location. I can't go into any more detail than that."

It is the sincerest best wishes of the staff of the Apple Grove Gazette that the case will be solved.

Notice: Stray Animals

Due to recent reports of several stray animals, the Humane Animal Shelter will conduct a sweep of loose animals. Under City Ordinance and by order of the acting mayor, all collarless and unidentified cats will be picked up and held for ten days and be tested for cat scratch disease. After which time, any unclaimed animals will be destroyed.

Advertisement: Mea Cuppa

Come in for a quiet visit with all the things you love,

A good book, conversation, and delicious coffee.

Try our new pecan and fudge fine candies — just right with roasted pecan coffee

Take some home today.

16

I let the newspaper fall to my lap.

"Hey! I'm not finished with the last paragraph," Adam complained.

We sat on my sofa, companionably reading the latest edition of the Gazette. His hand felt warm on my shoulder as he leaned forward to finish the article.

"Yolanda outdid herself on this one," he commented in my ear. "Oh, there's my ad. That looks pretty good. And on the front, right next to Bob's. I'm not used to seeing a newspaper put advertising on the front page."

"Hometown papers can do what they please, I guess. Yolanda dug out a few more interesting facts, but nothing much helpful. Does Margaret truly not understand what a 'wake' is? How can she have a wake a month after the funeral? And no one asked about Tut." I was going to tell Adam about my trip to Chicago planned for the next day.

He distracted me instead. I surely did have trouble keeping my hands off that man, let me tell you. He wasn't putting up much of a fight, either. I nuzzled his jaw. I came up for air for a couple of seconds. "Hey."

"What?" His lips trailed over my cheek.

"Thanks for leaving chocolate on my doorstep this morning. It was so sweet of you." I pressed my mouth against his.

He pulled back and stroked the hair from my temples. "I'm sorry to disappoint you, but I didn't do that."

"Then who did? It was the good stuff, you know — like from your store."

He grinned and kissed the tip of my nose. "Maybe you have a secret admirer. Or someone just wanted to thank you for the multiple kindnesses I hear you're guilty of." He brushed his lips over mine. "I saw you hold the door of the pharmacy open for Mrs. Lichtner."

"Anyone would do that."

"Mrs. Engelbrecht is over her tiff."

I pulled his face closer to mine. "Yeah. That was neat how she came up to me in church and apologized. Said she'd heard we had some sort of cult going, but realized that wasn't true because a real cult member wouldn't come to the ladies Bible study or join the Altar Guild." I nibbled at him, teasing his lips.

Adam's mouth turned up in a smile even while my lips were on his. "She came in to the store. Once she saw I stocked regular books, and Bibles, she apologized to me, too," he managed to get out before we locked lips.

"Mmm, Ivy. Wait a sec. That's the second time I heard sirens." He set me away from him and got up. He pulled the drape of my picture window aside to look toward downtown, even though it was dark. Adam's phone buzzed, and he reached absentmindedly into his pocket to check the screen. He frowned and pushed a button. "What?" Adam replied after listening for three seconds. He leaned over as if he had developed a pain in his gut and clutched the arm of the chair. "I'll be right there."

I caught the frantic note in his reply. "What's wrong?"

He straightened, all color drained from his face. "That was Bob. His tenant called him. He's been evacuated because my building is on fire. I've got to go now."

"I'll come with." I started after him, trying to recall where I had left my shoes.

"No, Ivy. Just wait here. I don't want you mixed up in that mess down there." He slid the phone back into his pocket and fished out his keys. "You won't get close, anyway, and there isn't anything you can do. I'll call you. Just — please, stay here, safe."

I stood on the threshold between the living room and kitchen, watching the door close behind him. *Pray,* a little Voice whispered through my rattled nerves. I went into the living room and plopped right down on my knees in front of the picture window. My forehead touched cool glass behind the drape. "Please, God, please, please." Words deserted me. I folded my hands like a little girl while the tears pooled on the windowsill. "Don't let anyone be hurt," I whispered. "Please, don't let anyone . . . burn."

Then I realized Adam needed me. He confessed that he sometimes still experienced nightmares about the accident that killed his wife and daughter and left him scarred. Fire. I wanted to be with him. I wouldn't get close as he said, but I didn't care. I jammed my feet into loafers, found my house key, and hurried out the door. It was only six blocks.

"Ivy!" Martha Robbins called to me from her stoop next door. I stopped at the end of the driveway. "Do you know what's going on?"

We could see the orange glow in the sky. Her kids were huddled with her in a blanket. "Dale was called to the station, but he didn't say where the fire was."

"At Mea Cuppa," I ground out. "I have to go."

"Oh, Ivy. I'm so . . ." Her voice faded as I started to jog. Two blocks later I realized that loafers were a poor choice of footwear and I slowed to a very fast walk. The evening was still plenty warm, and I was . . . glowing. Soon I met up with throngs of people who gathered to watch and wait. I slowed down. I headed toward the alley behind Adam's place only to find the entrance taped off.

A squad car, lights stabbing the night, sat empty, close by, as Officer Larken spoke to people a few feet away.

I moved in their direction, dodging sightseers.

A spray of water arced high over the building, which stood sooty but intact, billowing black smoke from broken windows and vents.

My eyes watered, and my nose grew stuffy at the acrid stink of burned wiring and drywall. At least any flames appeared to be out. "Officer! Officer Larken! Where's Adam?"

"Miss Preston. Good eve—"

"It is not!" I snapped. "I need to know

what's happening. How bad is it? Where's Mr. Thompson?"

Adam's voice called from our left. "Here, Ivy. I'm here!"

"Oh, thank You, Lord, thank You!" I rushed to him. "I was so worried. I just ran. Are you all right?" I cupped his face in my hands. "How bad is it?"

"The fire burned mostly upstairs, my apartment. The firefighters did a good job. Lots of smoke damage, and of course, water damage. I don't know about the store stock, but I wouldn't be surprised if —" He stopped to catch his breath. The front of his shirt wiggled.

"Isis. Oh, baby." I had not even felt her when I had grabbed Adam so roughly. He opened the edges of his vest, so I could see her. I reached my hand out to stroke between her ears. "She's safe, oh, she's safe." Isis had no intention of letting Adam go. She even nipped at me, which I would have done too, under similar circumstances, but I did back off.

"She was already outside," Adam said. "She wouldn't let anyone grab her, but came to me when she saw me."

"I wonder how she got out?" The prickly sensation at the back of my neck, when I had last been in the basement of Mea

Cuppa, returned.

"Mr. Thompson! There you are. Miz Preston." Chief Hackman touched his cap to me, then to Adam. "Our condolences. Captain Reed says they're nearly finished. I've roped off the place and as soon as it's a go, we'll begin processing. Can you think of anyone who'd want to do this?"

Adam wobbled with shock, then stiffened in anger. "You think arson? You're sure?"

"Mr. Thompson, I understand you were not at home when the fire broke out. Could you tell me where you were, sir?"

"He was with me, Chief," I said. "We were out to dinner at Lo Mah's, then we've been at my place," I replied, puzzled and upset at his tone. "You can't honestly think Adam had anything to do with this?"

"I just need to verify everyone's movements tonight, ma'am," Hackman said.

"I can vouch for them." Jeff Hanley walked up behind Adam to join us. "I saw them there at Lo Mah's."

Adam shook hands with Hanley.

"And after dinner, Mr. Hanley? Were you at home?" Hackman queried.

"Yes. With my wife, Renee." Hanley put his hands in his pockets. "You know her. What's this all about, anyway?"

"Chief is asking why anyone would do

this, Jeff," Adam said.

Hanley swallowed. He twisted swiftly toward the alley, as if he had heard a noise, and then turned back.

With the water blasting, the siren, the loudspeaker, and shouting going on I could hardly hear the person next to me, so I wondered what caught his attention. I tried to focus on the spot where he had looked, without trying to let on that I was doing so.

"It's pretty early to have suspicions like that, Chief," Hanley said. "Shouldn't you wait until there's an official report? From the fire department? No need to make the insurance people nervous over nothing, now, is there?"

"Mr. Hanley, Mr. Thompson, you must have misunderstood my usual line of questioning. I apologize for any confusion. You'll be contacted as soon as possible. All of you." Hackman touched the rim of his hat again and strode away to confer with the fire chief.

"You have a place to stay tonight, Adam?" Hanley eyed his business partner.

"I'll check back into the Prairie Center."

Neither of them looked at me. I was exhausted, as if I had been fighting the fire myself.

Smoke hung heavy everywhere.

"Why don't you stay with my wife and me?" Hanley offered. "Our son's gone for the weekend, a camp outing, so you can use his room. In the morning, we'll figure out what to do."

Cal Stewart dashed up.

Just in time to save the day, I thought sourly.

"Hey! What's going on?" Stewart asked.

Apparently, the quality of the conversation, like the smoky air, was not about to improve any time soon.

"Thompson's coming home with me tonight," Hanley told him. "Why don't you stop in for a while, too?"

"Uh . . . sure." Stewart said, his attitude eerily similar to Hanley. They were plotting something.

I could tell.

"Can I drop you off at home, Ivy?" Hanley asked.

Adam stared at me, as if willing me to do something. But what?

"No thanks. I walked here. I'll just walk back. Clear my head. Good exercise." Adam nodded ever so faintly, so I had guessed the right answer. Goody for me.

"Can you take Isis for me?" he asked. "She knows you and you have food and supplies."

"Sure. Fine."

Adam came close, transferring the unco-operative feline from inside of his vest to me.

She settled under my chin, dug her claws in enough to make me wince and growled low, just to make sure we understood she was upset.

"Don't believe everything you see," Adam whispered while he kissed me on the cheek, his touch lingering in my hair.

"Good night, Ivy," Hanley said, leading Adam and Stewart toward his SUV. Stewart waved, while Adam walked sideways so he could keep an eye on me a little longer.

As soon as the three of them drove off, I puttered toward home. A second later I realized Adam was not the only person with an eye on me.

"Psst!" A raspy voice coughed once, twice.

What was that?

"Psst! Ivy! Over here!"

I looked around furtively to see who else might notice if I tiptoed toward a dark alley. Wait a minute! Was I nuts? I stopped moving and peered into the dark as best as I could. What was that? Another cat? Bob's tenant, I think I heard they call him Toad, must have had a pet cat, too. I squinted. I could barely make out the shadow of a hunched figure against a brick wall. In the light a cat with patchy spots posed. Like Memnet. Or . . .

"Ivy!" Hoarse-sounding voice. Sneeze.

Tut.

And his keeper's cousin?

17

"God bless you, Mr. Grimm. Ronald." I moved closer, leaning to my left to observe the crouching figure in the alley. "Is that you? And Tut?"

"Shh!" The man hissed, finger to his lips. "Just — Just c'mere, will ya?"

I advanced another step, careful not to get too close. After all, Adam had just told me —

"Toad? Are you Toad? Here, Tut. Come here, boy." As if a cat would obey me. It must be the smoke.

"Tell the others, I stopped it, won't you?" The raspy voice captured my attention again. "I saw what they were doing, and I chased 'em out. Sorry about the damage, but it could have been worse, see?" Another sneeze.

"Chased who? Ronald, if that's Tut. . . ." I clutched Isis until she frantically wiggled and got her paw loose. I managed to avoid her swipe at my cheek, but then I lost sight of — Ronald? Had that really been him? Or Toad? I saw no cat now, either. A wave of smoke blew across the alley. The scene was surreal.

Isis let out one of those ripping yowls that about gives a person instant gray hair and bit my hand.

"Isis! Calm down," I tried to soothe her.

She'd had enough excitement for the night and wriggled until she dropped through my arms. She shook herself, swiveled her head for one recalcitrant hiss at me, then trotted in the direction of my house.

"All right! Just a minute, I'm coming! But for a cat who doesn't get out much — wait!" I turned toward the alley once more, just hoping. *Don't believe what you see.* But who was that man in the alley? He'd had Tut with him, hadn't he? Unable to decide between making sure Isis was safe or following a stranger in a dark alley, I opted for Isis's owner, who'd already lost enough.

"Isis, wait!" I caught up to her. She allowed me to pick her up and carry her the final five blocks.

When we arrived home, I saw a puffy envelope on the rubber mat by my screen door. "Ivy" was typed on a white generic label. I probably should have been nervous about it, but right now Isis and I were tired. If someone wanted to hurt me, he or she had ample opportunity during my walk home.

I unlocked the door and went into the house.

Isis hit the floor running, claws clattering on the linoleum as she bounded toward what I assumed was the scent of fresh Memnet in the living room. The yowl and a corresponding hiss confirmed my suspicion. I waited for a couple of seconds. I heard some low-throated growling. If they got rough, I could separate them.

I turned to examine the package. I tried to pull on the tab but found it stuck fast. I got out my kitchen shears to cut it open, hoping to avoid damaging the contents. I shook the items onto the table. A shiny gold-wrapped package of Featherlight Confections chocolates — the same kind that were left for me earlier. They were the ones Adam offered on his sales counter as samples, so that's why I assumed he had sent them. What followed the package of chocolates stole my breath. My missing coin purse.

Rather, my stolen coin purse. I wondered if I should touch it. There might be fingerprints. The purse was made out of a couple of small squares of woven cloth sewn together with a zipper. The thought of calling the police yet again made me shudder, but I needed to.

Larken answered the phone at the station.

I told him about the package on my doorstep.

He sounded tired. "Miss Preston, are there any other items in the package? Any strange odors or powders or liquids of any kind?"

"No, nothing like that. I didn't open the wrapped box, so I don't know for sure what's inside. I did touch it, though. I'm sorry."

"That's all right. I'll round up someone to stop over to pick it up and get your statement. Quite an evening, doncha think?"

"You're not kidding," I replied and hung up. I knew better this time than to mention my strange encounter with the guy in the alley.

"Yow!" Memnet raced into the kitchen, barely halting in time to avoid a head-on collision with the back door.

Isis prowled behind sedately. She swung her head from side to side while her hind quarters swaggered. If she'd been my daughter I would have had to come up with a suitable punishment to wipe that smirk off her face.

"OK, guys and girls. That'll do." I opened the basement door for Mem, who made a beeline and pattered down the steps. I closed it to protect him from further annoyance from Isis. "You can stay up here tonight, Isis," I told her. I'd have to get another litter box set up, but I could live with that. "I hope you eat the same kind of stuff Memnet does," I told her.

She offered me her version of a purr.

About fifteen minutes passed before Officer Dow knocked on my door.

"Nice to see you again," I said, hoping it didn't seem like I enjoyed having on-duty cops visit my house all the time.

She jotted down my very brief comments regarding the latest offering from the anonymous chocolate giver.

I had eaten the contents of the other box and thrown the wrappings away, so there was nothing left from the earlier gift. I hadn't gotten sick.

"I need to take this box as evidence. Someone will be in touch, Miss Preston. Good night." She went out the door, carting my coin purse and the pretty box of candy.

I chained and bolted the door, then

checked the locks on the front. If Adam was not gifting me with chocolate, then who was? And why? What about the little matter of seeing Ronald Grimm? I had not mentioned that to the officer, as it didn't seem real, and that certainly wasn't pertinent to her reason for coming. Was it? Adam told me not to believe what I saw. But what had he meant? I wandered restlessly, pacing the rooms of my house, checking under beds, in closets, behind the shower curtain.

Isis came to check on me every once in a while.

I'm sure she wondered what kind of a nuthouse she'd landed in. After an hour, I had exhausted myself enough to sleep.

I awoke the next morning to the buzz of my phone. Sunlight streamed in ribbons across my bed. Smoky-colored ears twitched in the valley of the rumpled quilts down toward my knee, I noted, as I reached for the receiver. " 'Lo?"

"Ivy! You'd better come downtown to city hall as soon as you can."

"Good morning to you, too, Adam. What's all this about? And are you OK?"

"Sorry. Good morning. Um, I guess I'm OK. Just come quickly, all right?"

"Got it. Give me — oh, fifteen minutes." I

hung up.

A disembodied tail rose from another valley in the covers. This one was silver. What? Memnet heaved himself up and high-stepped toward my head.

I pulled myself into a sitting position, so I could see Isis lolling on her side, whiskers flickering in the sunlight. I scrubbed at Mem's ears. "How did you get up here? And why aren't you guys trying to kill each other?"

Mem chortled in my ear and licked my hand.

"Well, I wish I could stay and chat, but I gotta scoot, my friends." After a quick shower, I fed the cats and checked my board before grabbing toast and juice. "Be good," I admonished the kids before I carefully locked the door behind me. I barely made it in my promised time limit.

Something big was happening. I had to park three blocks away on Lombardy, down past Tiny's.

People were standing outside of city hall where a loudspeaker cranked out some kind of speech. From this distance, the words were jumbled.

I had slept late, and it was after 9:00. I counted three media vans set up for business. Someone alerted them far enough in advance for them to get here.

Mrs. Lichtner stood vigil on the sidewalk, hunched over her cane, the ever-present rain bonnet tied over her head.

"Mrs. Lichtner, what's happening?"

She waved a knobby hand. "I heard someone say there's to be an announcement from the mayor's office, so I came to see. I was at the drugstore, you know, to pick up my pills."

"Thank you. How are you today?"

She only got to the second of her woes before the loudspeaker blatted again. "Good morning. Thank you all for being here. This is a press conference called by the office of the mayor, Apple Grove, Illinois." Letty Grimm's voice.

Oh, boy.

Mrs. Lichtner and I shared worried glances. I supposed Adam to be inside the building, but I still searched the crowd, picking out people I recognized. A trench-coated man, whom I guessed to be a reporter, wandered, stopping to ask questions and make notes.

"Citizens of Apple Grove, Mrs. Bader-Conklin," Letty announced.

A harshly curt voice followed. "Good morning. First of all, thank you for your prayers and support these past weeks. It's been a trying time for all of us."

I stared at the loudspeaker tied in a horse chestnut tree outside the front door, as if I could see Margaret's face in it.

A few uniformed officers worked the crowd, eyes alert, hands on radios.

"I'm sorry to have caused so many problems with my unexplained absence. The truth is, my husband's health had deteriorated. I did not want to worry anyone, not my family, nor you good people, with our troubles. After his terrible and tragic death, I took time to get away and formulate plans of my own." The unpleasant tinny wired voice of Margaret Bader-Conklin went on. "I was the deputy mayor, as you all are aware, and will now carry out my new duties as your . . . regular mayor. The first order of business is that we must find my poor late husband's precious kitty, whom I'm certain did not mean to kill him. Letty will organize a search party immediately. That is all for now."

A squeal made us cover our ears. After the click, I wandered over to the west corner of city hall and the big municipal parking lot. Donald had been perfectly healthy, mentally and physically, the last time I saw him. And now she was blaming Tut? Even though the autopsy report confirmed death by cat scratch fever, we'd have to test Tut to see if he was the carrier. I couldn't shake the sensation that Margaret wanted Tut for other reasons. After all, she had called him "precious." I didn't believe a word Margaret said. Shakespeare said it best: this was much ado about nothing.

Adam appeared, coming from the direction of the front of the building. "Ivy! There you are." He caressed my shoulders "How's Isis?"

I ignored his question. "What did you mean last night when you said 'don't believe everything you see'?" I demanded.

He grimaced and looked at our shoes.

"What's going on here? I saw Ronald Grimm last night behind your store. With Tut. He said —"

"Shh!" Adam held out a hand to someone behind me. "Doctor Bailey, hello. Quite a ruckus. What do you think about all of this craziness?"

I didn't turn around. I folded my arms. "Addy is Margaret's best friend," I heard my voice say in an acid tone I hardly recognized. "I'm sure the doctor is pleased."

"Actually, I'm not," Addy said. "I came here to tell you that I want to help. My confession may hurt me and my daughter in the long run, but it's the right thing to do."

Adam's wide-eyed expression would have made me laugh in any other circumstances.

"Help what?" he asked the doctor.

"You didn't tell Mr. Thompson my story?" Addy asked me.

"Your story is none of my business," I told her stiffly. "You didn't give me permission to share. Besides, I don't know how much to believe. You seem to have waffled there toward the end. I don't have any proof of what you said, and frankly, now I don't care." I turned around to stare at her defiantly.

"I — I'll tell you all about it," Addy said. "But maybe now's not the best time."

Marion, with Bob's arm around her, walked up to us, followed closely by an animated Jeff Hanley and his sidekick Cal Stewart.

Rupert Murphy, the hopefully temporarily deposed acting mayor, stormed out of the front doors of city hall trailed by several council members. From my vantage point at the side of the narrow building, I saw Murphy's jacket flying around him, making him look like some overgrown buzzard. His mouth gaped, but from this distance I couldn't hear what he said. He drew the crowd in our direction.

"What's your next move, Mr. Murphy?" A reporter from a high-profile local television program hustled in Murphy's wake, microphone held out.

"She'll never get away with this. NAM is on my side. We'll just see!" He slammed his car door and rumbled off, slowly threading through packets of lingerers.

18

Hanley invited us to the conference room at State's Bank. He acted keyed up and kept strutting back and forth at the head of the table. If he'd flapped his arms, I expected feathers to fly out from under his tweed jacket. "The first order of business," he finally said, when we all were seated, "is to protect those funds. Marion, can we move the money into a sheltered account where Margaret, acting as the mayor, can't touch it?"

"Excuse me!" I piped up. "I strongly advise that we include Officer Ripple in this discussion!"

Everyone stared at me. Everyone, that is, except Adam.

"What are you talking about, Ivy?" Addy asked.

"Aren't you in the least bit concerned about what happened to Donald's murderer? For all we know, he could still be lurking, waiting to kill again. Except . . ." I trailed off and clammed up.

"Murdered? Donald was . . . but I heard the cat got him," Cal Stewart said. "He wasn't well."

"He was fine, Cal, and everyone knew it," I growled back.

Hanley frowned and folded his arms. "The case is open, and the police are working hard to uncover the truth. But we have to move quickly on the money for the best interests of Apple Grove."

"Except what, Ivy?" Addy Bailey was the only one in my corner at this point.

I was not sure I wanted to trust her. I hated feeling so insecure. Adam still wouldn't meet my eyes. "I talked to Ronald Grimm in the alley," I said. "Donald's cousin. After the fire at Mea Cuppa was out last night. He knows something, I'm sure of it. He had Tut with him."

Adam's shoulders slumped. His whisper from last night echoed: "Don't believe everything you see." I still couldn't understand what he meant. Why wasn't he saying anything?

"Sorry I'm late!" Yolanda rushed in, shutting the door behind her. Hanley must have invited her to join the party at some earlier point. A buzz out in the lobby indicated that business had picked up at the bank after the commotion of the press conference. "What's happening?"

"Ivy says she talked to Ronald Grimm last night," Marion said.

"He had Tut with him," I added. Yolanda would understand that we thought Tut was a key witness to murder.

"Donald's cat? The one Margaret was wailing about?" Hanley asked.

"Toad Rumble, my upstairs renter, has a brindle cat. They look a lot alike, Ivy," Bob said. "Some folks confused Toad's animal with Isis. I used to get a lot of calls from folks worried that Adam's valuable cat was loose. Didn't you, too, when you first came?"

He nodded silent agreement, ignoring my pleading gaze.

"But Ronald said . . . he told me . . . to tell you, Adam, and Hanley . . . and Stewart, that he saw the arsonists and stopped them."

"Arsonists?" Hanley asked me.

"Those men in the shop. 'It could have been worse,' he said. He told me to tell you that."

"What do you think he meant?" Hanley asked, all oily, soothing concern, faking sympathy for the poor, insane woman.

"Why, about the fire, of course. What else could he have meant?" By now, I doubted what I had seen and heard. There had been smoke. "Of course he meant that," I repeated. "And Tut was there, too. Isis . . . Isis recognized him. Didn't she?" I felt my brows knit as I thought back. I had not gotten a good look at the man I thought was Ronald. And Isis wanted down, but she did not go to Tut. She moved away from the alley.

Hanley broke the silence. "Did the man say he was Ronnie? And you're sure it was him, not Toad?"

I was not sure. I closed my eyes briefly, confused.

Marion touched my hand. "We'll figure it out, honey," she whispered.

"But the police. Ripple," I protested, my voice faint.

"We'll call them when we're ready," Stewart said.

Just to placate me, I was sure. Or was I?

"Under the old city ordinances," Stewart continued, "Margaret Bader-Conklin was deputized at some point as assistant mayor, so she's first in line over the president of city council, Rupert Murphy. That's the way Apple Grove was organized and right now, that's what NAM has to honor. No one can change that."

"But that's arcane, absurd," I protested, my voice milder than my thoughts. "Who controls the money?"

"By the time Rupert's protest is filed and dealt with, this will all be over," Hanley said. "The National Association of Mayors can't possibly help now. We'll file notices with the grantors and get everything straightened out." He was obviously more concerned about the money than who sat in the mayor's office. "Yolanda, what can you tell us?"

"I brought the letter I received shortly before they smoked the Gazette office."

I felt as useful as a walleyed pike on a Saturday in Wisconsin and stood, intending to slip out. No one took notice of me as they all leaned over the table. I could see part of the paper Yolanda set out. Glittering, multicolor letters stuck onto a piece of lined notebook paper spelled the first part of my current mantra: "Don't believe every . . ."

I'd had enough and quietly opened the door and closed it behind me.

The new big bank building, which nearly rivaled the stately city hall in size, anchored the other side of downtown from the newspaper office. I suppose technically State's wasn't really in the "downtown" section of Apple Grove since it was separated by a cul de sac and a huge cement coulee meant to keep the Founders River from flooding the city, but I doubt anyone cared. I walked toward the older, smaller clusters of brick buildings, turned at Tiny's corner and headed for the river. I mostly wanted a quiet place to think. No one had stopped me from leaving the meeting. I didn't tell Adam about the second chocolate drop or how Isis and Memnet decided to be friends. Maybe I'd dreamed all that, too.

I thrust my hands deep in my pockets and bent my face to the ground. My sneakers hit damp grass before I realized I had arrived at the edge of the streambed. Miscellaneous scraps, old grass clippings, broken glass and general debris lined the bank, about six feet away from where the actual water dribbled along. I toed that line, lost in thought and time, remembering when Donald had invited Adam to Apple Grove and told him about a building Adam would like for the next franchise of his bookstore. I closed my eyes and smelled the coffee we each held in heavy take-out cups. Columbian dark roast.

"So, I have the perfect place in mind for your newest branch, Adam." Donald had bubbled enthusiasm as we stood outside an exhibition room at the last CAT convention last spring. We'd already gotten my little house ready for me to move into and I loved it. I was curious about where Donald planned to move Adam.

"It used to be an antique shop, next to the barber. It's the perfect location, right in the middle of downtown. The building is a bit rundown, but we'll take care of that. The last owner, a woman named Renata, moved out a couple of years ago. Her daughter had to put her at Trail's End. That's the fancy retirement home nearest to Apple Grove. Roberta's her daughter's name. She has the flower shop on the other side of downtown." Donald barely took a breath. He was in high form, performing a sales pitch for his beloved community. I sipped from my cup, loving that he showed so much enthusiasm for Apple Grove.

I had walked past the place Donald referred to a number of times before I moved to Apple Grove. A torn shade hung lopsided in the front window, which was cracked. And the dirty shelves lining the inside of the store were visible if people stopped and pressed their noses against the glass.

"Sure, Donald," I'd added my two cents. "No one really wants that old eyesore of a building . . ." *Oops.* "I mean, Renata's perfectly-located storefront, to remain empty. Makes downtown look less than prosperous."

Adam had shared his grin between me and Donald. He calmly drank from his paper coffee cup before replying. "Well, this smells like a set-up to me, but I'll swing by and check it out. Apartment upstairs, hmm? At least it has indoor plumbing." He winked at Donald over the cup's rim. "You did mean the toilet inside the building, didn't you?"

And we'd all laughed. I had felt such joy at the time, such release from my old life of being chained to a man who took me for granted, and from an apartment with escalating rent in a neighborhood that had gone stale.

A gust of wind drew me back to the present. I kicked at the remnants of a smashed and dirty paper coffee cup that had washed up along the bank of the river.

I had made friends in Apple Grove. The neighbors were nice and cared about each other, sending casseroles to folks under the weather and issuing friendly hellos from the sidewalk. People at church enthusiastically welcomed me, especially after they found out I had been willing to teach Sunday School. I wanted to be part of Donald's cure, not add to the disease of discouragement. And Adam was nothing like Stanley.

I walked along the bank of the Founders River, kicking aside some of the bigger piles of debris. Searching for treasure, I guess. Looking for answers. Both Donald and Adam let me down — big time. Donald by getting himself killed and Adam by his current lack of support, which I did not even pretend to understand. And then there was my so-called friend, Marion. I could not decide whose side she was on, if she even knew. Was there something wrong with me? Was I bound to make bad choices, trust the wrong people all of my life? Could I be content, single?

Self-pity burned in my eyes. I stopped walking and hunched my shoulders, staring downriver toward the bridge. Why had I come down here at all? Had I thought I would see Tut along the river bank, as Jenny had? Wiping my eyes across my sleeve, I faced the opposite direction. Adam was heading for me. Resolutely, I turned away from him to face the water.

He did not say anything at all for the first couple of minutes. I wasn't about to give him the satisfaction of speaking first. Finally, he bent to pick up a smooth piece of cloudy green glass. "Wonder how long this has been here?" he said. He let the bit fall then gripped my shoulders. "Ivy —"

"Were you in on this little charade from the beginning?" I asked, addressing the middle button of his shirt. "Because you sure have played your part well. All this time, you've been hiding him, haven't you? Where is he?"

"What are you talking about?"

I shot my glare upward, past his chin to his eyes. "Stop it! Last night you told me not to believe what I saw. Right before Ronny talked to me in the alley."

"That wasn't what I meant. Are you sure about what you saw?"

"Of course I'm sure." *Wasn't I?* "Donald's cousin . . . the guy from the newspaper articles. And Donald's cat, Tut. Aren't you hiding them out in your store? In your basement?"

"What? No! Ivy, what in the world gave you that idea?" His grip changed to a little shake of my shoulders. "All I meant was, well . . ." He let go and snorted a mixture of frustration and dismay. "I'm sorry. I want to find Tut just as much as you do." He put his fists on his hips and watched my face while he spoke. "Ivy, Hanley and Stewart offered to buy out the remaining contract and take back the store. I'm considering letting them."

"You haven't even had the grand opening. How can you just —"

"Not 'just'! Ivy, this whole thing hasn't worked out the way I planned." He made a rueful grimace and took a deep breath when he saw what must have been shock on my face. "Except for you, of course."

"Of course," I mimicked. I began to walk away.

"Ivy!" He came trotting after me, rounding to stand in front of me. "I've had enough trauma in my life. More than enough. Is it too much to ask for a normal, quiet, collected and calm, happy little life? With someone I love?"

Love? Love? A person who loves someone else doesn't run out on her. "I prayed for you. Last night. I felt as though I needed to be with you when you were at the fire. I rushed to be with you in case you were hurt. . . ." My eyes went to his throat, hidden under his usual turtleneck. "Or burned."

His face paled. I whispered, "I haven't prayed like that since Donald . . . since Donald and I prayed about his plan. Adam . . . I like living here. Apple Grove is nice. I'm starting to fit in. I think, all this stuff that's going on is just . . . an aberration. After it's over . . . I don't know. I want to settle down, too. Here. I don't want to go backward."

I watched while he struggled to get words out. He swallowed several times. "If Margaret gets her way, this will not remain a nice little village. Donald wanted better for Apple Grove. If he's not here to make sure there's proper sustainable growth, Margaret will ruin it with a big, smelly factory and all kinds of people who come and go, who don't care about things as we do. You know that's what will happen."

Whatever I expected from Adam was not that speech. I sidestepped around him and continued to walk. "I thought you were going to confess to helping Ronald Grimm hide out in the tunnels, using the entry in your basement. Keep him away from Margaret. Once Hanley found out what Margaret was up to, that is. Using him as a substitute for Donald, at least until she got the money. That's why Hanley, Donald's best man, has been so keen on setting you up in that store to begin with, wasn't it?"

Adam didn't answer.

I turned around, letting the wind whip my hair across my face. "Well?" I demanded.

He stood, staring at me.

"It's so obvious!" I yelled in anger, frus-

312

trated more by the fact that I wasn't making any sense at all. It was a long shot, accusing Margaret of trying to pass off her husband's cousin as the mayor. But I couldn't stop now. "How could anybody not see?"

Adam shook his head and stared out over the eroded, gravel stream bed. "I can't believe you think that I would be involved in something like that."

I could barely hear him.

"I didn't even know there were tunnels before Lucy told us. And who would believe a substitute mayor?"

I took a few paces in his direction. "I'm sorry. I'm confused . . . and upset. But don't you agree? That has to be where they're hiding. Jenny saw Tut down here. I saw them both last night. Ronny Grimm's here, Adam. He's got to be."

"But why would he be hiding out? If you really believe that, I'll help you look. Sometime. Right now, we're not safe in Apple Grove." He came closer to me. "Come on, let's just leave. We don't really belong here. We can go anywhere we want."

"He's got to be hiding from Margaret, don't you see? If they committed arson, it isn't a far stretch to murder."

Adam shook his head.

313

"I don't want to go anywhere else right now," I said. "But if you need to run, you need to run. I'm staying, at least until I know what happened to Donald. And Tut." I walked until I left him behind.

Now who's running? I sped up. I needed the comfort of my own house and Memnet.

Both cats padded in to greet me when I arrived home. I was immediately suspicious. "What have you two been up to while I was away?" I did a brief search but found nothing out of place. Hmm. "Well, I'm hungry. How about you? Want some lunch?"

Isis was the first to reply, followed by Mem's chuckling agreement.

I set out some of Mem's soft, smelly tuna treats, which Isis decided she liked, too. I poured out fresh water then watched while both cats drank out of a single dish. I could like this. Two cats weren't more trouble than one.

A clunking sound came from my front stoop, a signal I recognized as a mail drop. I opened the door a few inches to reach out to pick up the circulars and notes from the box attached to my house.

Janie, the neighborhood mail carrier stood on the sidewalk, sorting a few envelopes before walking to the next house.

I stepped out to greet her, but nearly

314

tripped over a familiar-looking gold package. "Hi, Janie." I stooped to pick up the box.

"You must have a secret admirer," the chubby woman responded, echoing Adam's comment from last night.

"This didn't come with the mail?"

"Nope. Nearly tripped over it myself."

"Oh. Did you hear the news?"

"About Margaret? Sure! From everyone who's been home today."

"You think things will change much?"

"Nah, nothing much happens in Apple Grove," she said. "See ya tomorrow, Ivy."

I wish Adam had heard that. I closed the door on Janie's cheerful comment. One thing I knew, no way was I turning this chocolate over to the police. This was mine.

19

The aroma of seared sirloin burger I cooked for my solitary dinner that evening drifted on the air, aided by my swirling spatula. The doorbell rang. "Who could that be?" I asked Memnet. Together we answered the summons. I would have been disappointed had my visitor been anyone but Adam.

"You really prayed?" He asked as soon as I opened the door.

I nodded. "On my knees and everything. Right there." I waved the greasy spatula toward the front window.

"Can we talk?"

I took a deep breath and couldn't refuse his sweet plea. Besides, I still had his cat. "Sure. C'mon in."

"I hope Isis is behaving herself," he said, closing the door behind us. "I didn't mean to interrupt your dinner."

"I'll make more, if you'd like to stay."

He flashed a grin. "If I say yes now, does

that mean you'll feed me no matter what happens?"

I laughed. "Got me there. Maybe I'll wait before I ask again. Have a seat. I'll get us some coffee."

Isis trotted up to him from the hall, where I'd left her lazing on my bed. He bent to pick her up.

I walked slowly over to the stove to check the food.

He went into the living room and stood in the spot I had occupied last night, on my knees, praying for his safety.

I turned down the heat and covered the burgers before going after him with the promised coffee.

He turned and moved close to me. Too close. He smelled so good, the pine-scented soap I associated with him just noticeable underneath the clean hints of outside.

"Oh!" I said. He had me addled. "Yes. I wanted to tell you . . . I forgot to say earlier, that is, that it seems Isis and Memnet have become friends."

Memnet crawled out from behind the sofa and gingerly approached, as if he was a nervous teenager meeting his girlfriend's father for the first time.

Isis jumped gracefully to the floor.

We watched while our pets touched noses.

"Ivy. I don't know where Ronald is. If I did, I would say so."

I buried my face in my hands. "I'm so sorry. I can't believe what comes out of my mouth sometimes. That was unforgivable. And I believe you. I'm not even certain just who I saw." I moved my hands and studied him. "I haven't even asked you about your place. Can anything be saved?"

His hands wound in my hair, stroking the back of my head much like he did with Isis as he urged me close. "The worst damage was upstairs. The equipment and store inventory are smoke-damaged and have to be replaced. My apartment will have to be rebuilt."

"I'm so sorry. That's terrible. You lost all your personal stuff?"

"Odds and ends. I kept my place in Chicago. I've lived there all my life."

I nodded, numb with suspicion and sorrow. "Right. This was just a temporary gig for you."

"You have to understand my other businesses are still in the city. I couldn't just jump blindly and give up everything."

As I had. "I do understand. And I'm sorry. I accused you of some pretty terrible things. You don't owe me anything, but I owe you an apology."

"Ivy, look at me."

I raised my head slowly, reluctant and shy to see his face.

"I believe you," Adam said. "Don't you think Donald would have trusted us if he was worried about something? He thought we'd make a good couple, and I don't want to prove him wrong. Let's just let things play out for now without jumping to conclusions." He stroked the hair of my temple behind my ear. I watched his lips form the words.

"What did you mean last night, when you said, 'don't believe everything I see?' "

He watched my lips, as if he could see the words as I spoke them, before answering. "Just that you might wonder what Hanley and Stewart and I would do about the store."

"Oh." I focused on his mouth moving closer. "Um, so that's when they said they would buy you out?"

Adam's momentum halted. He raised his eyes to mine. "Yes." But it was a question.

I leaned back. "You asked me what I thought of Apple Grove once. I had a hard time answering then. But now I have to tell you that, despite the weird things that are happening right now, I'm serious when I say I like living here. I have my own house for the first time in my life. The neighbors are nice. I know the mail lady, Janie, by name. Marion and I are going to play on the women's volleyball team at the Rec Center after Christmas. I'm helping at the newspaper office. I like church. Pastor and Mrs. Gaines are nice people. They've invited me to Bible study, and I would like us to go. Together."

Adam turned away from me to reach for his cooling cup of coffee I'd set on an end table.

"My business is picking up," I continued. "I can pay my bills on my own without getting into my trust fund. I miss Donald and Tut. The next meeting is soon, and I want us to go together."

"You may not get everything you want, Ivy." Adam stared out the front window.

"My mother said that every day for a year after my father died. I realize that. But the things I mentioned are in reach. I'm not hurting anyone. I'm happy." I bounced a little in irritation, crossing my legs. "Or at least I was." I heard Mem and Isis batting some object around the kitchen floor. "Even Mem and Isis decided to get along."

Adam turned to me. A frown line appeared between his brows. "Getting along isn't the issue, Ivy! You see life through your little rosy glasses. You think it's enough to be happy and not hurt anyone."

"So, what do you want, Adam? What makes you happy?"

He glared at me, his mouth set in a straight line. "My stores, and my customers. And when someone threatens my business, I'm not happy." He paced around my little living room, three steps one way, four another. "What if we'd been there when the fire started? If you'd been . . ." His voice choked.

I waited, trembling and upset.

Adam said in a stronger, decision-made voice. "I talked to my sister this morning. Marie oversees my other stores. I told her I was coming back for a couple of weeks. The condo complex I live in is undergoing some remodeling. She invited me — us — to stay with her. They have a big house, lots of guest rooms." He continued his restless journey. "I want you to come. Meet her. Our folks are . . . well, Dad's been gone for ten years. Mom's not in too good of shape. She has Alzheimer's, lives in a nursing home. I need to be there for her in case anything happens. Will you? Come?"

"I can't leave my work that long. Most of what I do is time sensitive. You know that."

He stopped before me and leaned close,

hands resting on either side of me, not touching me. His whole expression pleaded. From his gentle, smoky gray eyes to the cleft of his chin, he begged me. "You can work from practically anywhere. Please. I don't have anywhere else to go and I couldn't stand it if you . . ." He couldn't finish.

I felt the single tear spill over and run down my cheek. "I can't. I'm not ready to give up."

He bent his head, exposing the back of his neck to me with a vulnerability that nearly made me change my mind.

A yowl from the kitchen broke the spell.

He righted himself, stretching his back.

I sidled away from him and went to turn off the stove.

Mem stood at the back door, hair raised along his spine, tail twitching.

"What's wrong, my friend? If you want to go out, you know how to ask politely." I opened the door for him. Glittery paper caught my eye. Another package. "Ah. You saw the delivery!" I said. "If only you could tell me who it was." I opened the door and looked both ways along the street, seeing no one. I brought the box inside.

"What's that?" Adam stood in the opening between the kitchen and living room.

I held the box from Featherlight up for

him to see. "Remember when I thought you had dropped off some candy here? Someone's been making regular deliveries. Would you like some?"

"No." He came into the room. "You've eaten some before? Are you sure it's safe?"

"Yes. The police have been informed. In fact, the last package — no, the one before that — had my coin purse with it. The one that was stolen."

Adam watched me through narrowed eyes.

Good. Let him think about this. Maybe even be jealous.

"You have no idea who's behind this?"

"None. Now, do you want a burger with me, or not? I'm hungry." I didn't wait for him to answer, but bustled around, getting dishes and silverware out.

Adam helped finish the place settings and, at my direction, rummaged in the fridge for salad fixings. After we ate, he sat at the table watching me, Isis on his lap. Our meal had been silent.

Even though I was angry, I feared losing him. I didn't know what to do.

We cleared away the remnants of the meal with the minimum of talk.

I was not ready to let him leave. "More coffee?" I asked.

He inclined his head.

A few more minutes of polite small talk had me ready to scream.

"Ivy, I need to take a break from all of this — mayhem," he said quietly, clinking his coffee cup back into its saucer. "I want you with me, but I accept that you aren't ready to leave. I'm worried about you, but you have friends who will look out for you."

I stared at him, absorbing his features, trying not to cry.

"My niece is allergic to cats. Can I ask you to keep Isis while I'm gone?"

"Of course."

When he was set to go, we stood arm in arm at the door. His leaving was a physical rip in the fabric of my being that not even having Isis could bandage.

"I'll call you," he whispered against my lips, the brevity of the kiss making me quake.

I quickly closed and locked the door behind him, then leaned against it. Two weeks, two weeks, two weeks, he'd said, the words echoing in my mind. Two weeks to breathe and sleep and pretend to live with my heart in shreds.

20

Two weeks turned into three. Adam's mother experienced a health crisis. Then a hiring issue at one of the stores took up his time. One excuse, then another. His calls got shorter and shorter.

Stop day-dreaming, Ivy! Move on with your life. Think of finding Tut.

Mayor Margaret canceled the Fourth of July parade, calling such a celebration unseemly with the recent demise of the former mayor.

My Chicago trip had been sloughed off long enough. I set a date of August 1 for the trip. A real sleuth would most certainly have investigated this important angle long ago. I reminded myself that I was just a tech nerd, not a PI. The preparation for my journey would have made a veteran of safaris laugh. I packed a half dozen granola bars, bottles of water, recharged my dusty I-Pass I thought I'd never use again, and even took an extra gallon of gasoline. I studied the map as if I were attempting to locate a moving target instead of a large stationary building, and double checked all the surrounding exits of the target in case the never-ending construction blocked my chosen route.

I headed toward a brilliant mauve sunrise, hoping to get into the downtown area before the lunch time rush caused me grief; not that there seemed to be any time less crowded than any other in that great city. I wound my way to Highway 30 and hit the west beltline a couple of hours later. Another hour of anxious sign-checking, exiting and merging, and I arrived at the intersection of my goal. Naturally there was no place to park within sight of the good-sized lime-stone building. As I cruised slowly past on the third circle, I noticed there were no windows on the ground floor, which leant an aura of mystery right from the start. I found a parking ramp three blocks away. Great. Only fourteen dollars to park. In advance. I handed my cash over to the bored, young, tattooed, and pierced man plugged into some music machine, and hoped to find my car intact when I returned.

With the sound of squealing tires echoing off the dirty chipped cement columns and the smell of oil heavy in my nostrils, I prepared for my adventure. I carefully gathered my coin purse and key, stuffing them deep into my front pocket. I clamped my hat on my head, grabbed the cell phone, which I held like a security blanket and tried to orient myself with the map. Donald's picture was inside a cardboard sleeve, so it wouldn't get too rumpled. Trying to appear as if I knew exactly what I was doing and where I was going, I headed toward the Summersby building. As I tromped the sidewalk, I noticed the two stately towers that kept changing names framed the Summersby like nesting dolls. The Chicago skyline really was a fascinating sight. Maybe I'd get a puzzle for something to occupy my evenings since Adam didn't seem inclined to return any time soon.

The doors to the golden-hued business tower were nondescript. Only the address was decaled in anonymous numbers across the double glass entry. Fortunately, there was a receptionist at a round desk in the dingy tiled hall, which boasted two elevators.

Cherry, her name tag said, was dressed in a pinstriped professional business outfit and wore an earpiece. She calmly asked for my credentials before agreeing to look at the picture of Donald.

I wasn't prepared for that. I certainly wouldn't lie. "Um, my uncle was a bit confused. I think he just wandered away and I thought he might once have come in here by mistake." My uncle did get confused and lost once downtown on a tour. Was it still a lie? *I'm sorry, Lord.*

Cherry's expression softened. "My grandfather has dementia." She reached for the picture. "How long ago, do you think?"

"The man in the picture may have wandered in and out of this building any time over the last few months. That's why I'm asking all around."

The skeptical look returned, but her eyes flickered across the photograph. "He doesn't look familiar. I'm sorry." She handed the picture back to me, expression flinty.

Score one. Now how did I get up to Merris Corp?

"I have another reason for stopping in," I told the woman. "I'd like to get a backyard security fence for my cat. Someone told me that Merris was the place to come."

Cherry frowned. I had never seen lipstick painted on so beautifully before and I stared at her lips, fascinated. A second later I realized I had not been paying attention. A little snort from her had me refocused.

"Merris usually does custom jobs and sends representatives to your home. Can I take your name and address?"

"So, they don't usually see walk-ins?"

"No. What is this about?"

"I'm from out of town. I didn't know how it worked. I'll just call them to set up an appointment later." I backed away, afraid she might call security any moment. "Thank you for your time, Cherry." As I left, I noted the building directory posted on the wall. Oddly, "Summersby" was stenciled over a fresh coat of white paint that didn't match the surrounding color. But there was my goal. "Merris Corp" occupied an eleventh-floor suite, just as the message said: "eleven-oh-four." And Cherry told me walk-ins were not customary.

Because I wasn't a professional snoop and didn't know what else to do, I decided I might as well get my fourteen dollars' worth of parking lot time and walk around the block. Casual-like. I adopted what I hoped looked like a fascinated tourist stroll. As if there were any tourist attractions right here, far away from the lakeside square that was surrounded by the museums, aquarium, observatory, and shopping. I could always ask for directions. If anyone looked at me closely, they would have undoubtedly been able to see the thumping of my heart right through my blouse. The wind off Lake Michigan made my eyes smart and tear. I rubbed my arms and bent my head and clamped the hat around my ears as I rounded the corner to the rear of the building.

Through a tightly woven security fence I could just make out a dark-colored van, backed up close to the building, paneled doors open wide. I stopped, checked around me to see if anyone was nearby, and peered in between the slats. Along one side of the van was lettered: "Merris Pet Security, Systems for your peace of mind." Now where had I seen that before?

A figure in dark overalls slammed the van doors closed. I shrank against the fence, then decided that was stupid. I resumed my stroll past the gate, which slid open to let the van through. I turned to watch, as if I had never seen such an invention before. I pulled my hat over my eyes, so I suppose that was why Letty Grimm, in the passenger seat, didn't appear to notice me.

Half a block later I realized my feet were still moving. Carefully, I let myself sag against a storefront. The door opened, releasing a pair of chatting customers and the enticing aroma of steamed milk and freshly ground coffee beans. I made a decision to dock at this port until the storm of my emotions coalesced to a comfortable level.

Another great mistake, Ivy Amanda McTeague Preston.

I did a double take at the chime of the door. The tone exactly matched Adam's at Mea Cuppa. I closed my eyes and sniffed. It even smelled the same. My eyeballs were the only thing not paralyzed for this moment in time. It was Mea Cuppa; Adam's downtown Chicago branch. *Oh, Lord,* was the only prayer my gelled brain waves could recycle.

I remembered to breathe, and then turned to leave. And saw Adam's unmistakable profile in a room along the side wall. He laughed at something apparently said by the person on the other side of his desk who crossed her endless legs and wiggled her shoulders. I didn't even grab a cube of complimentary Featherlight chocolate from the dish next to the register on my way out.

A half-formed scheme to pretend that I was not just a tech geek and somehow get into the offices of Merris Corp on the eleventh floor of a secured building to confront possible murderers or at least find evidence that Donald Conklin had, in fact, been there, died in a vapor of Lake Michigan fog.

Over the next few days at home in Apple Grove I contemplated my misadventure to Chicago. I had a hard time establishing a connection between Summersby and Donald's death. Letty Grimm could have been there for any number of reasons on behalf of her boss, the temporary mayor, which had to do with the company establishing a MerriFood presence in Apple Grove. There was nothing I could share with the police. I didn't even bother to tell my mother, at least not yet.

Adam . . . had probably been conducting an interview. But if he hired someone who looked like that, why would he settle for mousy me every night after work? Maybe it was her he referred to when he said he wanted to settle down with someone he loved. When I heard through the grapevine, Bob, that Adam's mother had to go into assisted living, my heart sank and for the first time he called me. He said his mother's affairs might take some time to wrap up, then he'd come see us. He was sorry he hadn't called me first, but he'd been in regular touch with Bob about the reconstruction on his building, and just let it out.

I'm sure.

I struggled to keep up with my work projects. I even gave a talk to the Chamber of Commerce one evening. I pretended to be enthused and think I passed.

August back-to-school sales were on before Marion finally broke her silence with a visit to my house. I met her in the driveway. "Please, Ivy. I have to tell you what we're doing. Please!"

I realize that I sounded like a nutcase during the meeting that day after the fire. "What do you mean, Marion?"

"Listen to me. Jeff Hanley was one of Mayor Conklin's biggest personal business partners. You knew that, right?"

"Only recently."

"When he first lost touch with the mayor, he suspected a problem, even before you did, Ivy."

"Why couldn't he just say so?" I was exasperated. "First nobody believes me about Donald, and then I find his body, and now everyone's on my side? And why was it that Yolanda, Adam, and I were victimized, again?"

"It's not like that, Ivy. Can you blame Hanley for not trusting you? You and Adam show up at a council meeting, spout about all this money that Mayor Conklin and Jeff secured for Apple Grove businesses, and he had no idea that the mayor talked about their plans so freely. Jeff thinks that whoever stole your computers and hurt your cat was trying to scare you. Yolanda obviously got too close to the truth, and Adam, well, as a newcomer, I suppose he was next."

"What about Donald's cousin? Ronald Grimm?"

She put her chin in her hand and stared hard at a crack in the cement. "Grimm — you mean, like in Letty Grimm?"

"The same. They've all been friends since high school. Did he mention that little tidbit of information? I hate to tell you this, but I don't trust Jeff Hanley."

"What do the Grimms have to do with anything?" Marion asked.

"Ronald Grimm happens to look enough like his cousin Donald that it might be hard to tell them apart."

"You're kidding. Jeff is older than Bob and me. We weren't even in school together. How did you find out?"

"Remember when those students were here? And the newspaper office attacked? Some back issues of the paper were stolen. Bob's mother happened to have copies at the historical society. Sonja, Lucy, and Elvis found pictures of Donald and his cousin both in some club and later, saw Donald and Margaret's wedding announcement. Hanley was best man and Ronald was in the wedding party. I think I suspect what Margaret was up to with her look-alike husband's cousin."

"You do? You're . . . kidding, right? Replace Donald? Tell me you don't think that. Oh, my goodness. But there's worse news. MerriFood is in deep trouble with the Federal Trade Commission. If Margaret's involved somehow, then she's got problems, too. Remember when you asked me about Summersby Building Company? Well, I looked them up and —"

"I know. It's a place and has to do with Merris Corp. Elvis found that out," I told her, not wanting her to think I had been idle, either. I invited her inside to tell her about my visit there, where I last saw Letty Grimm.

"Oh." Marion sat quiet at my kitchen table for a rare moment. "I don't want you to feel bad, Ivy. As though we've left you out. We haven't. It's just that, well, this is Apple Grove business and we want to handle it our way."

"I am part of Apple Grove now, Marion."

She put her hand on my arm. "You're

right, Ivy. Donald wanted you here. That's good enough for Bob and me." She sat back and crossed her legs. "So, you went to Chicago all alone? You shouldn't have done that, Ivy."

"No one there knew anything, anyway. A fierce-looking woman named Cherry guards the entrance of the Summersby building and she said she'd never seen anyone like Donald."

"Did you believe her?"

"I don't think so. She didn't really even look at the picture."

"That's why you wanted a picture of Donald?" She laughed. "I knew you weren't going to hang it in your office. Of course, you told the police what you found."

"What? That I know where the building is that I got a creepy call from? And then what?"

"Well, officially, Donald died from a disease he got from his cat that's been lost so long that it's probably dead." Marion was a dog person.

I forgave her for calling Tut "it."

We were quiet for a few moments.

"So, what's the plan you wanted to tell me about?" I asked.

Marion's face cheered considerably. "You know how Georgine Crosby's not just the city engineer, but also sits on the zoning commission? She alerted the state authorities about the illegal work being done and MerriFood contractors spent all day pulling their people and equipment off the site. They'd started a structural skeleton over their cement pad, too, all without the approval of city council or even the permits. Margaret took their fee, but the permits were denied. She didn't tell them."

"Wow. Margaret must be really annoyed."

"We hope this will force her hand by making her try for the rest of the money by funneling it through her fake companies. Then we can catch her. Or make her leave town. Jeff said he knows about her financial state, but he can't say anything due to privacy laws."

That made as much sense as usual. "I still think Tut's involved some way. Adam and I found all these fancy collars at Tut's house —"

"Tut's house? When were you there?"

I squinted. "Um, forever ago, I guess. Before we found Donald."

Marion's eyes were full of melted sympathy. "But what does a cat have to do with it? If he has the disease, he'll have to be destroyed, if he's still alive. And you shouldn't get in the way of the police." She popped one of my chocolates in her mouth.

"Oh, Marion, you can't believe Donald died of a disease that's not known to be fatal? There has to be more to it. Are you watching how Margaret's using the community improvement money?"

Marion pursed her lips. "Yes. So far, we've just paid out the bills that were approved before . . . before . . ."

"Then why is MerriFood building? They must think they're getting money somehow."

"There's been nothing wrong done at city hall so far, Ivy," Marion insisted. "I gotta get back and pick up the kids from Bob's mom."

I saw her out. Donald's death must have taken place at Merris. But how? He must have been moved then back to Apple Grove. Ha! I remembered that van. And where I had seen it before — both at city hall, and later at Tut's house. But where was Tut? If Margaret didn't have him, maybe Addy Bailey could help me figure out more hiding places for a cat in Apple Grove. My thoughts unraveled. If Margaret didn't have him did that mean Tut hadn't been with Donald when she . . . killed him? Had Donald hidden him? Why? And now . . . Tut had escaped but was too afraid to go home?

Oh, boy.

I hoped Addy Bailey, Margaret's good friend, really meant it when she said she was tired of keeping her secret. Maybe she'd already gone to the police and told them everything. Only one way to find out. I'd have to ask her. Once I figured out what to say.

The first time I went into Tiny's Buffet last April, I only picked up a take-out box. Tiny's regulars stared their silly heads off at me. Jeff Hanley had been right to poo-poo Tiny's coffee at that long-ago council meeting. I threw it out when I got home.

I'm not sure why, when Marion asked the next day after our chat about Margaret's business woes and my trip to Chicago if I wanted to go there for an early supper, I agreed. Loneliness can make a person goofy.

"If you can find something not too greasy, the food's really pretty good," Marion said. It was Ladies Night, which meant we could order a free appetizer. We chose onion petals with a horseradish sauce that wasn't half bad.

"So, what have you heard from Adam?" Marion asked.

I stared at the faux granite laminate table top. A mental image of Adam's laughing profile and the other woman's long legs flashed in the gloss of the surface. I rubbed at the place with my finger. "Nothing since the other day when he came to talk to the builders and took me out for a quick bite," I replied. "He said it would take a while to go through his mother's business."

"That's sad." She shuddered. "I just hope I don't know it if I ever lose my marbles."

I agreed. "So, how're the election plans coming along?" I knew that would keep my friend occupied for a while, telling me all the latest news. I enjoyed attending Bobby's summer football league games and had even gone to a swim meet to see Colleen Bailey compete. Just because I wasn't a parent didn't mean I couldn't enjoy community events. Bob and Marion and their kids made up a great family in my opinion, fun and Godly people who, by example, made me long for a husband and children of my own. But with whom?

Marion might enjoy talking, but she was no mean gossip. "So, the election will be held next February," Marion said. "Both Margaret and Rupert wanted it earlier, due to the emergency and all, but NAM said the procedure was in place to prevent spur-of-the-moment decisions or revenge elections. They sent a representative to check over the ordinance book. Some of it was plumb falling apart, I tell you. I needed to photocopy the whole thing."

I tuned out of her prattle while I scanned the dinner crowd.

Jeff Hanley raised his glass to me.

Great.

". . . she's managed to alienate half the board. The ones who are still on it, that is," Marion said. "That Fourth of July cancellation was a bad publicity stunt. So far, let's see . . ." She ticked off on her fingers: "Knute Granger, the communications officer, resigned when Margaret tried to pass an ordinance that called for the mayor to oversee all advertising. She tried to separate and outsource the printed materials to a new copier place she wants to bring in, and use some new specialty envelope-stuffing firm to take care of mass mailings. Nobody knows where these companies are coming from. The Chamber of Commerce already says they're cutting ties with city hall. As far as the council goes, that makes Arnie Cappler, Needa Jones, and Gretchen Peterson, four who all quit so far. Soon they won't have a simple majority to do business. And did you hear the latest?"

"No, what?" I prompted Marion.

"Oh, hi, Jeff."

"Evening, ladies. May I join you?" Hanley asked from behind my shoulder.

"Sure. Have a seat," I said.

He slid onto the booth beside Marion.

I wasn't about to mince words, no matter who could hear. "So," I said. "How's your best friend Ronald these days, Mr. Hanley?"

He winced and held up his hands. "You got me. But Ronny and Letty split up a long time ago."

"That's not what I asked."

"I haven't seen him lately, if that's what you're after."

"I'm not after anything, Jeff, except to find Donald's killer. I think your friend might have some answers. Do you know how I can get in touch with him?"

"No, Ivy, I don't. Donald contracted an infection which unfortunately killed him. And I wouldn't count on Ronny Grimm for anything. That's one of the reasons Letty left him."

"Where'd you get the money for investing in Mea Cuppa?" I asked, trying to throw him off balance, poking for weaknesses in his armor of smugness.

"You're asking fairly personal questions. If I answer, can I ask you a personal question?"

Touché to you, too, buddy. "Sure."

342

"I'm a banker. I make a good salary and I know how to follow safe markets for high returns. The more I invest, the more I make."

I stared at him, willing him to blink first. "So, you didn't use any of the community grant money?"

His smile didn't reach his eyes. He folded his hands in front of him on the table and leaned toward me.

Marion squirmed, but she might as well not have been there, for all the notice we took of her.

I'd make it up to her later.

"That's two questions, Ivy," Jeff said. "My turn first, and then I'll decide if I want to keep playing this game."

I twitched my lips to the side. "All right. What do you want to ask me?"

"How did you get Donald to tell you about the twelve million dollars? He didn't even tell his wife."

Easy enough to answer. I was puzzled at his tack, though. "He didn't tell me. He told Adam Thompson, and Adam told me. Me and my mother, that is."

The muscle at the side of his smooth-shaven jaw clenched. "Why would your mother be involved in this?"

"Ha! I didn't say you could ask another.

My turn."

Marion grabbed her purse and twisted in the seat. "Excuse me! I need to go to the ladies' room."

My heartbeat suddenly skipped. "Wait, Marion, I . . . will you come back?"

She looked as if she wanted to cry. She blinked, checked the door, the other patrons, and slowly rested her gaze on me. She nodded. "Yes."

Hanley was already standing, and she slid out. He reseated himself and folded his hands once more.

I didn't think I wanted to play poker against this man.

"Why shouldn't the mayor include his wife in a plan to shore up Apple Grove?" The thought haunted me. I didn't care if their marriage had been crummy. Bad marriages were common enough, although usually divorce, not murder, took care of those issues.

"Margaret's run through her money and most of Donald's. I've been using my position at the bank to hide the facts, but the truth is, she's about to lose the house. Donald didn't want anyone to know."

Marion returned almost immediately and sat beside me.

Hanley barely spared her any attention

before saying, "He figured he'd lose the next election if certain information got around."

Marion bounced us a little as she got settled. "Rupert Murphy's been after him for years," she said, as if she'd heard the entire exchange. "Always challenging his position. Donald didn't win by that much in the last outing," she muttered reluctantly.

"That's a moot issue now, isn't it?" I couldn't keep the asperity from my voice.

Marion and Hanley stared at each other.

"What will happen if Murphy wins the election?" I asked.

"Nothing much." Hanley snorted. "He's all gas and no gumption. Tell me why your mother is involved."

Marion cut in. "Her mother teaches crime classes. She sent Elvis and the girls here."

Hanley leaned back, the plastic seat making a scrunch sound.

Tiny's one tired waitress came to refill our cups and ask how we were doing.

I told her we were fine.

When she left, Hanley said, "So that's what those kids were up to."

"They were here for their fieldwork credits," I snapped, upset at Marion's revelation of information to Hanley.

He eyed Marion. "So, what did Elvis come up with, Marion?"

"Well, he found those newspaper pictures."

"Marion." I tried to stay calm.

Her face lit up. "Oh! And the tunnels. Jeff, you remember. Underground. I heard you guys had all kinds of parties before they —"

"Were blocked. Yes, Marion, I remember." Hanley's speculative gleam turned to me. "Some of us kids knew that when you went to the antique store, all you had to do was pretend to use the back exit. We turned the old key to the basement door, went down the steps, slid past the old store dummy, crawled through the broken mirror frame into the back room and pulled open the trap door." He nodded his head, chuckling. "At least, that's what we called it. Big adventure. But not anymore. Those tunnels are out of reach. A generation of kids ago." Hanley leaned forward across the table once more. "So, what about the tunnels, Marion?" He asked her, but his eyes never left mine.

I took a chance. "I think that's where Ronny may be hiding out."

"Who else did you tell, Ivy?"

"Adam Thompson."

"And now he's gone," Hanley said, his voice dropping into an intimate range that was out of context with time and place.

"He's keeping on top of the reconstruc-

346

tion. He's coming back!"

Hanley merely smiled.

347

21

The hazy humid August morning fueled my gloom. Going home to my mother sounded like a decent idea about now. Apple Grovers could keep their little village of horrors.

I sighed. I wasn't about to crawl back home, no matter how much I craved my mother's love and protection. I wouldn't yield my independence. It had taken me long enough to find it. And maybe cost me the love of my life, who only appeared for half a day earlier in the month to talk insurance and remodeling with his partners. He'd taken me to lunch, then left right after to get back to work. Swell.

While vacuuming, I recalled Elvis's claim that Officer Ripple had spent a lot of time on the case. I should talk to him. But what would he do if I told him I suspected the vice president of State's Bank was holding the mayor of Apple Grove's look-alike cousin hostage in the inaccessible tunnel system under the city? So that he and the mayor's wife could funnel twelve million dollars into their own pockets?

Ripple would not simply tell me to call the hospital this time. He would probably take me there himself.

I thought about exploring the tunnels as I watered the philodendron I'd had since high school and the parsley that Mem liked to nibble on. I couldn't access the tunnels from Mea Cuppa while the store was closed. Cal Stewart had begged the police for permission to reopen, even while remodeling was going on upstairs, but had been denied due to safety concerns.

I switched chores.

Brandishing my feather duster, I thought about the city council meeting I attended last night out of curiosity. I heard first-hand about the planned expenses of the upcoming special mayoral election, the high school's request to block off Main Street for the Homecoming Parade next month and the emphatic denial of the requested zoning change from agricultural to industrial for MerriFood. No one from the company represented its interests, and Margaret had been livid. She wielded that gavel as if she possessed a superhero's hammer. Only four council members showed up, so the council couldn't do official business. That meant not being able to bludgeon through a final vote on the zoning board's recommendation to deny the change, but neither could the change be accepted. If looks could kill, Georgine Crosby would have been a steaming puddle on her seat.

Chores completed, I headed for the computer where I worked steadily until lunch. In between fixing bugs in Tiny's website, not the restaurant, thank heavens, and correcting Netty's posts on her flower blog, I thought up an approach to ask Addy Bailey for a last-ditch effort to help find Tut, even though I had to believe he might have died. I must have reached for the phone half a dozen times until I finally emailed.

Addy, you said that you wanted to help me.

Can we meet later today to discuss a matter of mutual concern?

I'm flexible and can get together at your convenience.

Thanks . . .

At noon, the emptiness of my house finally caught my attention.

Isis lounged under the kitchen table on the cool floor.

"Where's our Memnet?" I asked her, squatting to stroke her head.

Isis twisted to her feet and trotted to the

350

back door. "What do you mean, girl? Memnet! Mem! Treats. Where are you?"

I had never known him to completely ignore me. What if he was sick? Trapped? I raced to the basement, up and down the stairs to my office, looked in all the closets, under the bed, in the bathroom. "Memnet!"

Isis remained poised at the back door in the kitchen. "If you want to go outside, Isis, you'll just have to wait until we find Memnet." By 2:00 I needed to face the fact that Memnet was not in the house or the yard.

Panic. Memnet had never been so . . . gone before. I glanced at the kitchen clock for the third time before the pointed hands of my grandmother's rooster-shaped time-piece registered. Was Mom done teaching? Or at least in between classes? What day was this? I made a concerted effort to focus and thought I could try to call anyway.

"Hello, daughter."

Ah, the comforting voice of Mom.

"Ivy Amanda? Are you there? Are you all right?"

The words just couldn't cross my tongue. "Mom," finally came out as a shaken whimper.

"Darling, what's wrong?"

"Me-Memnet."

"Oh, sweetheart. He was getting up there in cat years. It was bound to happen. I'm so sorry."

"He's not dead." My voice sounded stronger. "At least, I hope not. He's — he's missing."

"Ivy, there, now. I'm sorry. When did you notice?"

A rational response I could work for. "Um, about noon or so. I was working." As if I could excuse myself. I could not imagine being a mother and ignoring a living child so completely. I'd better stop daydreaming about having kids of my own.

"And of course, you looked everywhere inside." She wouldn't ask the obvious questions.

"Do you . . . do you know . . ."

"Where to call?" Mom guessed.

"Mmhmm." Sniff.

"You could try the police station. If they don't work with missing animals, they might direct you. Does Apple Grove have an animal control department?"

That's when I started to cry. All the strays were still being rounded up for disease control. Maybe they'd confuse Mem with Tut and . . . and . . .

"Ivy! Ivy, listen to me. You should call that vet. She would know something. Weren't people supposed to turn in cats to her? Ivy!"

"I hear you." I could hardly get the words out. "Thank you. I'll try her now."

"You let me know what she says, or if Mem turns up. I'll call you later. I'm sure he's just confused. Cats probably have senior moments, too, you know."

"Thanks, Mom. I love you."

Mom had good instincts about people. Better yet, I could visit Addy's office with a really good excuse. But should I leave the house? Do not cry again, Ivy Amanda Mc-Teague Preston!

Telephone. Definitely. I left a message with the receptionist on duty, who assured me that the doctor would contact me soon. The elderly-sounding man who said he volunteered at the clinic for Addy told me that the city police do not handle missing pets. He saved me one embarrassing phone call, and then surprised me. While I waited, could I make posters? He said he would recruit some of his volunteer friends to help hang them and to search for Mem, as soon as his shift at the clinic was over.

Tears again. "Oh, thank you! Thank you." A last thought occurred to me before I hung up. "Um, you've been so kind, and I don't even know your name."

"Virgil Toynsbee. Jim from the newspaper's uncle. Call me Virg."

"I'm so grateful, Virg."

"You sound like a nice lady," he told me. "Lady" wasn't as bad as "ma'am" so I forgave him. "We'll find your friend, don't worry, Miss Preston."

"Thank you."

He understood! Mem was more than a pet, he was my friend. Virg's mention of the newspaper gave me an idea. I could take out a missing cat notice. A reward might help jog anyone's memory. It was early, but I was certain this was the right thing to do. *Is that You, Lord? Your ever present help in time of need? Thank you for the suggestion.*

I felt an immediate peace. I was growing in faith moment by moment and this automatic turning to prayer felt natural.

Isis wanted to come along. A couple of gray hairs later, I managed to convince her to stay inside the house and carefully locked the door. Had I been this vigilant last night with the front door? Guilt threatened to overwhelm my precious peace. *Back, guilt!* I would not let it in. I drove to the Gazette office and found a parking spot only a couple storefronts away.

There was nobody in sight. "Yolanda! Hello?"

The sound of her tennis shoes clapping

the wood floor boards preceded her.

"Ivy! Is this business or pleasure?" She wiped her mouth with a napkin. "Sorry. Late lunch."

"That's all right. Business. But first, how's Jim?"

"He's doing very well, thank you for asking. Jenny's a really good girl around him, too."

The little girl popped from behind the tall counter. "I am, I am! I'm good and quiet by Grandpa."

"Well, here's our Jenny. You scared me!" I picked her up and hugged her.

"You're sad, Ivy," she said earnestly, squaring my face with her sticky little fingers.

"You're right. That's why I'm here." I set her down, but she stayed close with her arms wrapped about my leg.

Yolanda pulled her stool over and sat, pen poised. Her acumen was reassuring.

"It's Memnet," I started, businesslike, until her silver curls shimmied with her double take.

"Oh, dear. What's wrong? I'm so sorry."

"He-he's missing. From the house. I noticed around lunchtime. I don't know why I couldn't tell before. I don't know how long he's been gone. I searched everywhere.

I called . . . I called the vet —"

"OK. You're OK. Come, sit." Yolanda came around the counter as soon I started babbling and led me and my leg ornament over to a seat at the work table. Moving books of wedding invitation samples aside, she settled her hip on the tabletop next to me.

Jenny kept a rhythmic stroking of my arm while her grandmother murmured sympathetically.

"Jim's uncle was so kind," I croaked out, when my voice returned.

"Good. You talked to him. Virg and his Seeds group was one of my first recommendations for help."

"Seeds?"

Yolanda grinned. "They call themselves the 'Good Seeds, a Core — that's c-o-r-e — of Apple Grove Volunteers.' There's a dozen of them, all retired seniors. They're a well-organized group of do-gooders and even have a phone number and a desk in Virg's den. He's the leader, but he'd tell you they're all leaders."

"Clever. How do they work? I haven't heard of them yet."

"They don't make a lot of noise, for sure. I guess if you don't need them, you might miss them. They keep their eyes and ears

356

open for places to help. Some have their pet projects, like Virg at the clinic, some help at the library or the rec center, others help at school."

"Wow. That's wonderful. Virg told me to make some posters, and he'd organize some of his friends to put them up and help look for Memnet."

Yolanda nodded and smiled at Jenny. "I bet we can help, too, can't we, Jenny?"

"Memnet ran away?" the little girl asked. "Why would he do that?"

"I don't know, Jenny."

"Maybe he went to look for his friend. Don't worry any more. I'd better go make a poster of him."

"That's right, Jenny," Yolanda told her. "We need a picture."

Out of the mouth of babes . . . had Mem gone to search for Tut? I shook my head. I couldn't imagine that scenario. Besides, Mem wouldn't know where to go, would he? Cats don't track like bloodhounds. Someone might have nabbed him. Maybe someone confused Mem with Tut. Margaret.

After we watched Jenny skip toward the back room, I turned back to Yolanda. "I thought I'd put an ad in the Gazette. Offer a reward. Maybe that will help."

Yolanda cupped my shoulder in her warm palm. "Yes. How about I put in a notice? We can even put in a couple of paragraphs about how Memnet is special, like the mayor's cat, Tut, and Isis. I can dig up some of the old copy, reuse it. Oh, and we'd better mention that he's not wanted for the general round up . . ."

"Right. The strays." I shuddered. "You don't think anyone would hurt him, do you? Even if he was confused with Tut?"

Yolanda was already on her feet, headed for the computer. She shook her head. "Let's make a poster, first. If I know Virg, he'll be raring to go come four o'clock. How 'bout we meet at your house?"

"Thank you, Yolanda." We. "How many should we make?"

I alternated between thankfulness for my new friends' willingness to help, dismay, and fear for Memnet, and anger that he was missing. The thought of someone taking him made me physically ill. If I ever found out Margaret was involved, I'd . . . I'd . . . scratch her myself!

When Yolanda designed the poster to our liking, she told me to go home while she printed them. She'd call Virg to let him know when and where to organize his cadre.

Giving into the urge to check on Isis and

see whether Memnet had returned on his own, I dashed home. Business messages were left on the machine, along with one from Addy assuring me I was in good hands with the Seeds. No one had called or turned in a cat like Memnet, and she would put the word out with other pet owners, who had been equally disturbed by the mandate that all cats be tested for CSD. We would get together later to discuss our mutual concern. *Thank You, Lord.*

I faced a wrathful Isis who had not appreciated being left alone and took sour note of the fact that I had not brought Memnet. I debated whether to call Adam but did not want to lose my momentum. Besides, it wasn't his cat that was missing. I gathered a hat, gloves, and four flashlights.

I met Virg and the Seeds at the end of my driveway about twenty minutes later. The Robbins family from next door decided to help, too, once I told them what happened. The three-year-old twins, Taylor and Timmy, carried matching toy flashlights. Dale called in a few of his buddies from the fire department, and soon I counted twenty people who wanted to search for Memnet.

Virgil and four of the Seeds, two men eager to be helpful and two white-curly-haired women, handed out photographs of

Memnet that I'd printed. They had already divided the neighborhood into search grids and were partnering off.

Virgil Toynsbee inspired calm confidence. Tall and lean as the proverbial string bean, with receding gray hair, he also possessed an air of authority about him, which made me believe he wasn't often disappointed.

"No one goes alone," Virgil called out. "Especially when it gets dark. 'Bout nine or so. Every group have a flashlight? Good. Now, Ivy says Memnet usually answers to his name. Everyone say 'Memnet.' " They all complied. "Good," Virgil continued. "Remember, Memnet has spots, not stripes or patches. I don't want you to bring back every sort of tabby out there, got that? Even though you shouldn't find any cat that doesn't belong to somebody already, since most of the strays have already been rounded up. Ivy, do you want to say anything before we head out?"

"Um, thank you. You're all so very kind. Memnet means the world to me. Maybe, would you all mind, if we — said a prayer?"

"That's a good idea, Ivy." Virgil rescued me from another bout of weepiness. He made a show of folding his hands, closing his eyes and lifting his face to the darkening sky. "Lord Almighty, protector of all living things, help us find this missing pet and keep us safe while we go about Your business. Amen. Now, everyone meet back here at eight thirty and there'll be a drink and snack ready for you."

I thanked Virgil in a whisper. Amazed, I watched neighbors, friends, and strangers set out calling for Memnet, searching under bushes, shining their lights into trees. Gradually the lights and voices faded as the groups moved out.

Virgil gently suggested that I stay back in case someone flushed Mem out and he ran home.

Yolanda would be here soon, armed with paper cups and brownies.

After she arrived, she watched me out of the corner of her eye as we filled jugs with lemonade. Eventually we had nothing left to do but wait. Isis allowed Yolanda to stroke her head as they sat together on the sofa in the living room. "Jenny was terribly disappointed to miss out on the action tonight."

"Oh? Mem likes her. Is she home?"

"Yes. My son came to get her, so she could sleep at his house tonight."

Yolanda had shared the separation news with me earlier. "Have your son and daughter-in-law started marriage counseling yet?"

Yolanda stroked Isis's head a few times. "Yes. I think things are progressing. They don't sound quite so vitriolic when they talk about each other anymore. Jenny doesn't cry like she used to when she went with either of them."

"It's a sad time for all of you. I hope and pray they'll make their marriage work."

"Yes. Seems more families break up than stay together these days." Yolanda shook her head. "I can't imagine why we can't get along in a nation that's supposed to be Christian."

"To be honest with you, Yolanda, I think that's part of the issue. People think that if they profess to be Christian, they're safe from bad things. Pastor Gaines at New Horizons is teaching through the gospel of John this fall. Last week was about Jesus's prayer before his crucifixion, a part I hadn't really known was there before, where Jesus says to his disciples, 'In this world you will have trouble.' Jesus doesn't mean to scare us, Pastor said, but to prepare us. Those whose faith is weak will turn and blame God when bad things happen."

"So those who have strong faith know who to blame?"

I smiled. "I think blaming others isn't right. I realize more and more that because my former fiancé, Stanley, didn't like to go to church, I was willing to give it up to please him. When our relationship didn't work out, I went back. My faith was always inside of me. But I have to work at it to keep it strong. Sort of how muscles atrophy if you don't use them."

Yolanda nodded her head, watching Isis twitch her ears and chortle her rough purr. "Like Jim, in that hospital bed. The doctors didn't want him to relax too much or he'd have trouble getting around later. His heart was damaged, and some of it won't ever work right, but it's still there." She looked at me. "Do you suppose a person can still have faith, even if it's damaged?"

I thought of Adam, watching his wife and daughter die, helpless to do anything to save them. He had lost the desire to return to the church they'd attended as a family. In fact, he had not gone to a worship service until he came to Apple Grove, he'd told me. His faith muscle had atrophied, but I believed he could strengthen it again if he wanted to. "Yes," I told Yolanda, "Even faith that's been terribly tried and tested can become strong again. With God, all things are possible."

"I'll keep that in mind."

The search teams returned, filling my

small house with stories of "I was so sure that was him under the bushes at Mrs. Crabtree's," or "I heard him, I'm sure I did, but when I pulled him out of the shadow, it was just one of those . . . whadd'ya callits? Tabby. Yeah, that's right. Stripes. Never seen one with spots."

No Memnet.

If it had been so easy to find my Mem, I would have done it myself. Nevertheless, I put on my game face and served lemonade until the pitchers were empty. Yolanda's brownies went just as quickly. I had Virgil and Dale write down everyone's names for me, so I could send thank you notes.

Yolanda was the last to leave. "I'm mulling over what we talked about earlier. I've been worried about everything for so long, and with Jim being sick, I can't even begin to imagine how much more peaceful I could have been if I had thought about relying on the Lord. Maybe we can talk about our faith more?"

"Of course. Any time. And I'm so grateful you were here tonight. I think I would have panicked without you."

"Does your young man know?"

"My what? Oh, Adam?" I pictured that groove beside his mouth deepening in amusement if he'd heard Yolanda call him a

young man. "No, I haven't called him yet."
I glanced at the phone, blinking with business I would have to take care of. "I've been
worried, too. I guess I just hoped Mem
would be back and I wouldn't have to say
anything at all. At least it isn't Isis who's
missing. I couldn't face him then."

Yolanda set her hand on my forearm. "Ivy,
call him. It's been my experience that woes
are best shared. Good night."

"Thank you. Good night. I'll be in touch."

Adam's and my last conversation had
been desultory. He told me his lawyer had
taken care of most of his mother's estate.
The lawyer also reviewed reports from the
investigation of the fire. His apartment had
been a total loss, though insurance would
cover it, since arson hadn't been proven.
Jeff Hanley was eager to buy off the contract
and he wanted to sell. One of the coffee
shops needed a new manager, and until he
could hire one, he would need to stay and
run it himself. His usual process took a
month, after he advertised for applications
and did background checks. Adam's condo
remodel complete, he had moved back
home. And that's how he put it: home. Not
home in Apple Grove. He hoped Isis wasn't
causing me any trouble, and he'd let me
know when he could spare a day to come

and get her.

Now that Mem was gone, I was glad Isis was here. I wasn't compelled to return her to Adam just yet, anyway. If nothing else, maybe he'd let me keep her as a parting gift from a relationship that never blossomed.

Sleep would be a gamble. Even through the stress of the last day, my clients deserved my attention. Up in my garret workroom about midnight, I stopped the tapes and cocked my head toward the steps. There it was again. A scuffle, creak noise came from the kitchen. Too big for a mouse. Memnet? Could he have come back? Or was Isis trying to get out?

I crept down the steps holding aloft my electric pencil sharpener, the heaviest, most portable object in my office. Crouching in the entrance to the kitchen, I let out a scream and lost my grip on the thing when a shadow moved. A flash of brightness caught in the light of my overhead stove, which I'd left on.

"Hello, Ivy."

"Stanley!"

The pencil sharpener fell on my toe. While I hopped on my good foot I felt that more than my toe had broken.

22

"What are you doing here? How did you get in my house? Don't you know what time it is?" I should call the police instead of asking inane questions.

"Ivy, Ivy, I've missed you." Stanley Brewer held out a foil-wrapped box. "I brought you these."

"Stanley, you can't just walk inside a person's house."

"I didn't mean to scare you."

Isis came from the direction of my bedroom. I wondered if Stanley might have accidentally let Memnet out during an earlier foray.

"I see you still have that old cat." Stanley tried to make nice.

"That is not Memnet," I replied.

Isis curled her ears back and the tip of her tail twitched.

I folded my arms. "Stanley, how did you find out where I live? And what are you doing here? How did you get in?"

"I jiggled the handle. It turned. Can we sit?"

"No."

"I've been driving for hours, Ivy. This isn't my normal route. I'm tired."

"So'm I. You mean, you sell this kind of candy now? You used to work for —"

"I've changed companies. A lot of things, actually. Ivy, I just wanted to see you, talk to you."

"At midnight? By breaking and entering? Yes, I see things have changed, and not necessarily for the better."

"It's not like that. I . . ."

I tapped my slippered foot on the linoleum. It didn't make the annoying sound I desired. I sighed. "Stanley, this is not a good time. Come back later. At a decent hour. And call first."

His receding chin lowered until it disappeared inside the collar of his coat. "I don't have your number."

"You know where I — oh, never mind." I marched over to the phone on the counter and picked up a business card. I thrust it in his direction. "Here. Take this."

He accepted the card, turning it over and over, staring at it. "I'm sorry. I'm sorry about everything. I . . . I'll call you."

Famous last words. Again. My life was turning into one big cliché. I closed the door behind him, and set the deadbolt. With all the commotion, I suppose I could have forgotten to latch it earlier.

I leaned my head against the coolness of the door and let my eyelids meet. That satchel he hitched over his shoulder. Something about it seemed familiar. Exhaustion swirled around me like fog. "Isis, I'm beat up. I lost my best friend Memnet and found Stanley. Not an even trade in my book. I can't think about this anymore. Bed!"

In the morning I woke to Isis pouncing on my feet. In my dream, I had been walking quickly along the bed of the Founders River but running to or from a man carrying a salesman's sample bag, I did not recall. One thing was clear, however. My guest from last night had not found my house by chance.

"Good morning, Isis. You're in a playful mood, aren't you?" She bounded up to nip my hand, but gently. "If you're telling me to be careful about our midnight visitor, I agree. He was the perp who stole my purse. Right before the candy started showing up. I remember where I ran into him before. On the sidewalk."

An internal debate over whether or not to

call the police backlit my entire morning routine. I should not have spent this much effort making this decision. I knew what my mother would say. She had not been openly hostile to Stanley, but neither had she been welcoming; not as she behaved with Adam Thompson.

As I washed my breakfast dishes, I decided to give Stanley the benefit of my doubt and hear him out.

Virgil telephoned about 9:30 for a consultation about Memnet. "We just finished hanging up the rest of the posters, Miss Ivy," he told me. He sounded out of breath and I wanted to urge him to take it easy.

"Thank you so much, Virgil," I said instead. "You and the Seeds have helped me love Apple Grove even more."

"If only we could organize and find out how Mayor Conklin contracted that disease," Virgil replied.

That surprised me. "I agree. Donald invited me to move to Apple Grove. He was a constant friend and I'd dearly love to know what happened to him and to Tut. The mayor's cat has been missing a long time, too."

"Well, well. I think we have a lot to talk about. Can we meet up some time to discuss this?"

I wondered for an instant if he had read my email to Addy. Even if he had, I instinctively felt that he was on our side.

"Yes. I agree. I'd like to talk to you."

"After we find your cat."

"Yes."

"Until then. Good-bye."

The next call I answered was, if possible, worse than finding out Memnet was missing. Little Jenny had apparently decided to look for him herself. According to her frantic grandmother, no one in the neighborhood or the family had seen her for several hours.

Yolanda was in shock, I decided when I heard her strained announcement. "I — we — oh, Ivy, Jenny wasn't in her bed this morning. Her daddy called me all in a panic, thinking she might have come here or even that he'd forgotten if she really had been with him. He's so confused. All I can think of is that she went to search for Memnet."

"Yolanda, I don't know what to say. Who told her we didn't find him last night?"

Raw emotion vibrated over the line.

"Yolanda. We'll find her. She can't have gone far. Everyone will help. I'll be right there."

The thought nagged at me that we might

end up near the river. Had Jenny been around when we talked about the tunnels? She was quite a resourceful little girl. Where were the other entrances? I'd wait before I brought the idea up to the authorities, see if we found Jenny safe and well first. Just in case, I grabbed the flashlights we used last night, pulled out my old backpack and began to fill it with water bottles, crackers, and matches. What else? Rope? It might be melodramatic, but I wanted to be prepared for anything. I rummaged in the garage until I came up with the remaining plastic-coated coil I used to restring the clothesline. Cell phone. I pulled a whistle out of my purse. How about chalk to mark the walls? Well, it worked in the movies. Backpack full, jacketed and gloved, I was ready. We were to meet at city hall in ten minutes.

Stanley stood in the driveway.

"I thought you would call!" I was thoroughly worried and irritated. I kept walking to my car.

"Your line was busy. Where are you going? On some hike? I didn't know there were any trails around here." Stanley followed me.

"This is still not a good time. There's a little girl missing. She's trying to find Memnet and now she's lost, too, and I have to help search for her."

The hairs Stanley combed across the middle of his forehead blew in the breeze. "But I saw Memnet last night."

My Christian charity was down to a trickle. "I told you, that was not Memnet."

His pale brows wrinkled as he tried to work this new problem. "Now you have two of those weird cats?"

"Stanley! I don't have time for this!" I slammed my door and started the engine.

He put his hands on the car. "I want to help, too."

The stubborn knight to the rescue routine was also new for him. I rolled down my window and leaned out. I glared pointedly at his linen suit, his shiny leather shoes. "You can't wear those clothes on a search and rescue mission," I told him. "And you'll get filthy. Stanley. I'll talk to you later."

"I don't care. I can help. I want to help."

I started to back out, but he ran around the car, grabbed the passenger door and managed to open it on the run.

"Stanley!" I jerked the gear shift to come to a halt.

He got in and closed the door, then pulled the seatbelt across his chest.

"You used to be more meticulous about your clothes than my roommate freshman year. You recall Amy, who was in fashion design? The one you used to ogle when you thought I wasn't looking?"

"I told you, I've changed."

I drove downtown in tight-lipped silence. When I stopped at the four-way, I said, "You stole my purse."

"I can explain that."

"Really?" I found an empty parking spot behind the hall. I turned off the engine and eyed the milling crowd at the municipal parking lot. We had a minute or two before the search began. "I'd like to hear your side. But maybe I should just talk to the police." Seeing two uniformed men, I started to open the door.

Stanley put his hand on my arm. "Ivy. Wait. Please. I heard someone say that you'd moved. Just random, one afternoon when I had lunch. I don't even know who . . ."

I rolled my eyes and got out.

He scrambled too. "I just needed time to think. I wanted to make changes in my life, but I was afraid you'd laugh or something. We were so used to doing the same things the same way. Then, this other career move came along —"

"Are you telling me you're not a chocolate salesman anymore?"

"There's more to it! We have a great

374

product line. More than candy. It's coffee —"

"It's not different, Stanley. I never cared what you did for a living, only that it was something you wanted to do. Now, what about my purse?"

"I couldn't believe it. I searched for you for weeks, and there you were. I got close enough to talk to you, but then . . ." he flushed an unattractive cream of tomato soup color. "I chickened out."

"How did you . . . ?"

"Well, I didn't reach my hand in your pocket, in case you were wondering. It, um, I heard something fall, and after you went past, I went back to look. I didn't take anything, Ivy. I just wanted to see where you lived. That's all!"

"You waited a long time before you returned it. And why didn't you just call? Oh, yeah, I remember. You didn't have my number. Excuse me, but I need to go help my new friends."

Stanley followed me to Virgil, who held a clipboard he used to check in and pair up volunteers. Stanley stated his name to Virg in a deep voice and offered his services. Virgil looked my former fiancé up and down. In the end, I took pity and vouched for him. Virg's eyes narrowed, but he handed Stanley

375

a whistle and told him to join Marty and Wilbur, two guys from the senior set whom I had met last night. Limp-fingered handshakes were applied to Stanley. Marion and Bob and the Gaineses made up another group, and I recognized quite a few people from church or through my work.

"You know that guy from where, Ivy?" Virg asked me out of the corner of his mouth.

"Previous life." Ignoring Stanley, I went to Yolanda and hugged her. "We'll find her."

Yolanda held on to me, her whole body trembling. "This is so hard on Jim."

A whistle blast caused us to straighten and turn toward Virg.

He held up a whistle in his right hand and the clipboard in his left for attention. "Folks, Yolanda thinks little Jenny went to look for Miss Preston's spotted gray cat named Memnet. Some of you remember, Memnet disappeared yesterday and hasn't been found. Yolanda also told me that the little girl thought she saw a cat near the Founders River earlier, so we'll start our search there. Now, we'll do it like this: spread out in pairs but keep the next closest group in your sight at all times. Walk slowly and carefully and use your whistle if you see anything suspicious. We'll work both banks before we move inland. Any questions?"

He dealt with "what if we just find her clothes," or "what if we find her dead" with a swift instruction to "stay put and holler for someone to come and don't touch anything" and sent them out.

While the others went and searched along the river, I told Yolanda and Virg that I'd just walk up and down the streets of downtown, and look in all the alleys on the east side. Many of those businesses long ago fled, leaving gaps of empty darkened windows along vacant storefronts. Yolanda and I shared a lingering gaze, telling each other not to feel guilty. Small comfort, but comfort none the less.

I wouldn't admit that I had an ulterior motive. I wanted to check the alley behind the barbershop where I had spoken to the mystery man the night of the fire.

Yolanda and Jim's neighbors all came to help, as well as several teachers from the elementary school. The day was overcast, adding to the sense of gloom. I could hear calls of the searchers echoing along the riverbanks and under the bridge as I strode briskly along the sidewalk into the downtown shopping district. I realized I was close to Adam's when Tiny's deep fryer aroma clashed with the spicy scents from Lo Mah's. I walked up Lombardy to Main Street, where I could see the blackened bricks of Mea Cuppa's upper level. New windows and a power washing would take place one day next week, according to Bob Green. The roof had already been replaced and drywall hung. I ducked into the various alleys along the east side of Main Street.

When I got to the barber shop, I paused, then crossed the street. Mea Cuppa was the middle of three shops, and the alley between Bob's and Odds 'n Ends did not go all the way through. A tall fence discouraged anyone passing from Main to First. I walked back around the block behind Odds 'n Ends to First Street and then behind Bob and Adam's.

A fire escape to Toad's apartment ended at the alley. Adam's metal stairs zig-zagged down the wall. Big, dark green waste bins lined a brick wall. The mystery man had hidden in the shadow by one of them. I moved closer, tilting my head at a speck of color on the ground. I glanced along the pitted, mottled cream city bricks to Mea Cuppa's back door and then Bob's. Bob had a window overlooking the scenic bins. I toed the item, which turned out to be a turquoise crayon. I kept my hands deep in the pockets of my coat. Anyone could have left this here. Any child with a penchant for coloring. A child, perhaps, named Jenny.

I didn't touch the crayon but instead hauled out my cell phone and called Ripple, then Virg.

23

The almost-detective had only four blocks
to come. Ripple, lights strobing, pulled up
in his squad car only two minutes after my
call.

Virgil and Yolanda took three minutes
longer, enough time for Ripple to take some
pictures and start me talking.

Yolanda positively identified the crayon.
"See, it's the way we tear the paper off as
Jenny wears it down. Jim always does it like
this, with the stub of his thumbnail. Those
little ridges . . . see, it's his nail impression,
I'm sure of it."

Ripple bagged the crayon, shone his light
under the bins and in all the recesses. The
search crews gradually reported in as the
news was passed along. Other teams reported crayons and went back to guard their
finds until Ripple could meet them. Purple,
silver and green crayons lined the way
toward a great cement culvert overshadowed

by the hulking State's Bank. The grill covering the opening had rusted, a crackly voice
came over the officer's shoulder mic.

*One end of downtown, one of the tunnel
system's egresses.* "Officer Ripple?" He
looked startled when I explained about my
suspicion that the little girl may have gone
into the tunnels, either by choice or force.

Yolanda never relaxed her grim expression
and stepped in when Ripple questioned me.
"Officer, the tunnels have been plugged for
years. You're not originally from Apple
Grove, so I don't expect you to know about
them. But Ivy's right. It makes sense." She
nodded at the culvert. "Building the bank
might have caused some of the stuff we used
to come loose."

"Let me get this straight. Apple Grove is
riddled with tunnels?"

"Not exactly riddled, Officer," Virgil said.
He squinted at the culvert as if he could see
into it. "A couple of generations back our
ancestors had the foresight to provide
protection and storage in case of trouble.
We were glad for the tunnels during the last
big war. But when a young rascal came to
grief, the city council, of which I was a
member, I might add, took matters into our
hands and blocked off the entrances." Virg
nodded his corduroy beret-covered head for

emphasis.

"But now you think they're open again," Ripple asserted. He glared at the culvert and got on his shoulder mic.

Stanley approached hesitantly, blinking in the late sunlight as if he wasn't used to it. "Any news?"

I didn't see the harm in repeating the theory about the tunnels. His shoes were no longer shiny and his shirt tail hung loose. He did not complain, though, or even perform his favorite trick: going to wait in his car and listening to music. The fact that he stayed by my side almost endeared me to him.

Several uniformed officers showed up at that point. Must have been all of Apple Grove's force, and then some.

I acknowledged Larken and waved at Ann Dow.

Behind the last car was the city's main utility service vehicle. A man jumped up next to the folded crane arm and began unspooling yards of electrical cord attached to a wire-caged utility light.

We were drawing a crowd.

Margaret Bader-Conklin, resplendent in a short summer skirt and dark sunglasses, spoke to Gene Hackman.

I managed to inch close enough to see her

mouth tighten in displeasure at whatever he was telling her. He gave her a wide berth when he strode away to confer with the khaki-overalled and helmeted crew preparing to enter the culvert.

Virg organized several of his Seeds into refreshment detail. Stanley got someone to take him back to my place to pick up his car. He contributed boxes of sample chocolates and packets of coffee to brew. He also pulled out a couple of camp chairs from the back of his company SUV and we sat waiting, as close as we could. A fresh respect for him grew as I watched him chat with my neighbors and acquaintances from church.

Marion even gave me a furtive, questioning smile.

Just as I wondered if the townspeople might break out the grills and start cooking supper right in the parking lot, a cheer went up from those gathered near the culvert.

I saw Larken first, the big light held aloft in his hands. Dow followed, then Ripple, holding Jenny in his arms. From my vantage point, which meant standing on tiptoes — and I realized later, hanging on to Stanley's hand — I saw Jenny gibbering non-stop.

Yolanda folded her granddaughter into her arms.

Jenny took her grandma's face between

her little hands and earnestly nodded her head up and down, lips moving and moving, eyebrows knit.

Hackman came last, a huge torch in his hand. He handed that to Ripple, then began to coil a rope attached to a loop of his uniform belt.

Stanley and I made our way to the little group.

Yolanda's face was pasty white. Beads of perspiration decorated her hairline and I reached for Jenny when her knees buckled.

Hackman helped her to a seat and wrapped my sweater around her shaking shoulders.

Jenny immediately transferred her attention to me. "Ivy, that man. You have to go back. He was nice. He shouldn't be left in there. Ivy. Ivy, promise me you'll help him and the other kitty." Jenny's voice began to go hoarse.

I shifted her in my arms. "What man, honey? And a kitty?"

"In there." She continued to bob her head up and down vigorously, as if that would help us understand.

Ann Dow approached, clipboard in hand. "Did that man hurt you in any way, or touch you, Jenny?"

Jenny put her lower lip out. "He helped

me. He said, 'don't be afraid.' He's so lone-some. You have to go get him. I think he's scared. Memnet made him sneeze, so he said the kitty needed to go with me. But the other one ran away. I just went in there when I heard him."

"Memnet? Did you say Memnet was in there, too?" I began to search the area near the front of the culvert, turning my bundle this way and that. "Where is he, honey? Did he come with you?"

Officer Dow wrestled the questioning back to her clipboard notes. "Did you go in there by yourself, honey?"

"Yes, yes. I heard him." She pointed to the culvert.

"Heard who? The man or the kitty?" Dow persisted.

"Kitty. Crying." Jenny spared no more patience on the officer and grabbed my face, just as she had her grandmother's. "Ivy, your kitty is coming out. He had to say good-bye to the other kitty. Memnet ran away when all the policemen came. He didn't want everyone to see him."

Only a child would have understood my Memnet as well as I. Tears welled, and I had no doubt she meant what she said. Memnet would come when he was ready. But who was the man she spoke of? I had my suspicions of that, too. Ronald Grimm. And the other cat must be Tut, feeling threatened and anxious to hide himself so carefully.

Margaret passed through the fringes of the crowd to us.

The newspaper photographer, Gregg, snapped away.

"Stop that!" Margaret commanded Gregg. "Little girl, what did that man look like? He had a kitty?" Margaret put a manicured hand on Jenny's arm.

Jenny twisted violently, and I nearly dropped her.

Hackman saved us both from tumbling to the ground. Jenny transferred to his arms and hid her face in the policeman's shoulder.

"That's enough, Mrs. Conklin!" Hackman hissed.

Margaret recoiled.

I sought out Ripple and repeated what Jenny told me. His skepticism was not quite as pronounced as the first time we spoke on the telephone, and I could tell he did not completely discount Jenny's story.

"I think I'll suggest we move this investigation and questioning to the station. Thank you for your help and good afternoon." Ripple tipped his cap and sauntered to join his boss under the streetlight.

Stanley followed me, a silent shadow, absorbing the conversation. He couldn't have understood the situation, but I appreciated his show of support.

Hanley, the second to last hold-out on the city council, approached us. "And what do you hear from Adam Thompson these days, Ivy? I understand he moved back to Chicago permanently. I made a good offer, you know."

I glanced at Stanley. His lips tightened, and he bent to brush at burrs stuck to the hem of his pants.

"Hello, Jeff," I said, ignoring his taunt. "Let me introduce you to an acquaintance of mine, who insisted on helping search for Jenny, despite the fact that he didn't even know her." I rubbed Hanley's absence from the search in his face and felt the satisfaction of seeing his nostrils flare momentarily.

I kept one eye trained on the culvert.

Jeff and Stanley shook hands and started that wary male assessment dance around each other.

I turned away completely to watch for Memnet, whom I could almost feel come closer. Someone touched my shoulder and I jumped. "Oh! Stanley, you startled me."

Hanley must have left. The streetlights

came on. The horizon developed inky purple and orange waves. The utility truck's backlights flashed, then pinged as it pulled away.

I took Stanley's hand. "You've been so very patient today. How can I thank you?"

He smiled in a way that I had forgotten, quirking just the right side of his mouth. He cleared his throat and said, "Let's get something to eat. I like that buffet downtown. The one called Tiny's. There's this huge man behind —"

"Wait just a minute, will you, Stanley?" His companionable arm across my shoulders dropped when I bent over a gray streak leaping up at my waist, clawing my shirtfront. "Ah, Memnet, love. What took you so long? Where's Tut?"

24

Even though we waited another twenty minutes, Tut did not appear. We took Memnet home before we went to Tiny's. Isis padded into the kitchen and greeted Mem calmly, nose to nose, before checking the empty water dish and giving me the evil eye. My cat had been hungry and grouchy but allowed Isis to groom him.

I let Stanley come back to my house after we'd eaten a silent supper, but I wasn't sure what to do with him. I hoped he wouldn't stay long and didn't waste much time worrying about where he was staying, 'cuz it wasn't here. Especially after the way he'd kept calling Tiny's red-headed evening waitress over to refill his water glass.

My answering machine flashed like a disco ball, practically humming. I groaned.

Stanley closed the kitchen door behind us and set the lock. He glanced from me to the equipment. In a routine from the old days, he knew to give me room for my business. "I'll just leave you to it for a bit," Stanley said, bending slightly to brush my temple with his mouth. "Your bathroom's down this way?"

Forty-five minutes later I flopped on the sofa.

Stanley sat there looking way too comfortable catching up on back issues of the Apple Grove Gazette.

After dealing with my personal messages in the kitchen, I had gone up to the office.

Memnet remained within sniffing distance of me at all times.

Stanley tried to make nice with him on the way home, but Memnet buried himself under the blanket, creeping up my chest to put his nose in my ear, his favorite resting position. There had been no call from Adam, either personal or on my business line. Surely, he could have gotten hold of me somehow. I left a message for him on his cell, telling about Jenny and Memnet's great adventure.

"Thanks again for helping us out today," I repeated to Stanley, starting the "isn't it about time you go home now" ritual.

He dipped the side of the pages to peer at me. "That Thompson guy. He's the one at the bookstore, right?"

Isis hopped up on my other side. Distracted, I stroked her ears, so I wouldn't have to look at my former fiancé, who had no right to question me about Adam. Isis sat on her haunches and stared at me.

"Yes. A bookstore and coffee place. You had business with him. At least, before the fire."

"Yeah, too bad about the fire." Stanley put the paper down on the coffee table. "He made a big order with me, though. I get partial credit for the Chicago sales. You been seeing him?"

Why exactly had I let Stanley into my house again? I wanted to close my eyes and pretend that everything from mid-June until now was a bad dream. Maybe if I ignored the Stanley nightmare, he'd vanish.

I focused on my cat instead of nosy Stanley. Mem and I played a little game, which involved him following my wiggling fingers until he nipped at them. I wished he could talk, so he could explain to me what he'd found in the tunnels. I still thought Stanley had accidentally let him out yesterday.

"Ivy? I asked —"

"I heard you." I set my mouth in a straight line. "Why are you here? Now?"

He appeared puzzled. "I'm adding Mea Cuppa to my new route. I don't mind driving out here to Apple Grove. It's not bad. Now I know you're here."

I shook my head. "I mean, here, at my house. Why did you go to the trouble of trying to find me?"

"I missed you." A crevice of a line appeared between his eyebrows. "I apologized about keeping your little purse. I'll pay you back for the cost of replacing your driver's license and all. Knowing you, you went right out and got another one."

I hated that he had me parsed so well. "We said good-bye. A year ago. Why are you back?"

"I told you. I changed. It's like I woke up. After I started going home so much at night with the new route, I realized how lonely every night seemed with no one else there. Then I thought, that's how you must have felt."

He was only a little correct. I'd had friends to spend time with. "Stanley, I've changed, too."

Stanley barely paused. "Then I started hanging out with some of the new guys. Well, I was the new one, but besides that, I got to know other people. I had fun going out after work. I even joined a health club." He showed off a biceps.

So, this was new. I sat up.

392

Memnet jumped off and went exploring as though he had been gone longer than a day.

I grinned. I had never seen Stanley so animated before. He almost impressed me. He had never acted as if he enjoyed being alive, something I came to wonder about during our five-year relationship. Even though I asked myself why I spent so many years waiting for him to pop the question, it was because I'd been comfortable with him. Not passionate, but comfortable. He didn't boss me around or force me out of my niche to do anything I didn't want to do. He never cheated on me. Boring. Safe. Could I make myself believe differently now? If I didn't have Adam, that is?

He continued to jabber about movies, a book he'd read, some of the new dishes he had eaten at places he stopped at while on the road. "But, mostly . . . lately, I think about you all the time, Ivy." He reached out to touch my face with his soft fingers.

I hated to burst his bubble. "What about before, when you just weren't sure? About us — about me? What made you change your mind?"

"I figured you'd ask. I think I just wasn't ready before. Now, the guys, they all talk about their girlfriends. Wives. Kids. I even stood up in Doug's wedding last month. I wondered . . . well, maybe now it's the right time."

I just stared, willing my lower jaw to stay hinged.

"With the new job and all, more money, I think I can swing it. I can set up almost anywhere, although it'd be nice if you wanted to live back . . . but that's OK. And this job with Featherlight . . . it's not like before, with Maribel Candy," he told me. "This route has more volume, less road time. I can do phone calls, fax. I'm only overnight every other week."

I listened. Maybe I didn't pay attention to every word, but I sat there and let him talk. I stared out the window at the dark street and wondered what Adam was doing.

I leaned my head against the back of the sofa.

Stanley rambled on. His mouth moved, his lips formed words, his eyes sparkled. He did have nice eyes, Stanley. Blue. Invisible eyelashes, though.

Adam had been gone for weeks. I wasn't sure he even cared about Isis anymore.

"So, what do you think?" Stanley broke into my reverie. "That other guy's been gone a while, right? Can I call you again? I'll be back next week. I can schedule . . ."

His rambling dribbled to a stand-still.

I said something non-committal. It might have been "we'll see," but I don't recall my exact words. Then I stood. I walked him to the kitchen and waited while he put on his jacket and jingled his keys. He hesitated at the door. "I've changed, really I have. You'll see. Please, can we . . . will you give me another chance to prove it to you? Those were nice folks today. I can see why you like it here. I don't mind . . ." He finally stopped jabbering and swallowed loudly. "Ivy." He pulled at my shoulder.

The thought of kissing anyone but Adam made me unbearably sad. Adam's face loomed in my mind when Stanley came close and I pulled back at the last second. I lifted my hand to cover his on my shoulder. "Not yet. Stanley. I . . . thank you again for today, OK? Thank you."

I closed the door on his "I'll call you later" and leaned on it.

Isis came to rub against my calves.

I crouched beside her so I could run my hand along her soft back as she wound herself back and forth.

Memnet held a paw on my knee.

I gave myself a mental shake and decided to put Stanley on the back burner. "Memnet, Memnet. What I'd give to hear about your adventure. Why did you go there, anyway? To find Tut? Was he there?"

He yawned a fishy-smelling mouthful of air at me and began to bathe.

I glanced up at my kitchen clock. The hands pointed to the long side of 9:30 and I decided to wait until morning to check on Yolanda and Jenny.

The next day I went to Addy's office. She agreed to talk to me over supper after work. In her cheerful waiting area, I read with interest the edition of the Gazette, which reported Ripple's search in the tunnels for Jenny's mystery man. Jim had done the interview and article himself, so he obviously felt better after his recent heart trouble.

"Officer Tim Ripple of the Apple Grove Police Department reported on his findings in the defunct tunnel system. Although there was clear evidence of a fire having been used for possible cooking and heating, and a few newspapers scattered, it is impossible to determine if more than one person had been using the tunnels for habitation, or for how long."

Wouldn't dates on the found newspapers have been a big clue? Well, they always held evidence back in these investigations, to catch the real perp in the act.

"Apple Grove engineers are in the process of reshoring the loose wall," Ripple said. "I cannot say often enough that the tunnel system is dangerous. No one, and I mean no one, should ever try to enter those tunnels."

A later brief mention was made of the great cat hunt: "Dr. Bailey reported a total of sixty-eight cats without licenses had been brought in. She enlisted the aid of Colby's Humane Animal Treatment Center. Testing for CSD resulted in thirteen cases. Those cats have been treated and await adoption."

Between patients, I set the paper aside to talk to Virg about how Memnet came back and about Maus in general. I thanked him again for his help and told him that he could call me next time the Core was needed. I would be proud to do what I could for Apple Grove.

Even Virg had gone home from his usual station at the reception desk by the time Addy had seen all of her patients.

At last Addy came out of her office, locked the doors and shut off the lights. "Thank you for waiting."

"No problem. Are you about ready to leave?"

"Yes." She took off her white coat and

hung it over the door. I could see her mentally tallying her close-up procedure. I'd done the same often enough with my own business. We planned to drive into Colby to a family restaurant that boasted high-backed booths, in the hope of having an undisturbed conversation.

Jansburg's Family Eatery was as nice as Addy said. We slid on either side of a glass table into black-cushioned booths that loomed a good seven feet toward the high ceiling. Fresh baby's breath and guttering candles on each table were a simple touch of elegance. The booth provided the intimacy we wanted for our talk. After choosing our meals and giving our orders, we leaned in for a discussion.

I opened. "I'm pretty sure I know where Tut has been hiding."

"He's still alive, then," Addy said.

I nodded. "He's hiding. Probably he got scared when the round up started."

"Makes sense. Where is he?"

"The tunnels. Jenny Toynsbee saw him when she was lost."

"Ah. I heard about that. I'm glad she's all right."

"Yeah, me too. Did any of the cats you tested so far have a severe enough case of

CSD to cause a healthy grown man's death?"

She shook her head, her eyes troubled and mouth pinched. "I just got caught up on some of my journals. A former colleague is involved with a genetic engineering project I think you should be aware of."

Whatever her news was would have to wait. The waitress arrived with our food. When she left, I told Addy I planned to pray. She waited, and I'm not certain if I saw her lips moving, too, after I raised my head, feeling a little more calm and able to hear her story, which ended with "So that's why we have to get to Merris Corp headquarters in Chicago. I think that's where they did away with poor Donald."

My fork shook in my trembling hand. It seemed fantastic that I had been that close to the place where research into manipulating the bacteria that causes CSD harmless had taken place. Addy had read about it.

The food was getting cold. We began to eat.

Addy glanced around after a couple of forkfuls of her fragrant chicken tetrazzini. "I talked to Margaret. She said she didn't have to worry about Donald acting crazy anymore."

My lasagna tasted like dust in my mouth

and I forced myself to swallow. I took a hasty gulp of ice water. "Wasn't she upset that he was killed?"

Addy studied me, her face showing the depth of her concern as strain lines framed her lips. "Ivy, I'm afraid —"

"How's everything, ladies?" Our cheerful waitress interrupted us. We assured her the food was delicious and she trotted away again after clearing the bread basket.

"Of what, Addy? Afraid of what?"

"I think she thought I had no business asking about Donald's death. I asked if he'd been in good shape physically, and she said yes. Then later, she changed her mind, you know, as if she'd thought about it. It doesn't feel right."

"Did she tell you why she was so anxious to get MeriFood here?"

"I didn't ask about that. I did ask how the search for Tut was going."

"And?"

"She got mad, big time. Absolutely furious. Said she had to have him back — her one tie to her beloved husband."

I swallowed hastily, before I choked. "Beloved! She hated Tut. Donald always said so. Wouldn't even let him in the house."

I sipped coffee to give myself time to formulate my next thought. "She must have some reason to want Tut."

We ate in silence for a few minutes.

"Adam and I found Tut's collars," I said, eventually; really just thinking out loud. "Some of them were pretty fancy and had hiding places."

"Right." Addy frowned. "Pet owners find them handy for a hide-a-key or to keep change in when they take their animals out, so they don't have to carry a wallet or purse." Both of her eyebrows rose. "You don't think Donald hid something in Tut's collar?"

"I do."

"Something Margaret needs."

Our food cooled. I no longer had an appetite. We huddled closer over the table while I explained my theory about the look-alike cousins as well as what I had seen in downtown Chicago.

Addy plopped back against the seat and took a shaky drink from her glass, the ice cubes clinking. "Why didn't I see this coming?"

"You can't blame yourself, Addy."

Addy sat up straight. "Who else knows about this?"

"The Greens and Jeff Hanley. Yolanda, too."

"Ah. At that meeting after Margaret's

return, at the bank? Some of their talk makes more sense to me now. But what can we do?"

I slowly pushed a forkful of lukewarm lasagna into my mouth. I wished I could have trusted her right from the beginning. "Right now, all we have is a collection of loose bits of suspicions and no organization."

"Wasn't Adam Thompson in on this? Is he doing some undercover work in Chicago?" She grinned and winked.

Adam was a tender subject with me. "I don't think he's coming back to Apple Grove. Why should he, when his store burned?"

Her mouth opened, and her eyes rounded. "What? Didn't the chief declare the fire accidental? Faulty wiring behind the new stove, I heard. He's rebuilding. I've seen it. Don't you have his cat? I thought you two were an item. So, now you're not? Who's taking over the store? It's nice of him to cover Colleen's pay for July. What's he doing in Chicago?"

I didn't like the sudden gleam in her bachelorette eye. "Hanley and Cal Stewart own the building. You can ask them." I sounded short and apologized. "It's just that I'm disappointed he left."

"Virgil said your old boyfriend's in town."

"Stanley has visited. He's a traveling sales-man," I said evenly. "But back to Tut. I'm sure he's in the tunnels, but he's proving hard to flush out."

"Even with Memnet's persuasion?" Addy smiled. "Give me some time to think about that."

"Meanwhile, I have a theory about Merris Corp headquarters." I stopped as our wait-ress silently left a check face down at the edge of our table, her lip curled at our barely disturbed plates. She set takeout boxes next to the check and turned on her soft-heeled shoes.

I set my napkin on the table and pulled the check toward me. "Feel like a drive soon?"

25

"We have to plan out how we'll say this, so the police will accept our evidence," Addy said as we left the restaurant and returned to my car. I was glad she believed we needed to go to the authorities.

"What about Margaret? She'll bring up all kinds of dirt to cast doubt on you. Everything you were worried about will come out. You know that."

Addy's humorless smile tipped off the extent of her rage. "Margaret's dug her own grave. She's made no friends in Apple Grove. MerriFood is in serious trouble and if she tries to defend them, she'll go down, too. Virg told me the governor has been called in to look at the mess Apple Grove's in. He's got the authority to appoint a temporary emergency government. Since Virg used to be council president, he's offered to step in and help. He told me, because he thought he'd have to stop volunteering as my receptionist for a while."

Virg's interaction delighted me. From what Marion told me about the current state of affairs at city hall, someone had better do something, and quickly, or Apple Grove would soon turn to chaos. Most of the council members had quit, the Merri-Food building skeleton sat like a rusty eyesore in the middle of an unpicked bean field. Every issue of the Gazette featured some sort of letter or editorial about how the city was in shambles. No one could get their questions answered, no new building permits were being issued and licenses were lapsing left and right. There were rumors that taxes would skyrocket so no one could afford to live here anymore.

"Does Virg realize what he's stepping into?" I asked. "From what Marion says, city hall is a mess." I started to feel better about what I was planning to do to bring justice for Donald.

"I think so." Addy composed herself for the drive back to Apple Grove. This time we talked about ourselves, our families, our hopes. "For the first time I feel like I have a future," Addy said. "If I can get past the mistakes I made —"

"If Margaret will let you," I corrected. "I hope she will now. Will you tell Colleen?"

"Sometime. I want to see what happens first. What shall we do about our theories?"

"I think I know just the right person to talk to."

By the time we pulled into the parking lot of the police station in Apple Grove, Addy and I felt we had a reasonable collection of facts to present to Officer Ripple.

"But not enough for a search warrant," Ripple said. By 8:00 that night it was nearly dark outside.

We were hot in the station and thoroughly frustrated.

"Look, ladies . . ."

Whenever someone started with "look, ladies," I just knew we wouldn't be taken seriously. And I was right.

". . . you're not trained. You wanna be cops, investigators, go to police school. Leave the serious stuff to us. You could get in a lot of trouble." He held up his hands at Addy's protest.

I felt too tired by then to argue.

"This is dangerous. If there were guns or something involved, you could get hurt, or killed."

Addy started again, patiently. "Merris was developing an agent meant to change the structure of Bartonella henselae to eventually eradicate it. I read about it in the professional journal I get. I believe this work is going on at the Summersby building, where Merris Corp recently moved the laboratory where I used to work. I can find the material used to infect the late mayor. If it's there. I'm the only one qualified."

"You know as well as I do, Doctor Bailey," Ripple said, "if you ladies even consider going onto Merris Corp property without express permission from the owner, nothing you find there can be used for any purpose to help Donald's case, and you will, in fact, be prosecuted for trespassing. And you will, in fact, get any case we've built thrown out. Do you understand me?" He put a hand behind both of our elbows and escorted us out. "Good night."

Undaunted, I got out my car keys and headed for my car. Addy hesitated before trotting to catch up, her heels echoing on the pavement under the floodlights around the building. "What's next?"

I was glad she was with me. "I'd like to talk to Yolanda."

Addy nodded and slammed her door. "I'm in."

"Well, I'm glad Jim's not here tonight," Yolanda said, " 'cause he'd either say 'no' or want to come. Jenny's with her mama for a few days before school starts." Yolanda bowed her head, then raised it and cast us a determined expression. "What can I do?"

I looked at Addy. "Well, for starters, we need back up."

Yolanda grinned and pulled off her half-glasses. "I always wanted to drive the get-away car. When do we leave?"

So that's how I ended up going on a ladies shopping trip to Chicago, the weekend before Labor Day. In reality, we were three women who were determined to protect our community. On the way, we went over our strategy and came up with a plan.

"We'll show them the newspaper articles about the outbreak of CSD and the strays round up in Apple Grove. Then I'll ask about how the new antibacterial agent is coming along. Hopefully Cole is still working there. He'll talk."

"So, Yolanda will circle the block," I said, "and I'll distract Cherry, while Addy goes up to the eleventh floor."

"Remember, we have to have permission to look around the lab," Yolanda cautioned.

The doctor snorted. "I'll just call now and find out if Cole is there." Addy put her fingers to her lips and pushed the speaker phone button on her cell.

Yolanda and I held our collective breath in an effort to remain quiet.

Addy put on a cheery voice and made poor Cole believe that she was just in the neighborhood and wanted to see the new lab.

Cherry had not been particularly pleased to see me again. I could tell. Those beautifully decorated lips poofed in annoyance. She reached for the phone, probably to dial security.

"I have an appointment," Addy said. She squinted at Cherry's name tag. "Cherry," she added belatedly with a smile that made me doubly glad she was on my side.

Cherry knew her business and dialed anyway, her stare keeping us skewered to the front desk. How much did she know about what went on in this place? Murder, for one. Kidnapping. Potential bioterrorism.

I shuddered and glanced around the dim lobby again, wondering where the back door was. There were a lot of doors.

The transport van angle troubled me. But how to prove that, one — Donald had been murdered by use of a lethal dose of bacteria, and two — said murder took place here, and three — Donald's body had been moved to the men's room of his own office suite across the state to take suspicion away from MerriFood.

"Thank you, Dr. Webster." Cherry hung up. "Dr. Bailey, you have permission to visit Merris. Follow me and I'll open the elevator for you." She made a performance out of collecting a big noisy keychain and inserting one of the keys into a slot next to the elevator doors. They swished open, swallowing Addy when they closed.

Cherry returned to her round desk. "What can I do for you, ma'am?" she asked, not even looking at me, but busying herself by booting up a computer.

I locked my hands behind me and raised my chin. "I'll just wait for my friend," I said, and began to saunter around the lobby as if fascinated by the miniature squares of black, white and turquoise tile. I meandered slowly toward what I judged to be a position behind Cherry to covertly examine some of those many egresses, when a glance at her revealed why her desk was round. She swiveled to keep me in view at all times. I felt like whistling, but I didn't. Something pinged on Cherry's desk, and while she attended to it, I managed to put my hand on three doorknobs, none of which moved.

The elevator was descending straight

down from the eleventh floor like an express train. Addy stumbled out, her face flushed. She grabbed my arm and took a deep breath. Flashing a Hollywood smile toward Cherry, she muttered out of the side of her mouth, "Keep moving and act natural."

I wondered if she had a clue how unnatural she was acting at the moment, with her hand deep in the side pocket of her lab coat and her hair mussed like she'd lost a wrestling match. I wondered just what her relationship with Cole had been.

We continued our stroll through the revolving door. "Where is Yolanda?" Addy grunted. She dropped my arm and held a hand up to shield her eyes from the sunlight. "Come on."

"What did you —"

"Shh! Not here."

Sirens wailed in the distance. I did a double-take and tried to relax, thinking that sirens were a normal everyday background noise in Chicago. Right?

"Here she is," Addy yelled. "Come on!" She pulled me into the back seat after her. "Drive, Yolanda!"

In Addy's lab, Yolanda and I hovered until the doctor told us to wait outside. Addy had recovered a bottle of the serum, after what had been apparently a more enthusiastic reunion dream on the part of poor Cole than Addy anticipated. Cole was the sole employee in the lab on Fridays due to cutbacks. Addy didn't share the details but mentioned that while he was indisposed she managed to grab a syringe and samples of what she thought we could use as evidence.

She came out of her lab a few minutes later, pulling off gloves. She sighed. "Well, girls, it's the same strain as we found in Donald. I kept a sample here," she grinned, "just in case I needed to examine it more thoroughly someday."

"Can we prove anything?" Yolanda asked.

"Scientifically," Addy said.

"We'd better show Ripple." I waved for them to follow me to the car.

Ripple watched us from his laid-back position in his squeaky roll chair, with his hands folded across his gut.

Yolanda did the talking. We all agreed she'd give the story the best spin, what with her powers of observation and reporting experience.

"You're kidding," he said.

"It all adds up," I said. "You don't need to be a detective to see where all the facts lead."

He gave me a tight-lipped snort and stood. Déjà vu — I knew what was next. "Please, ladies, how can I get you to understand that we have this investigation under control?"

"Will you at least take this sample from the Merris lab into evidence?" I asked.

Ripple pursed his mouth. "Yolanda? You tell her."

She hung her head. "We have only our word about where it came from," she said.

"But we have the security tape from the building that proves we were there. And that Dr. Weber — Cole — he knows . . ." My voice trailed off at the sheepish look on Addy's face. "And the van, and Letty," I whispered to myself. I straightened. "Well, I'm going to find Tut, anyway." I turned and left.

My plan might have worked, if I had gone to Margaret's earlier, instead of waiting for the next day. Even if Mrs. Conklin and I were at cross-purposes for getting Tut back, I figured if we found him together, Tut would come to me first, and I could run faster. My plan had been to see if she had some recordings of Donald's voice we could play at the entrance to the tunnels. Tut would hear it and be lured out. Pretty nifty, huh?

Except the cops beat me to her house. Ripple had been looking for an angle all along, and if FTC problems resulted in arrest, that worked for him. Sort of like Al Capone and tax evasion. He said it gave him more time to work on the murder.

Margaret's telephone records were subpoenaed. Between officials who were fed up with MerriFood trade troubles, and board of director members who were sensationally annoyed at what they called being taken advantage of, the story came out in bits and pieces.

"A trial is a long way off," Hackman warned us during the press conference. We sat in the council chambers, where Virgil Toynsbee would take charge of the emergency government until the elections next spring.

Television personalities from out of town were in force, cameras and reporters on microphones, electrical lines everywhere. The Bader family was absent. They were prominent in state business, and Margaret's downfall made for big news.

Stanley sat at my side for the show.

"I can't believe you were involved in all of this," he said again. "You could have been

414

hurt. Or killed." He held my hand and I let him.

Adam had not called for a while, although Marion said he had spoken to Bob.

The reporters were allowed to question board members who were present. "So, none of you really know if Mrs. Bader killed her husband?" A reporter called from the audience. He had a notebook raised, pencil in hand. I could see another pencil stuck behind his ear.

"That's Mrs. Bader-Conklin," Hackman said. "The evidence will come out at the trial."

Another question, this from a larger woman with an ugly hairpiece, whom I did not recognize, either: "What will happen to the money the former mayor amassed and hid from his constituents?"

Marion nudged my ribs and rolled her eyes.

Jeff Hanley took that one. "Nothing was hidden from the citizens of Apple Grove," he said, with some heat. "The grant funds were awarded to Apple Grove on the basis of Mayor Conklin's belief that Apple Grove could thrive with a little extra help. His vision for our community was that it would become an extraordinary place to live."

Hear, hear. Way to go, Hanley. He continued to impress the audience. I did not like him any more than I had before, but he could give a nice speech. And he had a lot to gain for his own business if Apple Grove became a thriving community once again.

"It sounds like a campaign platform, Mr. Hanley," a reporter shouted. "Are you running for mayor?"

A general chuckle ensued.

Hanley protested, mildly. "Well, I hadn't thought about it much. Until now."

The conference wound down and Virgil was introduced as the temporary head of government. "Let me take this opportunity to assure you, my friends," his voice rang out, "that we will continue to carry out the plans Mayor Conklin began. With the help of the good Lord we'll finish that race."

Any other person would probably not have gotten away with that religious remark in the hallowed halls of city government, but it seemed people had a lot of faith in Virgil Toynsbee.

I did. I clapped along with the others in the audience.

But Tut was still missing. The longer he was gone, the less likely we'd find him, but I was sure he was important enough to not have been killed.

26

October was a blur of emptiness, the kids in the neighborhood had been adorable for Halloween, and then, as if the next day, the leaves were curled up on the lawn and Thanksgiving Day came and went.

Stanley called or stopped over maybe half a dozen times. I wasn't totally sure. We somehow wound up at Tiny's three or four times where I couldn't help notice the new red-haired waitress had eyes for Stanley. When I realized I was only amused and not jealous, I could laugh, which took my mind off a certain coffee shop owner for a few seconds.

I helped Yolanda and Jim at the paper and babysat a couple of times for the neighbors. Once for the whole weekend, which made my ovaries rumble. My tech business was rolling along. People would be buying personal computers for the holidays and need me to set them up. One of the more popular avenues of service was acting as the funeral catch-all — as in, who was collecting what for flowers and memorials, without the donor looking nosy. I put a two-fifty charge on each order.

The good news was, Isis and Memnet were inseparable. Addy confirmed my suspicion about why.

But, yes, my personal life was a morass of confusion these days. For Thanksgiving I contemplated two invitations to dinner: Stanley and his parents, or my mother.

No, the parental units could not be combined. My mother had not taken the news of Stanley's return with her usual aplomb. In fact, I suspect she hunted up Adam to give him the good news, for he had left a guarded message one day last week, asking about Isis but making no promises to return for either of us. I chose, with righteous dignity, to ignore him. I barely managed to catch my childish mental burst of "so there" before it got all the way to my tongue.

Janie the mail carrier heaved a case of Feli-Mix Supreme dry cat food from him onto my front stoop not long after.

I couldn't explain to my mother or anyone else how I felt about resuming a relationship with Stanley. There wasn't anything wrong with him. I even felt glad for his attention to me, since nobody else of the male persuasion seemed to care. His manners remained impeccable, something I'd always appreciated. He even called me several nights of the week instead of texting, something he had never done before because of the cost, besides not having much of anything to say. I wondered if he had taken a class in self-expression. Twice he wanted to kiss me and twice I could not bring myself to let him. The visits to Tiny's, when he was in town, ceased.

That would have to change if our relationship was to advance. I just wasn't sure. Stanley seemed more interested in finding out what it meant to be in love, rather than really wanting to be in love with me.

We spent Thanksgiving with his family. I felt guilty about my mother, who airily said she had accepted an invitation to spend the weekend with a colleague, in New York. In my heart I admitted to jealousy of my mother's visit to New York while Stanley's mother and I made subdued small talk as we loaded the dishwasher after Thanksgiving dinner. Close by, the televised football game did not have much influence over the napping men.

Back in Apple Grove for the weekend, Stanley attended the Sunday service at New

Horizons Church with me.

I poked him midway through. With an unbecoming snort, he sat up straight. "Sorry."

We shook hands with the Pastor on the way out.

"Very nice," Stanley said. "Enjoyed the sermon a great deal."

I frowned, for he couldn't have heard more than five words of it before he started breathing too regularly. We were invited to the Greens for dinner at their house after church.

Stanley talked to young Bobby Green about the football game coming on later in the afternoon. They shared stats, and Bob stuck his two cents in every once in a while, from the dining room where he set the table.

Marion had a pot roast in the slow cooker, and I brought bread, so it did not take much time to get the food ready. Bob said grace.

Stanley seemed to take note of everything that went on as if there was a test on the subject of Normal Family Behavior in America next week.

"Pass the Brussels sprouts." Marion elbowed me.

I handed her the dish, while trying to gauge her expressive eyebrows, so I missed the first part of Bob's announcement.

". . . Grand Opening. You might want to come, Stanley. The stuff you handed out that time when Jenny Toynsbee went missing was a big hit. You could pick up a lot of contacts." Bob waved his fork.

"I'll think about that," Stanley replied.

"What's opening?" I asked.

"Jeff Hanley finally got the repairs completed at Mea Cuppa," Marion said, giving me a critical snort. "You weren't listening. They're opening tomorrow, Monday, with a party, and giveaways. The Chamber of Commerce has a big gift certificate drawing, and there's a contest. The kids and I are coming after school."

"Oh? Hanley's not quitting his job at the bank, is he?" I ate a bite of Marion's roast. "This is delicious."

Marion set the bowl of potatoes down with a thump.

I could tell my attitude bothered her. Hanley interested me not at all, although I wondered why Adam Thompson would let him keep the name of his popular franchise. I changed the subject. "Oh, hey, Stanley. Did I tell you that Marion and I are playing volleyball? After Christmas we're on the blue team at the rec center."

He grinned at us and passed the potatoes around again. We didn't stay long, as Stanley wanted to get back for a colleague's birthday party. He hadn't asked me to attend and I hadn't protested. I was glad for his new acquaintances and his new life, but we agreed that I should not feel obligated to share it. He told me he wanted to move up the company ladder and things were happening. It was time to make a decision about what was happening between us and we planned to talk about it later that night.

I didn't plan on talking long.

Marion had something on her mind I could tell by the way she lingered with us at the door. "I have to talk to you, Ivy," she said when I asked what was up.

Stanley, talking to Bob, did not notice us.

"I'll call you later."

"All I'm asking is, are you sure?" Marion chewed the subject like a terrier that wouldn't let go.

"I invested five years of my life in him. That's gotta count for something," I told her over the phone. I turned my toasted cheese sandwich over on the griddle. "Maybe I just want what you have."

"I'm flattered," Marion said dryly. "But honestly, Ivy."

"I thought you liked him. You gave him a thumbs up."

422

"For his chocolate. What girl wouldn't like a man who brings chocolate?"

"All right." I sighed and turned off the heat. "What should I do?"

"Just go to the opening tomorrow."

"Opening?"

"Remember? Downtown. Mea Cuppa."

"Why? I don't give a hoot about Jeff Hanley."

"Just go."

After she hung up, Stanley and I had that conversation. He'd applied for promotion and found out on Monday he'd gotten it. We talked it over. Stanley was learning to be content, and so was I. He planned to set up house on the east coast. I doubted we would cross paths again, certainly not on purpose. He deserved to start over as much as I. But the main point was I found peace where I was. Really. I had finally gotten over needing a man in my life. Certainly not one like Stanley Brewer, who made up his mind too late. Or Adam Thompson, who never made up his mind at all.

And there he stood, cutting the ribbon for the real grand opening of Mea Cuppa, Apple Grove.

I should have known. The past six months passed before my eyes. Marion! I wanted to cry. She could have warned me.

Adam Thompson smiled and waved at people in the crowd. Jeff Hanley joined him, as did Cal Stewart, the third partner. But today was Adam's show. He joked, shook hands, patted the heads of little ones too young for school.

I reached the head of the line for a free cup of coffee.

His face paled when he saw me.

My hand shook so hard the coffee sloshed over.

Adam handed me a napkin. He opened his mouth, closed it again.

"I thought you sold this place," I said in a rush. "I mean, I came here, but I didn't realize you would be here."

"Or you wouldn't have come?" He frowned with the words. His gray eyes were as chilly as the late November day.

I shivered. There were still lots of folks behind me and I stepped away.

Marion might have meant well, but I wanted to run and hide. I went home to pet his cat and my own, then left a blistering message on Marion's voicemail at city hall.

At ten after nine that night I hustled around the kitchen getting myself some hot cocoa during the commercial break of my favorite television show.

Someone outside clomped up to my kitchen door and rapped with gusto.

That figured. I wore my way big flannel pajama pants with the balloons and my hair was in a messy ponytail that showed all the grays at my temples. I let Adam in without comment.

He didn't take off his coat but leaned against the kitchen door.

Isis padded out and warbled her hello as if she had only seen him earlier in the day instead of months ago.

Adam picked her up, noticing the change in her shape immediately. He raised his eyebrows.

Memnet slunk along the wall behind the kitchen table as if he was afraid Adam would demand a shotgun wedding for knocking up Isis. He blinked his gooseberry eyes.

"I was so rude to you today, Ivy. The first thing I do when I see you is act like an idiot. I can't explain myself. I'm sorry, and I wanted you to know." He looked at Isis, ruefully.

"Um. Would you like some hot chocolate?"

Background voices emanated from the living room.

"I don't want to disrupt your evening."

"You're not interrupting anything." Just a host of daydreams, and a load of regret. "So, you didn't sell?"

He shook his head. "I told you I thought about it. Hanley and Stewart gave me a good offer."

"But you didn't? Why not?"

"After I was . . . back there for a while, I realized how much I missed . . . Isis."

Only her?

Adam felt Isis's burgeoning tummy before giving me a serious look. "You have something you want to tell me?"

My grin was self-conscious. I waved at the table and turned on the overhead light. "I told you they were getting to be good friends. Why don't you sit? Take your coat off." I pulled the band from my hair and fluffed.

He shrugged out of the coat and hung it over the back, just as he had done in the past.

I stared, dizzy with recall and longing. I pulled out a chair and managed to fall on the seat.

"Ivy. What's going on?" His voice sounded so gentle.

You left. I thought you were never coming back. You found a new girlfriend. "You heard about Jenny and Memnet getting lost?" I said instead.

"Yes," he nodded and lowered himself opposite. "Hanley told me. I talked to the Greens. I got your message. Later. There was some mix-up with my phone company for a while. That's not my only excuse." He hunched his shoulders, and he stared at the table top. "I'm sorry, Ivy. I really liked Donald. I owe him a lot." He set his gaze on me, the molten gray I remembered and loved. "The chocolate salesman. Someone from your past?"

"Stanley? Yes, what about him?"

"That's your ex-fiancé? Or your current one?" He rushed on without waiting for my answer. "The first time he came to the store, he stopped to read your ad when he left. I thought it strange. He stood there for so long I had to ask if he was all right. He wondered if I knew you, and was that a local address. I should have realized."

"Adam."

"Just, tell me, are you . . . do you want to go back to him?"

I was miserable. I pulled my knee up and wrapped my arms around it. "He changed. He was here when I needed him."

He ducked his chin. I did not exactly mean for the words to come out like that, but I spoke the truth. No, Stanley wasn't staying in my life, as we'd agreed at Thanksgiving. But I couldn't just let Adam back in like he never left, and I wasn't just acting out of revenge. A girl needs some respect, you know?

He pursed his lips at me for a couple of seconds, then got up and reached for his coat.

"Adam, please."

"Isis seems content here. If you want her —"

"Adam!"

"When is she due?"

"Around Christmas. Adam —"

"Will you let me see the kittens?"

"Adam Truegood Thompson, will you listen to me?"

He shook his head and retreated from me as if I was radioactive. Then he left. I glanced at the clock. Fifteen minutes. That was all the time he'd been here. Dazed, I sipped from my cup. The hot cocoa was lukewarm. Just like my life.

27

Ask me the real reason why I don't like Christmas. Go on, ask me.

I had just turned six years old. For the first time in my life I anticipated the lights, colors, sounds, smells and presents, oodles of presents, under the Christmas tree. And Santa Claus, who was really Saint Nicholas. Mom said he had been a real person who lived long ago, and loved Jesus so much he helped poor children. That's why we give each other presents now, because we love Jesus. I got up early, wondering about my presents.

What I found half-way under the tree had nothing to do with Saint Nicholas. My father felt cold to my touch and didn't answer when I called in his ear. Mom did not decorate for the holidays for years afterward. When I reached my teens, she asked if I'd like a tree. I always said no. We went to church and had dinner with friends.

Sometimes.

Yet I put up a tree this year, the first Christmas of my adult life that I lived in my own house. I made popcorn strands and a few of those cinnamon ornaments with the help of Martha and the kids next door.

Mem batted at the tinsel. I moved it to the upper branches.

Isis, heavy with her pregnancy, slept a lot.

I determined to show my mother that I had adjusted to my new life. She came to visit for Christmas week to see for herself. I weathered her war of subtle insults against Stanley all month. Yet I refused to tell her that Stanley and I had come to an understanding and he was no longer in the picture.

On Christmas morning, I woke about 8:00.

Mom and I stayed up late last night watching old movies and church would not happen until ten.

I smelled coffee. She was up. I pushed my arms through the sleeves of my robe and padded out to the living room.

The lower half of a human protruded from the base of the little tree.

My knees hit the carpet, but my shriek died when I recognized Adam's moccasins.

Mom sat on the sofa, still in her maroon

robe and drinking something steaming. She looked at me passively over the mug's rim. "Darling, what's the matter? And Merry Christmas."

She could not have appreciated my traumatic moment.

"Merry Christmas. And to you, too, Adam." I leaned forward, fists on my knees, to demand of his backside, "What are you doing here?"

"Ivy! Adam's our guest."

"I don't remember inviting him." I exhaled. My blood pressure was slowly beginning to recalibrate to normal.

"I've got some news for you, dear. Come. Sit by me for a minute." Mom patted the cushion to her right.

I stayed my ground, crossing my arms, still on my knees.

I ignored Adam, who had removed his upper half from under the tree, almost tipping it when I screamed. He emerged, blinking dust from his eyes, brushing dry needles from his hair and keeping too quiet. I paid no attention to the fact that he wore my favorite shirt of his, the cobalt-blue one that also happened to feel really soft under my fingers.

I took a deep breath. "Mom!"

"Stanley Brewer hasn't got a chivalrous

bone in his body."

"Mo-ther."

"I happened to be up last night when I heard your machine pick up a message from him."

My gaze cut quickly to the kitchen where my personal answering system blinked. "You listened in to my private business?"

Adam rolled to his feet.

Mom calmly drank from her mug. "I assure you I did not listen on purpose. He said Merry Christmas and best wishes. And that he met someone who made him happy." She rose. "But I did call Adam on purpose this morning, and for that I'm not sorry. Excuse me."

"It's pretty early in the morning for visiting," I said in his direction. I noticed his boots at the back door, his overcoat draped on the back of a kitchen chair. Right at home. I heard him breathing. Still, he said nothing.

Remembering to fill my own lungs, I got up and sat on the sofa, cuddling in my mother's leftover warmth. Afraid he might misunderstand my welling tears, I refused to look at him. I stared at the tree instead. Someone had plugged in the lights, which appeared like miniature swimming prisms until I blinked. "Stanley told me after

Thanksgiving that he'd been promoted and would relocate to Trenton. I never even considering going with him."

Adam strode to a side chair and sank into it. He cleared his throat. "When were you going to tell me?"

I stared at my twined fingers and sucked at my lower lip, scared of ruining this moment by saying something ridiculous. Like blurting out "I love you! Why did you leave?"

Adam got up to pace.

A moment later, the cushion sank as he settled next to me, his warm fingers brushing my cheek. "Ivy. I love you."

All the gooey feelings settled in a puddle at the pit of my stomach. Drat tears. "I love you, too."

"Then why are you acting so sad?"

"I'm not sad," I protested, weakly. I still could not face him.

"Does it have something to do with that . . . other guy? I won't stand in your way if you changed your mind and would rather go after him."

"Oh, stop it!" I faced him. "I told you, he's already gone. I couldn't even, I never let him . . ." My eyes strayed to his lips, which were twitching with amusement. I fell on him, batting weakly at his shoulder

433

until his arms enfolded me. I closed my eyes as our lips met and clung. This place, holding and being held by Adam, was more home than anywhere in the world. The last six months might never have been.

We broke apart.

"You said you'd only be gone for two weeks," I accused him.

He didn't let me out of his embrace but regarded me frankly. "You knew about my mother, and the store mess."

"I really am sorry about your mother. I wish you would have called me more to talk. And," I swallowed, "I saw you."

His grip loosened a bit. "What? When? And thanks, my mom's move to assisted living was really more of a blessing. I didn't want to make you sad."

"Oh." I took a deep breath. "I went down to check out the Summersby building. It's not far from one of your stores, only about six blocks from the lake. Why didn't you say you knew where it was?"

His eyes glazed over and he frowned. "Summersby? Like the message? I don't — oh, wait! You must mean my shop that needed a manager. On Fountain Street. But there's no office building close by with that name."

I wiggled, but he didn't let go. "It's big

434

and squarish, like twelve stories or something. Pale limestone, no windows on the first floor. To the south of your store."

"There's the Bluecity that sounds like that. Ivy. You mean you went there alone? To do what?"

"Never mind. I suppose they could have changed the name since you were gone. The lettering of the sign looked new. Addy and Yolanda and I went back later. But we can't use the evidence we collected there. Anyway, the first time, I saw you."

If he could follow my garbled speech, I knew he was the perfect mate for me. He shook his head a little, but gamely asked the only question that mattered now. "Why didn't you say anything?"

"You were entertaining."

Adam gripped my shoulders. "Ivy! What in the world are you talking about?"

"There was this gorgeous, young, woman with legs up to here," I indicated a spot on my ribcage, "who made you laugh."

He plopped back against the sofa, taking me with him. He tucked my head under his chin. "I interviewed several people for the manager's position. That woman you saw might have been one of them, I don't recall. You should have knocked on the door, or something."

Chastised, I leaned close. "I didn't even know it was your shop until I was all the way inside. Why did you stop calling?"

His hands stroked my back. His heartbeat raced under my hand. "Maybe I'm not so different from Stanley, after all."

I squeezed my eyes tight. "Don't say that."

"I was married a long time, Ivy. I loved my wife and daughter. When I realized that I had stopped missing them, that days passed by when I hardly even thought about them, only you, I wondered if I was doing the right thing. I even told myself no one could want someone like me, used up, old, and scarred. I'm ten years older than you, Ivy. I'd like to have more children, but then I think of being the oldest dad around. When my mother needed to move to assisted living, I used cleaning out and selling her house as an excuse to stay away. I missed you so much. I waited to see if the feeling would go away. And when I did come back. . . ."

Which feeling? Missing me or loving me? It hadn't occurred to me that Adam would have doubts about himself. Children? We never discussed the subject after he'd first mentioned it so long ago. I had pictured him the perfect father after watching him with Jenny. Wait a minute! "Did you say you came back? When?"

"A month ago, to see you and meet with the others about the store."

"You came, but didn't bother telling me?"

He got up and folded his arms. "I couldn't sleep or concentrate. Then Marion told me about that — guy. I came to see for myself. And there he was, car parked in your driveway. I saw him through the living room window. Looked as if he was going to church with you."

I twitched my lips. "You were jealous."

He didn't hesitate. "Yes. I was pretty beat up about it, thinking you'd moved on."

"I'm sorry," I said. "I thought you didn't want anything to do with me, or Apple Grove anymore. I never dreamed you felt like that. What made you change your mind?"

"My sister told me anyone who didn't want me for a husband would be insane."

I laughed. He didn't. How I'd missed him.

"Then your mom called."

That's all it took. I went to him and locked my arms around his waist.

I could hardly hear him say, "I thought, maybe. I hoped." He nuzzled his nose in my hair and hugged me tight.

I'd forgiven Mom already. I wanted so badly to stay wrapped in his arms forever. I planned to never move on. "Isis didn't like Stanley."

Adam perked up. "Really?"

"He never could keep Isis and Memnet straight."

"You're kidding."

"Nope." I pulled back to study his features. "What were you doing under my tree?"

Adam flushed scarlet as Santa's suit. "Oh, turning on the lights. Leaving presents."

"Presents?"

"Yep. Just like Saint Nick."

"Show me!"

He guided me over to the tree where he put his hand between branches. The hinged glass ornament with the diamond ring inside he plucked out and put in my hands was beautiful. But not as lovely as the look on his face when he asked me to marry him.

28

I got my wish to stay wrapped in his arms. I held my hand out, admiring the beautiful double diamond setting. Of course I'd agreed to marry him without even torturing him a second by pretending to stall.

"Why two?" I asked when he put it on my finger and we stopped kissing long enough to gasp for air.

"Oh, second chances. Pairs." He brushed the hair along my ear with the back of his hand. Smiling. "For me and you. For Isis and Memnet. It just seemed like us."

"Thank you."

Mom reappeared when we went into the kitchen later and started making cooking noises. I made French toast for breakfast.

Adam and Mom sat at the table, discussing the wedding, pretty much ignoring me. I loved to see them bonding like that. We hadn't decided on a date, yet, although Mom shared her opinion that Memorial

Day weekend would be perfect. New Year's Day, or even Valentine's couldn't be soon enough for me, but Mom wanted to be free from her teaching responsibilities so she could throw us a big party. Since I was her only daughter, she wanted all of her friends and our relatives to see what a good match I had made.

Every once in a while, Adam winked at me.

I felt so free to slip my arms around his shoulders from behind and let my cheek rest against his.

Neither of us minded Mom's company. Mea Cuppa was closed on Christmas Day. The three of us lazed after church. We created a small stir at New Horizons with our news, and the Greens, among others, were overjoyed for us.

In the afternoon, Mom went to read and nap in her room "for a few hours. I'll give you two some time alone."

"Mom, wait." With a backward glance at Adam, I walked her to her room. "Thank you. This was the best present ever."

"I hoped you would forgive me," she said.

"Forgive you?"

"For interfering in your life."

I started to smile before I realized I should be sober. "Well, you took a gamble. What if

I hadn't liked Mr. Thompson anymore?"

"He would have talked you out of it," she said complacently. I hugged her for a long moment, then returned to Adam.

He stared at the tree, stroking Isis.

Memnet huddled in the spot I had vacated. I lifted him onto my lap. "Margaret's trial is set for March."

"I heard. Are you nervous about testifying?"

"No. Adam, nobody seems to care about Tut or Ronald Grimm."

"The police have search warrants out. And by now I'm afraid we have to consider that Tut's probably dead."

I looked squarely at my fiancé. "I want to search the tunnels."

He regarded me as though he'd been in this position before — having to deal with a woman whose mind was made up. "I thought the police already did that."

I stared back. "Not like we can. From the store."

"Ivy, if a grown man was in there, don't you think I would have heard him moving around?"

"Maybe you did, but you didn't recognize the sounds. And what about Tut?"

He gave in, but I knew he just wanted to please me. "Tut would have come to me.

But, OK. We should notify the police."

"Why? It's your store. And I know what Ripple will say. That it's too dangerous."

"Ivy!"

I got up and showed him my survival kit I never put away from the time Jenny was lost. "We probably won't get far, anyway."

"Ripple said no one should go there."

"He didn't say you couldn't go in your own basement."

"All right! All right! What do we do if we find him?"

"Ask him for Christmas dinner. And find out if he knows where Tut is."

We left a note for Mom. The streets were deserted. Adam parked in the alley at the back of the store. Toad smoked a cigar out on his fire escape balcony. I couldn't believe he would do that, but when we wished him Merry Christmas he waved and said he treated himself once a year only and was extra careful this season.

Adam propped the door to the basement open with a handy brick. We treaded cautiously down the staircase. "Well, at least one other person knows we're here," he said when we approached the little door to the tunnel, which remained ajar. Hunched under the low ceiling, Adam shone his light along the smooth walls. We reached the blocked area quickly. I stood there staring at the stones. He would prefer to turn around, but he let me make the decision. The wall appeared solid. Adam lit the boards and medium-sized boulders. Shoving them aside did not seem terribly safe, but I wasn't ready to give up. I stood back, staring until I realized there was a pattern on the right side. An abnormal symmetry revealed that someone had carefully stacked the boards and stones so that they could be easily removed. I turned off my light.

"What are you doing, Ivy?"

"Shh! Just, turn off yours for a sec too. Humor me?"

I heard the click. I reached back to put my hand on his arm. "Feel that?" I whispered.

"Your hand?"

"No! Wait."

"Ah, yes. The air is moving."

We both heard the scrape.

Adam immediately put his light back on and tried to draw me away.

"Wait."

"Ivy!"

"Ronald? Is that you? We can hear you."

"Shh!"

"No, wait. Ronald? It's me, Ivy Preston. You talked to me the night of the fire. And

Adam Thompson, from the store. We won't bother you, or . . . or anything. We just want to talk. Margaret and Letty have been arrested. They can't hurt you anymore."

Silence.

"Ivy, come on."

This time I followed Adam out of the little room. We nearly reached the steps when we heard the sounds, the scrape and plunk of boards being moved. Adam pushed me behind him and aimed the light directly into the tunnel room. "Who's there?" he called.

A gnome of a man, dark with grime, held a hand in front of his eyes. He brushed at stringy gray hair.

I rushed from behind Adam. "Tut? Where's Tut?"

"Ivy, no." Adam grabbed me just in time. The man held his hand up to shield his eyes. Adam lowered the light. "Mr. Grimm?"

"Yeah." Ronald cleared his throat several times before he could make his weak voice heard. "I didn't do nothing. Really. Letty talked me into it. Said she'd pay me to pretend I was the mayor a coupla times, but I never saw a cent. I came back here to the tunnels. I can tell everyone what I seen. They did it all, both of them. I'll make a deal. I'm ready to make a deal. I'm tired and hungry. What day is it?"

444

"Merry Christmas, Mr. Grimm," I said, and helped him climb the steps into the light of the store. I looked back until I knew Tut wasn't coming. At least, not yet.

"I'm sorry to make you come out on Christmas Day, sir," I told Chief Hackman, who answered our call to the police station.

Once Ronald Grimm found his voice, he did not stop talking, even when Hackman read him his rights and told him to be quiet.

"All for the money. Scheming, they were. Did it all, too. Letters, phone calls. I saw 'em. 'Cept for the smoke grenade to the newspaper. Hired a boy for that. Ran fast to collect the back issues. Neither o' them ladies could run fast. I stopped 'em from torching your shop, Mr. Thompson. Wanted to smoke me out of hiding. Ruin your business. And for Donny. Just brung him home from Chicago in the truck. Nasty, that. Not proper. Donny shudda had beddar than being dumped on the can like that. That's when I told 'em I was leaving. I don't hold with murder."

Hackman shook his head at me, muttering. "Got anything else up your sleeve young lady? Just when I thought I'd seen it all. . . ."

Yolanda wasn't far behind, having the

445

police scanner to alert her to calls. She burst through the front door of Mea Cuppa, notebook, camera, and recorder ready. She had to have been the fastest interviewer in Apple Grove, clamoring for a statement all the way through the reading of the rights and the walk outside. We all followed in Hackman's wake while Grimm sputtered the whole time.

"Mr. Grimm, you should wait to say anything else until you have a lawyer," I said.

Yolanda was still waving her pen. "What proof do you have —"

"That's enough, ladies," Hackman said.

As Ronald was being shown into the police car, I yelled out a last question. "Mr. Grimm, do you know where your cousin's cat is? Did they hurt him?"

He shook his head. "Can't be around animals. I got an allergy. Alls I know is I sneezed and sneezed in the tunnels. Didn't do that as a kid. No, no cat I could see. Till that liddle gurl came. Said she hadda cat she followed into the culvert. Liked to die sneezing, I did."

We waved the police car off, spent exactly two more minutes telling Yolanda what happened and that we did not want to keep her any longer from Christmas with her family. Her quick gaze noted the ring on my finger, but she merely congratulated us with a hug.

After the others left and Adam locked up the front door again, I lingered.

"What are you thinking about now?" He asked, pulling me back against his chest.

"I guess I'm pretty transparent."

"Hmm. Pretty." Adam rubbed his chin in my hair.

"But, do you think if Ronald said he sneezed in the tunnels, maybe, just maybe there was a reason?"

He groaned. "We're not going back down there."

"What if we brought our cats here?"

"For them to get lost, too, trying to find Tut?"

"Aha! So, you think it's possible."

"I didn't say that. And you can't move Isis now, you know."

"I know. But sometime. Do you think sometime we could try?"

"Let's just get through one crisis at a time. Your mom's probably wondering where we are."

Addy Bailey's van was in the driveway when we got back to my house. "I can't believe I didn't take my cell phone!" I said.

Adam did not comment as he parked on

447

the street, but both of us hurried into the house.

Colleen and Mom sat at the table, talking. "Merry Christmas, Mr. Thompson, Ivy. It's so exciting! What a cool Christmas present! Congratulations."

"I just thought you'd rather be safe than sorry," Mom said. "So, I called Doctor Bailey. I'm sure Isis knew what to do, but this is her first litter."

"Thanks, Mom." I told her, caressing her shoulder.

Addy sat on the floor in the open arch between the living room and kitchen where she had access to the spot behind the sofa. Isis had made a nest for herself there the last couple of weeks, dragging in a couple of my socks that missed the laundry basket and a scarf hanging out of my coat pocket. I didn't begrudged her the theft once I realized why she wanted them. Addy wore a white coat and currently held a tiny creature in her gloved hands. "I didn't mind at all," she said.

"We were just sitting around," Colleen contributed.

Adam went to squat next to Addy, who quietly reported on Isis's litter and condition.

Memnet sat on the sofa, tail twitching,

regarding me with smug pride. I gently pulled on his ears and played with him.

"Two boys, two girls," Adam told me.

"Isis is just fine," Addy crooned.

"Not bad, old man," I told Mem, tickling his ear.

"You'll want to keep Memnet away for the first few weeks," Addy said. "Sometimes the father shows aggressive tendencies and stresses the mother. Either of them could harm the kittens."

I hated to think of that, but she was right.

"When can Isis be moved?" Adam asked. "I can take her back to my apartment."

"Give her a few days," Addy advised.

I tugged Adam's sleeve. "Why don't you take Memnet with you?"

He had my number. His eyes twinkled. "I suppose that makes sense."

"So, you two have been to the store?" Mom asked. "Any excitement?"

29

Two days later I got the phone call I'd been waiting for.

"Hello, Ivy, could you please come on down to the store? I've got something to show you."

"Hi, Adam . . . let me guess. It chortles, has big ears and spots, and answers to the name of Tut."

"Not much gets by you, does it?"

I'd almost let him get away, but I refrained from that chorus. "He's all right? I'll come now."

When I got to Mea Cuppa, the usual crowd had come: Ripple, Hackman, Yolanda, and Addy, who was in the midst of examining a very thin and ruffled-looking Tut. She removed his loose collar, which had made sores around his neck, and handed it over to Hackman.

I stood next to Adam. We watched together as Hackman twisted the collar in his hands, found the slit on the inside and removed the incriminating printed e-mail between Margaret and someone named Thurston at MerriFood that Donald must have managed to stuff inside before his death. If Ripple hadn't been able to use our captured bacteria or even all of Ronald's strange testimony, this piece of paper dead-bolted Margaret's jail cell.

On a Friday evening late in the middle of January, Adam made supper for us in his apartment after Mea Cuppa closed for the day.

We still needed to decide where we were going to live after the wedding. I loved my cottage, but knew its limitations. Hopefully someday we'd need a bigger house, but I appreciated that he did not expect me to give up my deed automatically. We kept his Chicago condominium for convenience as we planned to travel often to visit family and check on the urban shops.

With his sister so capably in charge, Adam didn't have much to worry about. I could not imagine what he would do with his time once his mother no longer needed him.

I cuddled Memnet, who'd stayed on batching it with Tut and with Adam, while I perused a copy of the newspaper. Tut had recovered well but tended to be a little wary. Basil and oregano scents wafted from the kitchen. Heaven could not have come much closer.

APPLE GROVE GAZETTE
Apple Grove, Illinois
Friday
Trial Ends for Bader-Conklin
by Yolanda Toynsbee, Editor
As of this past Thursday the defense rested in the murder trial of former citizen Margaret Bader-Conklin after three days of testimony. The jury deliberated only two hours before returning a guilty verdict.

Bader-Conklin and her assistant, Leticia Grimm, whose trial was already held, were convicted of several conspiracy charges as outlined in the January 3 edition of the Gazette. Extra copies are available for those who missed that issue.

The trial took place in the state capital.

The defense team has already filed an appeal, we're told. Further news will be forthcoming in the Apple Grove Gazette, your source for all local news.

Monument for Mayor to Be Dedicated
by James R. Toynsbee, Editor
Feli-Mix corporate officials have gra-

ciously agreed to the placement of a monument for former mayor Donald Conklin who was murdered last summer in Chicago.

Feli-Mix was the last corporation which took advantage of Conklin's invitation to set up business in our fair community.

The bronze likeness of Mayor Conklin was commissioned by the Good Seeds, Apple Grove's Core of Volunteers, headed up by Virgil Toynsbee, acting mayor of Apple Grove.

"We wanted the best for our far-seeing twenty-first century father of Apple Grove," Toynsbee said in a recent interview. "The Core commissioned the piece from Judith Abernathy studios in Chicago, one of the world's finest sculptors known in modern art."

According to photographs, the mayor is seen in full formal attire, pointing in the direction of Founders River.

Everyone is invited to the dedication ceremony, which will take place after the spring election.

"Indeed, the dedication will be the first public act of our new mayor," Toynsbee said.

■ ■ ■ ■

Race for Special Mayoral Election Final Field

by the Apple Grove Gazette staff

Meet your candidates who have decided to test the Apple Grove mayoral field, and don't forget to vote in the special election, only two weeks from next Tuesday.

Tiny Alnord

Age: 52

Family: Sister, Babs Gould, nieces and nephews

Occupation: Restaurant owner

Education: Chuck's School of Gourmet Cooking

Goals for Apple Grove: I'll make sure that everyone stays happy. Ladies Night will be expanded to include a free non-alcoholic beverage with the purchase of a meal, and we're considering offering a family package in the future, so that all you parents can make eating together as a family an important priority. Remember, the family that eats together, stays together.

Rupert Murphy

Age: 66

Family: Wife, Lannah, three grown children, all of whom attended Apple Grove's fine schools

Occupation: ret., City Council President (former)

Education: MBA from UNI

Goals for Apple Grove: I'll continue to do my best to make sure city hall runs smoothly, not like our recent debacle of last fall. As your mayor, good citizens, I'll run a tight ship, hold short meetings and make sure everyone has access to all the information they need from my office.

And . . .

I dropped the paper over Memnet's head on my lap. "Adam!"

He stuck his head out of the kitchen entry to see what I wanted. I waggled the paper as Mem jumped down. Tut stuck his head up from his spot on the cushion next to me, his tail twitching.

Adam wiped his hands on his Mea Cuppa apron and came toward me. "Oh. Right. Er, I guess I forgot to tell you something."

I reveled in the gooey feeling that rushed to my toes when he blushed like that. "Dearest Adam, we have got to work on our communication skills."

He crouched in front of me. "So, what do you think? Would I make a good mayor?"

I took his hands in mine. "I think you'll make Donald and me very proud."

ABOUT THE AUTHOR

Lisa Lickel lives in the rolling hills of western Wisconsin. Surrounded by books and dragons, she writes inspiring fiction. Her novels include mystery and romance, all with a twist of grace. She writes short stories and radio theater, is an avid book reviewer and reader, writing mentor, workshop leader, freelance editor, and blogger. She loves to encourage new authors and is a member of Chicago Writers Association and Novel-in-Progress Bookcamp & Writers Retreat. Find more at LisaLickel.com.

The employees of Thorndike Press hope you have enjoyed this Large Print book. All our Thorndike, Wheeler, and Kennebec Large Print titles are designed for easy reading, and all our books are made to last. Other Thorndike Press Large Print books are available at your library, through selected bookstores, or directly from us.

For information about titles, please call:
(800) 223-1244

or visit our website at:
gale.com/thorndike

To share your comments, please write:

Publisher
Thorndike Press
10 Water St., Suite 310
Waterville, ME 04901